I'M COLD, I'M COLD

He grasped the edge of the sheet and pulled it back.

A skeleton with tendrils of brittle brown hair attached to its skull lay where his wife had been sleeping.

Suddenly Brad remembered what she'd said when he'd sat up in a sleepy daze to watch the lightning crackle.

I'm cold, I'm cold.

The skeleton was wearing Sarah's pale blue nightgown. The teeth grinned, and from the bed rose the bittersweet odor of a damp graveyard.

"Oh . . ." he whispered.

I'm cold, she'd said, in a voice that had sounded like a whimper of pain. *I'm cold.*

Brad heard himself moan, and he let go of the sheet and staggered back across the room. The sheet settled back over the skeleton like a sigh.

Doom City

Edited by
Charles L. Grant

Doom City

TOR
HORROR

A TOM DOHERTY ASSOCIATES BOOK

*Many thanks and much gratitude to Melissa Ann
Singer, who keeps a kind and good watch eye on the
Bay and its unofficial mayor; and to Nancy Holder,
who graciously allowed me use of her artist.*

DOOM CITY

First printing: December 1987

A TOR Book

Published by Tom Doherty Associates, Inc.
49 West 24th Street
New York, NY 10010

ISBN: 0-812-51866-7
Can. No.: 0-812-51867-5

Printed in the United States of America

0 9 8 7 6 5 4 3 2 1

ACKNOWLEDGMENTS

CONTENTS

INTRODUCTION

by Charles L. Grant

THE SKY WAS CLEAR WHEN TOM REACHED THE HEADLAND, a forever sky over a forever sea, and he wondered as he often did why he bothered with a studio when he could have days like this. Out in the open air at the end of North Hill. The smell of the ocean, the smell of the marshes. The ordered stretch of Greystone Bay laid out below him. Granite sparkling. Windows flaring. The dash of a red car, the blob of a yellow one, slips and slides of pastels on the backs of slow pedestrians walking the beach, walking the streets. Trees nodding. Chimneys waiting. The muffled cough and roar of a fishing boat, a pleasure boat, adding white to the bay.

He unfolded his chair and set up the easel, and grinned at a curious sea gull coasting above him, black head darting, wings barely moving. There would be

1

others before the day was done and he was gone, wanting to know what he'd brought with him for lunch, not very patiently waiting for the scraps.

He would feed them, as always, and as always they would leave him, crying their anger that he hadn't brought more. But he didn't mind. These days they were about the only friends he had left, and probably, he thought with a wry smile to himself, his truest critics.

The time had passed when galleries called him; the time was long past when magazines here and abroad contacted him for opinions of new artists, or updates on his career, or requesting slides of whatever he had done recently. He didn't mind that either. He wasn't sure himself of the direction he was taking; and though it sometimes felt as if he were lost, without a map, in a land populated by dark things and dark shadows and dark light, nevertheless he was fascinated.

If nothing else, he couldn't complain that his work was boring.

Today the sun was above him, so he sat facing the east horizon, the distant dark of Jendick's Swamp beyond the marshland to his left, the beach below on the right, angling himself to put his shadow on the ground. Then he set the canvas on the easel and sat back, and stared, a finger to his cheek, a palm resting on his thigh.

Seeing nothing, hearing nothing, waiting for an image to come vaguely to mind.

He seldom made plans, and seldom painted what was around him; only once had he done a landscape of the swamp, but the images his hand had traced weren't the images he'd wanted; only once had he done an aerial view of Harbor Road, but the old men who kept intruding weren't the old men he had seen. And only once had he arrived in early morning, his back to the Atlantic, to put down what he saw as the bay stretched to the far hills. It stretched too far. It seemed less endless than never-ending, and he'd put that particular piece in the attic, with all the others that somehow never got finished.

He sat for nearly an hour.

The hand and finger never moved.

Then his lips parted in a silent sigh, and he shook his head in resignation. Today wasn't going to be right; there was too much sun, too much wind, the surf too much a warning as it slammed against the rocks.

It wasn't going to be right, and that did bother him because this was the fifth day in a row it had happened. As if whatever sixth sense he had when it came to picking his subjects had finally dried up on him, had finally withered and was gone.

Five days without working.

Five days closer to the hour when the money would run out and he would have to admit that his comet had flared out.

And he felt cold at the thought of it—not the cold that required a jacket or sweater or gloves for warmth, but a cold that filled him abruptly, as if he were falling into an arctic wind. The cold that came at thoughts of dying, being dead, that came at thoughts of being alone at the end, that came when he feared no one would come to the funeral except the preacher and the gravediggers.

He gasped, and grabbed for the edges of the chair.

He closed his eyes tightly and sought to hide in the spiraling lights, the clouds of red and the storms of green, the stinging that made him snap his eyes open again, and again grab the chair to keep from falling into the dark.

"The sun," he whispered, telling himself it was only his imagination that the sun was gone, the Bay was gone, that he was left on North Hill in a dark that let him see only the easel, only the canvas, only his hand slowly picking up a brush and beginning to work.

It wasn't right.

It still wasn't right.

But he couldn't stop and he couldn't think and he couldn't understand the colors he was choosing.

He watched himself, and he watched the canvas fill, and from the corner of his eye he watched the lights snap on in the town below. The stars above. The moon.

The touch of a fog damply on his cheeks.

And when he was done, canvas filled and hand cramping and acid in his stomach boiling toward his throat, he rose too quickly and the chair clattered onto its side; he rose too quickly, and he stumped backward, felt his ankle turn on a rock, felt the pain, felt himself falling.

And as he lay in the moonlight, unable to move, fire in his chest and fire where his head had struck something buried in the ground, he stared as the miniatures he'd painted caught the moonlight, one at a time—a wharf, a supermarket, a farm, a clinic, all of them washed over with grey as if veiled by the fog that climbed the bluff now and gave him a blanket.

It wasn't right.

They weren't right.

They were portraits in night and screaming, and he denied they were his until he saw himself in the high corner, surrounded by the dark.

Oh god, he thought.

Slowly, teeth clenched against the burning at the back of his skull, he rolled onto his stomach and put his palms to the ground. He must have blacked out, that's where the day went; not enough to eat, too much worry—he must have blacked out.

Knees up, and he took in the salt air, moistened his lips, blinked against the rise of the seawind. Swallowing a touch of bile. Allowing himself a weak smile when he realized that in spite of it all, he was working again.

After nearly a week he was working again.

He looked over his shoulder at the canvas, wondering about the nightmares he had spat out in oils, deciding that before he came here again it would probably be wise to have a word with Doc Johnson, maybe some tests, and listen to his lectures on decent hours and decent food.

A slow and deep breath, and a grin when he was standing.

A slow and cautious turn, and with hands on his hips he checked the canvas again. All in all, it wasn't bad, not bad at all, and a few minutes' work would take out that hideous self-portrait. It didn't belong. It would have to go.

Then a cloud took the moon, and the fog took the bay, and the moment he took a step toward the easel, the earth gave way beneath him, and the night and his screaming followed him down.

SHIFT

by Nancy Holder

HE IS THE LOBSTER MAN.

He is so old, such a fixture of Greystone Bay, many of the young inhabitants don't know his name. To the littlest ones, it doesn't occur to them that he has one at all.

But Allen Hill, the lobster man, has lived a life. Hard as it may be to believe, he walked the cobbles, worn even in his day, to Greystone Elementary School; worked a job in Mr. Lindquist's factory, married a local girl, and fathered a red-headed boy named James.

Hard for the young ones to believe.

Harder still for the lobster man to believe.

It seems he has lived this way forever:

One plate, one cracked china cup, a cupboard filled with tins of dog food. Doilies his wife knitted decaying on the worn arms of a single upholstered chair. A hot plate that works intermittently. A black-and-white television, a thick woolen sweater covering dusty old-man's pants and cheap socks his daughter-in-law sends from California.

Four walls, two uncracked. A separate bathroom containing a tub with clawed feet. Curtains wafted by so many summer breezes they looked like the moldy remains of a winding-sheet. Linoleum that crumbles beneath his brown corduroy house slippers. A daybed. A lamp. An empty fishbowl.

About the dog food: he doesn't have a dog, though it is obvious to his son and daughter-in-law that he should have one ("Keep you company, Dad, you're alone too much"). The shelves in the cupboard bulge with dog food. And each night, he looks them over, deciding—

—chicken parts? hearts and livers?

—because there are nights for scraps and nights for organs—he knows this to be true, though he couldn't have explained just why to another living soul. There just are, and this, the choosing of the dog food, is one of the few uncertain factors in his existence—one plate, one cup, one chair, but dozens of tins of kidneys and livers and other bits and pieces of sacrificial cattle.

He selects the tin of food, then takes up a large hoop almost three feet in diameter draped with a net of fine wire mesh, this lobster man, and leaves his single room to walk the fog-laden streets of Greystone Bay.

He doesn't feel the cobbles beneath his feet anymore; doesn't hear the keening of the foghorns out at sea. He doesn't look in the windows of the shops and offices as he passes: the ghosts are all still there, as are the faces of the men and women among whom he has lived and aged all these years, the changeless years of Greystone Bay. He carries his dog food in the pocket of his baggy, dusty trousers, a dark blue cap hiding his eyes from the misted streetlights. His grey hair curls around the collar of his pea coat. He never cuts it; it never grows.

Each night the soles of his boots—his feet are cold in the Californian socks—each night they buff the same scores of cobbles on his way to Waterford Tavern. For decades he has walked along Woodbine Street, holding on to the hoop, feeling for the dog food—and it occurs to him once that he must have rubbed and buffed and lightly sanded the cobbles of his ever-unmodified path, perhaps just one one-hundredth of an inch in his lifetime, but that he must have affected them. And yet, the cobbles look no different than when he was a boy—he had been a *boy*, once, that lobster man.

Nothing looks any different. Nothing in the entire grey town of Greystone Bay.

Except the faces of his friends. Lines etched like scrimshaw into ivory, where once-robust youth bloomed; lips as grey as Greystone fog; eyes rheumy, hands shaky. Old-man tremors, old-man talk. Old Man Death taking one now and again.

Allen Hill sighs heavily and walks along the quay, shifting the weight of the hoop. Then he pushes open the double doors of the Waterford Tavern and goes in.

His friends are there—there are four; he makes it five at the varnished circular table closest to the potbellied stove. Hiram, Wayne, Joe, Ken—bare, short names for men whose lives have been pared down by years and circumstance—one cup, one chair, the embarrassment of being taken in on holidays, or worse yet, being pitied because no one did take them in. Spare old men—whose lives have been long, perhaps overly so. With spare faces of scrimshaw ivory that don't exactly smile as Allen Hill walks in, but register his entrance and welcome him, in their way.

He sets down his hoop behind the door. Without being asked, Ruth, the daughter of the tavernkeeper and the only barmaid, brings a mug of ale and leaves it in front of one of three empty chairs at the table while Allen divests himself of his pea coat and cap. At the other two places, beer mugs turned upside down gleam in the tavern light.

The can of dog food thumps against the arm of the chair as he sits down and gestures his thanks at the woman. Once a girl, once an infant. He went to church for her christening. Now she looks like a young matron, as Anne was when she died.

"Evening," Wayne says for the four.

"What's new?" Allen replies, and they all chuckle grimly. Nothing ever is.

"Bagged a bufflehead today," Joe offers. "Big one."

The men nod. Then they drink their ale and sit in companionable silence. After so many years, words can be a nuisance. They have long ago told each other everything they ever planned to, and a few things they have not. The years of divulged secrets, blurted wishes, murmured regrets are their collective culture, the Old Men's Culture, set in stone like epitaphs. They are a society of five, though once there were seven of them, seven friends and old mates.

Each time one of them dies, they turn over his mug—there is a special rack over the bar for them, with seven hooks (though only five are used now, and those in the shape of a star)—and set it in front of his accustomed place at the table. Ruth washes them and sets them out each night before the survivors arrive. Tom Blouseter, the resident artist of Greystone Bay, painted the scene four years ago when they turned George Tooney's over after his funeral.

When touched with melancholy, Allen stares at the two empty, upside-down mugs and wonders, *When?*

On bad nights, he hopes, *Tonight?*

He drinks his ale slowly, for these days he takes only one because it makes him sleepy and he might have a long night to face. Across the room, a young man punches a song selection on the jukebox, something jumpy with a refrain that goes "all night long." The man raps a drumroll on the face of the jukebox, then dances back to his place at the bar.

"Kids today." Hiram gestures at Ruth, who comes for his empty mug and spirits it away.

Kids today. *Greystone Bay sucks, Dad.* That was how James said it. *You suck.*

No, he didn't voice that last part.

But he had meant it, his red-headed child who looked so much like Anne that it used to make Allen weep. James hated the grey town with its grey fog, hated his grey father for living there and for being grey. He hitchhiked to California as soon as he graduated from high school. There were some bad years, and then the boy straightened himself out. Now he works for a bank and has a wife.

—who sends Allen socks that make his toes ache with cold; but they are, in an indirect way, gifts from James, and so the lobster man wears them—

—who doesn't understand why a man with no dog has so much dog food, even after he explained it to her when they came—once, just once—to visit.

"I'd better shove off now," Allen says to the others. "I've got to get to work."

They all nod. No one says goodbye. They simply watch him drain his mug and push away from the table.

All night long, all night

Allen walks from the tavern and turns another corner. Now he is directly in front of the Atlantic View Hotel. Forty yards beyond, the pier stretches into the black marble water, its end dissolved in fog.

He hefts the hoop and feels for the dog food. There is a glow in the fog that tells him the moon is full, though he can't see it. The diffuse light rings the streetlamps and drizzles in pools of damp at their bases.

Four years ago, a young Jewish man from Manhattan visited Greystone Bay—jogging all the way down the seaboard, no doubt, attaché case in hand— and declared it the perfect site to develop into another Nantucket. He nearly swooned when he saw the cobbled streets; and the Atlantic View, where he stayed, threw him into a fit of ecstasy. He clasped his hands at the sight of the four old sailing ships bobbing in the water.

"Quaint, untouched, unspoiled!" he chanted as he viewed the old brick buildings. "Perfect! Look at that quay—I see shops! Boutiques! Those clapboards! I see condos on North Hill—I mean, *luxe* housing," he assured the Chamber of Commerce, who stared at him blankly. "I could make this town for you!"

Much discussion followed. There was talk of a referendum. Allen and his friends said little, except to shake their heads. And just when it looked as if Greystone Bay might have its quaintness restored by a quay filled with boutiques and a hill crammed with condominiums, the young Jewish man returned.

And saw the fog.

It rolled in that night like bolts of grey flannel, like silver cotton wool blanketing housetops and treetops and the illuminated sign of the hotel, rendering everything invisible. It swirled around Allen Hill's ankles as he walked from the tavern to the pier. In all his years he had never seen it so bad.

The Jewish young man lost all interest in making Greystone Bay. He couldn't see shoppers groping through the murk, cars grinding into each other like lost ships. He left for Manhattan and was never heard from again. Life went back to its original form, its unvarying texture, except for the death, seven months later, of George Tooney. Old age, the doctor said. A lifetime of bad habits.

The fog was light the day of his funeral. Afterward, Allen himself turned George's mug over at the Waterford Tavern.

His toes are stinging by the time he reaches the wooden box in the middle of the pier. His fingers have etched a groove in the lid and they fit into it automatically as he opens it. Inside lie a battered picnic cooler, a pair of gloves, a package of rubber bands, and a sandwich wrapped in cellophane.

He pulls the cooler out first, then picks up the sandwich and sets it on the pier. He isn't hungry yet; he might be there some hours and need it later.

About the sandwich: the youngest Peixe boy makes one up for him every night and leaves it with the emptied cooler. Lobster salad for the lobster man. "Best of the catch," Juliao assures him. "For you, always the best."

Which is, of course, only fair.

For here he stands in the cold, grey night, a few feet

above the black water that lap-slaps at the pylons that will never support Greystone Fashions and Greystone Creperie. He stands all alone, impassive, a granite man, while others sleep and drink and savor each other. But for him, solitude, a night swimming in fog, a hoop, a tin of kidneys,

a lobster salad sandwich.

A son who comes but once to see him, a daughter-in-law who doesn't want children because she is afraid of stretch marks. Two dead friends, four living ones, oh, please, four . . .

It is a calm night. A typical night. What's new? There, on the pier, absolutely nothing.

He fills the cooler with bay water by carrying it off the pier to the shore and dipping it into the bay. After he carries it back, careful not to slosh it on such a chilly night, he pulls his key chain out of his pocket —one key only, for his front door, and a can opener —and sets about indenting the can lid with six triangular-shaped openings. Enough to let a little dog food out, but not enough to let anything devour it.

He attaches the tin to three wire spokes that point toward the center of the hoop. He sticks the wires through three of the triangular openings and bends them backward. He makes the projections out of clothes hangers, which Hiram gives him every once in a while: Hiram used to own a dry-cleaning business.

The odor of dog food is on his fingers; he wipes them absently on his pants before he puts on his thick leather gloves. He lowers the hoop into the thick waters of the bay with a length of chain. A passerby (who is not a native of the Bay, and therefore would not know of the lobster man) would think he is fishing.

Down, down, until it rests on the bottom. After all this time, he knows exactly how far to lower it. Then he glances up at the whitest part of the fog—where the moon floats in the sky—and waits.

It usually takes about fifteen minutes. Sure enough, there is a tug-tug-tug, ever so subtle, that a less experienced person wouldn't notice.

But Allen Hill is the lobster man. Quickly he pulls in the chain and raises the hoop from the water.

Inside thrashes a lobster. Allen nods at it. With the unconscious ease of decades, he lowers the net to the pier without letting the creature out; grabs it, secures its tail against its body with a rubber band, and dumps it into the cooler.

Lobster salad.

He lowers the hoop and the tin of dog food back into the water.

And waits.

It takes twenty-five minutes this time. Well within range of his experience. After he drops the second lobster into the cooler, he eats his sandwich. He steps on the toes of his shoes to wake up his chilled feet, then lowers the hoop one more time.

Five lobsters are his quota. He doesn't remember how he and the Peixe brothers, who own the town fish market, decided on five, but five it is. How ironic. There are five old men now. Maybe if it were seven . . .

When? Tonight?

Three, four, five come in quick succession. Lobsters to the slaughter. The Peixe brothers suggested he leave the filled cooler in the box, which they retrieve the following morning, and he is always grateful he doesn't have to lug the heavy object home.

He unfastens the tin of dog food and plops it into the cooler—last supper—and gathers up his hoop.

Then he trudges home as he always does.

Always.

The lobster man.

The next night, he walks to the tavern, hefting his hoop. He lays it by the door; Ruth appears with his ale. His friends sit in their accustomed places; the empty mugs, too.

"What's new?" Allen asks.

"This duck," Joe says. He shakes his head a little before he sips his ale. "I tell you, there was something about it."

Allen looks at the others.

"He's talking about a duck," Hiram explains.

Joe goes duck hunting. One duck for Mendel the butcher, that is his quota.

"And there's something . . . different about the drake I caught." Joe pulls a pipe and a pouch of tobacco from his jacket.

They sit without speaking. After an interval, Hiram frowns, pulling his mouth down so slightly that a passerby wouldn't notice it.

"Joe, I looked at it. It was just a plain old duck."

Joe scoops out the wad of old tobacco and plops it into an ashtray, then knocks his pipe sharply on the side of the table.

"You're not a duck hunter. You don't see the things I do."

"I've hunted ducks, Joe."

"Not like I have. Not nearly every day, like me."

Allen is startled by the conversation. These are too many words for the Old Men's Culture, sliding beneath an undercurrent of tension—not much, but the ripples are obvious. The five never quarrel anymore; they are too old and they have settled all there is to settle among them.

"Well, then, tell us what was different about it," Hiram says.

Joe glances at Allen as if for assistance. The lobster man returns his look blankly—he knows less about it than the others, having come in last—then shrugs and picks up his ale.

Joe sighs. "I told you, I can't explain it. But I know that duck is . . . isn't . . . I threw it out. I didn't eat it."

"So it was diseased, then," Allen ventures.

"No." Joe wads the new tobacco into the bowl of his pipe without looking at the others. Yet his fingers betray his frustration as he tamps the tobacco. "I mean, I don't know if it was or not. I just knew I . . ."

He flushes. "I didn't want to touch it anymore."

Again he looks at Allen, who lowers his eyes to his mug. He wonders if his friend is getting senile. He wonders if that is what's behind the too-cheerful calls from California ("Weather's great out here, Dad! Why don't you come for a visit?"). Have James and his wife decided he is getting stupid in the head? He muses about the despair that washes over him at night

all night long, all night

and makes him stare at the empty beer mugs.

"There was something *wrong* with the damned duck," Joe mutters, and that is the end of the conversation.

About fifteen minutes later, Allen rises and leaves the tavern. No one has spoken another word.

* * *

The next day, Hiram comes knocking at Allen's door. (If at all possible, the old men never phone each other; they prefer to conduct their business in person. It is as if they do not trust the machinery, or do not believe the wires could pierce the fog sufficiently to carry their straining old voices to each other's houses.)

Allen has been in the pantry, contemplating his stock of dog food: he is fine; he won't need to call the market for some time. He seems to favor kidneys lately, though hearts take a close second.

"It's Joe," Hiram tells him. "He wants us all to go over to his place."

"Is he sick?" The image of Joe's beer mug flashes through Allen's mind. Down it goes, down and over

down and out

and Blouseter the artist paints another scene.

Hiram shrugs in response. Allen slides on his pea coat and cap and follows Hiram out the door.

Greystone Bay is a small town. Hiram and Allen both have walked the route to Joe's a million times, a hundred million. They walk without speaking, twisting and turning, and Allen thinks once to comment on the thinness of the fog for this time of year; but he never gets around to it.

Wayne and Ken are already at Joe's. It is Wayne who answers the door, face impassive save for one bushy white raised eyebrow.

"We're out back," he says, leading the two men through the cottage

one plate, one cracked china cup

and into the yard (one broken manual lawn mower, a thousand weeds, trees, a rotting teddy bear, a discarded gun rack).

Joe is crouched with his back to the men. He turns around and glances at the four, his gaze pausing at Allen. Then he gestures to something on the ground.

Allen and the others gather around him. Spread on a flattened plastic trash bag shimmer the remains of a small brown duck. Beside its severed but otherwise undamaged head lies a bloody hunting knife.

There is a long moment of studying the splayed carcass. Beady eyes, bleeding entrails. Allen bends down, winces at the arthritis in his knees, and straightens again.

Finally Joe lowers his head. "Can't you *see*?" His voice is low.

"No." Hiram nudges a wing.

"Don't touch it!" Joe cries.

Silence.

"What's wrong with it?" Allen asks. "Tell us."

Again a long look in his direction. "You're a hunter," Joe says. "You understand, don't you?"

A hunter. Allen has never thought of himself that way. He is the lobster man.

"There's nothing wrong with that duck." Hiram rises. "Not a thing."

After a while, they all go back inside. Joe halfheartedly offers everyone a beer which each man declines. They do their drinking at the Waterford Tavern.

Always have.

Allen is on the pier, waiting for the first lobster of the evening. He can see the lights in the windows of the Atlantic View, almost make out dim shapes in them

Listen, it is spring fogless night

and wishes himself inside the Waterford Tavern,

drinking more ale with his friends. Joe is looking
unwell these days; he says nothing more about his
ducks, and the matter has dropped, but he is clearly
troubled about something. Allen supposes that it is
the ducks, but he doesn't ask. It is not part of the Old
Men's Culture to pry.

("What's all this dog food for, Allen?" James's wife
asked in a high, shocked voice. Her tone took Allen
aback until later, after they had returned to California, he realized she thought he was eating it himself.)

He stands on the pier—why has he never gotten
himself a chair? More to worry about, more baggage
—and looks up at the moon, pale and thin behind
streaks of grey.

Spring, fogless.

He is waiting for the first lobster, and as he lowers
his gaze from the moon to the water he experiences a
sense of disquiet.

He cocks his head. He can't understand the feeling,
nor pinpoint its source. After a while, it fades, and he
frowns when he realizes how much time has passed
without a catch.

He smiles as much as the lobster man ever smiles
with his grey face. That is the source of his unease
—that no lobster has yet crept into his trap. They are
slow tonight, his lobster salads, but then, there have
been other slow nights.

The water is so calm. Still. He doesn't hear it
lapping the pylons. But then, he hasn't heard, nor
seen, nor smelled anything of Greystone Bay in years,
that lobster man.

But it seems calmer than usual, that black marble
sea.

There is a tugging. Allen grunts to himself and
hoists the lobster net out of the water.

A good, fat one. He readies a rubber band around his fingers and prepares to grab the spiny creature.

He catches it as if by the scruff of the neck, avoiding the claws and the wildly thrashing tail. He bands the tail against the body with the movements of a calf roper.

Then, just as he is about to put it into the cooler, he stops. It doesn't smell right. No, that isn't it. Doesn't look right. No. It doesn't . . .

It doesn't.

Without knowing why, he unbands it and throws the lobster back.

Spring and fogless, all night long. It is the first night Allen can remember that he doesn't fill his quota. After he throws back the first one, no more appear. He waits for hours, until his toes can stand it no more, and goes home.

The next night, he finds a lobster salad sandwich in his cooler, as always, with a note from Juliao: *Good* Sorte *tonight!*

But he has bad luck that night, too. Empty-handed once more, he pockets the sandwich and takes it home with him, but forgets to put it in his refrigerator and has to throw it away in the morning.

By this time, Joe has begun to watch Allen when he comes into the tavern. He says nothing, but Allen notes a flicker in the man's eyes when Hiram asks, "Feeling okay?" and Allen nods.

"Okay as an old man can feel," he responds, which makes the others nod (slightly, so that a passerby wouldn't notice).

They say little else. Allen drinks his beer. Then he leaves the tavern.

He wonders if a disease has killed off all the

lobsters. Nothing like this has ever happened before.
His cooler is still empty. He stands one, two, three
hours

  tug, tug, tug

and finally raises the net, rubber band at the ready
and he *knows* what Joe was talking about.

Something not quite right. But what? He stares at
the lobster he has just dumped into the cooler. A thin
chill skitters up his spine. What? He can't see anything different. He can only feel it.

He keeps looking at the lobster while he waits for
the next one. His stomach is heavy, as if from eating
too much, and after a while he pulls up the net
—empty, save for the can of beef hearts. He dumps
most of the water from the cooler, mindful not to
touch the lobster, and drapes the net over his wooden
box. One night won't ruin it, and he can't carry both it
and the cooler.

He takes the lobster home. He sets it on the floor
and sits on his bed, and stares at it. It is an ordinary-
looking lobster about a foot long, with two large (but
not unusually large) claws, antennae, and a stiff tail
fan.

After a while, he shakes his head. ("Weather's great
out here, Dad! Why not come for a visit?" There will
never be any grandchildren, ever, because James's
wife doesn't want to ruin her figure. He has a vision of
himself, mired in senility, feeding dog food to a
screaming toddler.)

There is nothing wrong with the damned thing. He
knows that now. Feeling foolish, he changes into a
pair of heavy flannel pajamas, brushes his teeth, and
climbs into bed.

But sleep does not come easily that night to the

lobster man. He guesses it is because he was in bed too early, but his consciousness is focused on the cooler, dimly outlined in the dark room. This lobster, this *thing*.

He turns on the light and peers into the cooler. Not a damned thing wrong. Maybe tomorrow he will cut it open and make lobster salad with it. He hopes the Peixe brothers aren't getting impatient with him.

Later, in the night, his peripheral awareness tells him of sloshing in the cooler, perhaps of scuttling . . . he thinks of his dog food, a pantry of it. He thinks of spiny legs, crawling beneath the blanket, creeping past his ankle, his calf, his sore, cold knees . . .

He wakes up and makes himself some chamomile tea, which he drinks from his cracked china cup.

About the chamomile tea: he doesn't remember buying it. He doesn't remember how often he drinks it.

He doesn't remember how old he is.

That lobster man.

The grey daylight shines on the shell of the lobster as Allen stares at the creature. Nothing wrong with it at all. He has been foolish. He decides he will take it to the Peixe brothers as a peace offering and catch twice as many lobsters that night, even if he has to stand there until dawn.

He dresses and eats, then hefts the cooler in his arms and starts toward the fish market. The air is brisk, the gulls wheeling above him in the fog. He can't see them, and he imagines himself inside a fishbowl, swimming through the fog; and above the mists, the clear surface of the world where the gulls and other creatures live.

Other creatures.

He turns this way and that, swimming through his fog, and then he stumbles on a cobble.

Stumbles, he who has worn those cobbles down—

and drops the cooler. The lobster flies out and rolls into the street, disappearing beneath the tires of the Peixe brothers' truck as it turns the corner.

An image flashes through Allen's mind, accompanied by relief: *Now he will see inside it.*

But he can't, because there's really nothing left.

In the tavern: a bad night, because he thinks they all are glancing at him, wondering about him. Joe looks pasty, almost angry, but he says nothing. He is working on his third mug of ale when Allen wordlessly leaves.

On the pier: a bad night.

Another lobster, and this one as . . . unsettling as the other. He knows how Joe felt, the frustration, the confusion—

and wonders if it is part of the Old Men's Culture, as he had wonders before about his despair (*tonight?*).

This time Allen sits on the pier, legs dangling over the side as when he was a boy—a *boy*, that lobster man—and looks at the lobster floating like a dead thing in the cooler.

The bay is too calm, the night too clear. For a moment he thinks he's in another town.

But there is the Atlantic View; there the never-to-be quaint quay of the never-to-be-made town, the fog-bound town of Greystone Bay, uneasily free of fog.

It is spring, fogless.

But no, even in summer there is fog; always, always some few wisps of grey cotton wool.

Always.

Why he takes the lobster back to his room he has no idea. And why he sits there in the night, peering at it. And why he is still up beside it in the sunlight. He doesn't move all day, keeping a vigil, as it were, with the thing that seems smarmy, not right, unnatural

thing

not diseased, not . . . *bad*

is it?

He crosses his arms as he scrutinizes it, hunched, his arthritic knees hurting as the room grows chilly. He balls his fists. He doesn't want to touch it. At the thought, he shudders, then goes to brush his teeth.

He sits all day beside the lobster. A few times, he reaches out his hand, then recoils.

He must have dozed; when he stirs, it is dark in the room

scuttle, scuttle-scuttle, no, he hears nothing in the blackness

and the hairs on the back of his neck stand on end when he reaches to turn on the light. Suppose the lobster has escaped?

Senile. He grits his teeth and flicks the switch. He takes a breath before he turns around to face the cooler. And the thing inside it.

A bad night: how on earth can he be lost? He knows Greystone Bay better than he knows his own son, his James. He knows each inch of each cobble, each building. He knows the shapes and forms within the fog—so thick tonight, but that doesn't matter. He can find his way blindfolded.

Yet the streets all look the same, as if they have melted into each other. One amorphous mass of grey paste, grey wax, melting and running—floating, really —and he, the maze-maker, stumbling inside it. How can he be lost?

He only wants to find the tavern, with its lights and its potbellied stove, tables of varnished wood

upside-down mugs

and his friends, who at that very moment must be sitting silently, drinking ale, perhaps wondering why he is so late.

For time moves inside the floating paste; he knows that, though he doesn't know the contents of the windows he passes, nor the texture of the cobbles beneath his feet. Time moves, and he is lost, and he can't understand it.

That lobster . . . and tonight he will try again, though he is beginning to lose hope. Tonight he will apologize to Joe, in his spare-old-man's way, perhaps with a mumbled word, a glance, a shrug. An implicit gesture, unrecognizable to a passerby, but understood within the society of the Old Men's Culture. He will apologize for not understanding about the ducks.

If he ever finds Joe.

For is he not moving in slow motion? Are the streets whirling past, breaking up, rising into the fog to surface in the clear world of the gulls? He flails for a lamppost to catch his balance; but it is gone, missing from the spot where it has stood for decades, for as long as Allen himself has stood.

Where are the buildings he knows so well? Where are the Peixe brothers' fish market and Mendel's shop with the sausages in the windows?

(Where he used to hang his exotic prizes, the ducks Joe shot for him, and which have been missing for weeks.)

Where is it all?

"Weather's great, Dad. Why don't you come for a visit?"

He labors on in the grey paste of Greystone Bay, searching. He thinks of the lobster, still floating in the cooler, and wraps his coat more closely around himself. His toes burn with cold.

Listen, it is spring

and then he rounds a corner and sees the neon sign of the tavern.

He nearly weeps with relief. With both hands he opens the door and steps into the room.

The grey paste swirls around him. Everything is different. The walls are a different color; the bar, no longer made of wood; the jukebox, no longer a left-over fifties consolidation of chrome and red plastic but sleek, streamlined, silver.

And Ruth, who stands at the different bar *en profil*: old.

Older than Allen Hill himself.

He gasps audibly, falling against the door. At that moment Ruth turns, sees him, and screams. He has never seen such a look of terror on anyone's face before.

Everyone in the tavern screams. They jump out of their chairs and back away, huddling together around the jukebox.

"What?" Allen cries, looking behind himself. He hurries toward the group. "What?"

His gaze leaps to his old table.

No one sits at it. In front of seven empty places, seven mugs rest upside down.

Seven . . .

"What? What?" Allen pleads, holding out his grey arms, his arms that once were pink and muscled from working in Mr. Lindquist's factory; that once held his wife and cradled his son; that lifted thousands of lobsters from the Greystone Bay.

That finally touched the one in the cooler . . .

And then he remembers: he searched the pantry before he left. The dog food was all gone.

The lobster was gone.

It is spring, fogless . . .

All gone, all gone.

"What?" he screams.

Ruth's father, the tavernkeeper—unbelievably ancient—raises a rifle from beneath the bar.

"Jesus, god, Jesus, god," the man whispers as he takes aim.

Allen begins to cry. As the man pulls the trigger, Allen flings open his arms.

"Why?" he shrieks in a thin, high voice.

Old Man Death coming for one now and again—
shift

He is the lobster man.

WAITING FOR THE HUNGER

by Nina Kiriki Hoffman

SALT SOAKS THE AIR, EVEN IN THIS TIGHTLY CLOSED LITTLE house. Through the shredding curtains I can see the moon walking the waves, bleaching the beach they whisper on. I have insisted on light; she found and lit three candles. The air in the house is so still the flames never waver. Her plump face hovers above the flames, the rampant spills of her curls touched with gold. The yellow underlight makes a winged shadow-shape of her upper face—the shadow of her nose its spine, the shadows of her cheeks its wings, outspread, below her eyes.

"When was the last time you let yourself feel your hunger?" I ask. My voice sandpapers my throat on its way out. I try to shift my hands, but my wrists are bound too tightly together. I feel my feet swelling. I am convinced she has cut off the circulation in my

29

ankles, though she insists she has had a lot of experience with ropes, and the traceries of veins and arter-
ies; she says she never cuts off circulation. In the midst
of my discomfort, I regret that she tied me up while I
was deeply asleep. I missed feeling the touch of her
fingers.

She looks down, the shadows sliding up her face.
The reflections of flames in her eyes brighten. I tell
myself they are only reflections; her eyes do not burn
with interior fire. What she has told me about herself
is only moonspinning.

I have trouble believing my self-talk.

The house smells of mildew and wood rot, with a
faint tang of marshland. No one has lived here for a
long time.

Ruby touches her belly. It is globed and full as the
moon. "Doctor, I feel hungry all the time," she says.
"I've talked to the others. They say it's not real
hunger. But it gnaws at me. I try to resist." She rubs
her temple, then glances up, the flames in her eyes
dancing. "Most of the others eat about every three
days, and they don't need much. But once I start
eating, I can't seem to stop until it's too late. I hate
myself." She twists her hands in her lap. "I hate what
I do. Sometimes I want to kill myself, but I'm not
strong enough."

"There are different kinds of hungers, Ruby," I say.
My voice comes more easily now that I am discours-
ing on my specialty, the treatment of eating disorders.
"There are mental, emotional, and physical hungers.
If you can listen to your hungers, you can learn to
differentiate between them. You can't feed an emotional or mental hunger with food. The more you try,
the less you satisfy yourself." I blink, and realize again

that this is not my office in New Haven, and Ruby is not one of my regular patients.

"I'm hungry for something else?" She touches her mouth, which is slightly open. Her teeth are not ordinary. Her lips are generous, a deep color I suspect would be red in normal light.

"You could be hungering for love, attention, satisfaction. You could be hungering for your true self, for all the things you needed and never received. Most of my patients eat when they're angry; they've never felt safe expressing anger, so they stuff it down with food. Anger is persistent; it takes a lot of food to keep it quiet."

Ruby rises and turns her back on me. Her full-length dress was once white; it is tattered and stained now, its hem muddied and stepped on. Through small rips in the fabric I catch glimpses of her body. It is smooth, pale, desirable. I remember why I decided to specialize in this field. I have always loved large women, an obsession I try not to analyze too deeply.

In college I deemed this perverse, so I studied how to cure their affliction, instead of working on my own. I majored in nutrition and psychology as well as general medicine. Now I live in a cauldron of uncertainties, as women I adore enter my office, learn what their fat is really trying to tell the world, learn to speak with their mouths as well as their bodies, and change into women I couldn't care less about.

Ruby is one of the beautiful ones, as lovely large as she will be thin. Her features have grace and clarity. I know this even though I have not seen her by daylight. Even under these circumstances—my wrists bound to each other and my ankles tied to this chair—I find myself falling in love with her.

"You think I'm angry?" she asks, turning back. For a moment she stands still, though I sense a lot of activity going on behind her face. Her hands tighten into fists. "I never get angry." Her voice shakes.

"Why not?"

"Anger destroys people. It reaches out and rips them to shreds." Her hands open. She stares down at her naked palms; then her fingers curve, her long nails poised like talons. "I watched what my father's anger did to me, and to the other kids. He twisted us all up. I got the younger ones away, most of the time, so he'd concentrate on me, but I vowed never to get mad like that and hurt people."

"You never got mad back?"

"Once, I did. Just once." She flexes her arm. "It never set quite right, but now it's okay," she says, looking at her forearm. "I thought maybe everything got fixed, this side of the grave, but my appetite's still out of control."

"Your appetite isn't a physical thing; it's other things, turned sideways. How many children in your family?"

"Four."

"And you're the eldest? You tried to take care of them?"

"Tried to? I *did* take care of them. Somebody had to, with Mama gone, and Papa—Papa . . . whenever they needed something, I figured some way to get it for them. I kept them clean. I bought them new shoes. I made their lunches and sent them off to school on time. We stuck together. I raised them good." She smiles, her eyes looking over my shoulder. "I wonder how they're doing now." She frowns. "I've been afraid to go back and check up on them. The hunger . . ."

Her arms go around herself. "I always took care of everything, Doctor. When this man, Darcy, started seeing my sister Linda, I tried to find out about him. Nobody knew where he came from or anything about him, so I told him to stop seeing her. After that, he came to see me. Papa couldn't stop him. Darcy told me he'd make me strong, like him. I thought if I was stronger I could take care of Papa and make the kids safe forever. But first I got sick . . ."

She paces away, stands with her face to the wall for a moment, comes back. "Everything changed when I got sick. The kids got mad at me, and so did Papa. They all thought the roof caved in. 'Ruby's not supposed to get sick. Who's going to take care of the housework? Who's going to pay the bills if Ruby's not working?'"

"Who's taking care of Ruby while she's sick?" I ask. Her story is familiar to me in outline; I have heard it from many women. Every time, though, it hurts me. Every time my own response confuses me.

Of course, I rarely get sick either.

"Why, nobody really knew what to do for me. I'd never been sick before." She walks to the window, lays her hand flat on the glass a moment, then lifts it away. Living hands leave a print on cold glass, yet Ruby's hand leaves no mark. "I felt so tired, and I felt so evil for watching them run around wondering how to take care of themselves. Linda brought me a rose, and all I could do was cry. I wanted to get better right away and get back to work, but I couldn't. Darcy came for me three times. He said he would give me power, and he did."

She turns toward me. Half her face is silvered by the moon, half burnished by candlelight. A tiny sob rises in her throat. "On the third day, I rose again, and I tried to go home to them. I wanted to make sure they were all right. I was walking home—I hadn't yet learned to fly—when the hunger rose in me, and I couldn't stop it. Three people died by the time I woke up. My hunger eats me up, and I can never escape it until too late." She looks at her hands. "It's been six years, Doctor. I can't go on this way. Most of the others like me survive on just a little blood—a couple mouthfuls—they can stay in one place a long, long time without people noticing. I can never stay anywhere more than a week—too many people die and the police start looking for me. I can't stand doing this anymore."

She puts her hands to her cheeks. "When I found that copy of the *Gazette*, with the article about your work, I thought—can you help me?"

I look down at my hands. Though I am certain the circulation is cut off, my long fingers are pale, not purple with congested blood. My class ring is heavy on the third finger of my left hand. I have married my career, since I cannot find a woman I love without working to make her unlovable. I look up at Ruby. "You want me to help you stop bingeing? I don't think we can do that in one night."

Her hands grip each other. She closes her eyes a moment.

She smells like very ripe apricots.

"Work like this takes years, Ruby."

"I don't have years." She stares at me, then comes back to sit facing me across the candles. She reaches out to touch a pulse point on my neck. "You don't either. Help me, Doctor. I feel the hunger waking, and you're the closest blood."

I hunch my shoulders, feeling exhaustion along the lines of my bones. I said goodbye to my last patient at five P.M., left my secretary to close up the office for the weekend, and drove two hours to come here to Greystone Bay. I have my retreat here, a converted apartment upstairs in one of the Victorian houses on North Hill; I spend my weekends here alone, walking the pebbly beach, into the fog and away from my work.

After I had some of the "best chowder on the coast" at the Golden Oyster, I went home to bed . . . and woke in this house from a sleep deeper than any I am accustomed to. I know where we are. Out the window, I can see Blind Point across the bay. We are in a deserted beach house north of town, between the sea and the marshes, one of a scattering of houses an ambitious developer built in the twenties, hoping to establish another Jazz Age getaway, but the lost generation did not want to get quite this lost; the project withered. I have walked past these rotting houses on windy days, when they seemed ready to blow away like paper. No one lived here for long, and no one lives here now.

No rescue will walk in off the midnight beach.

At first I thought Ruby was crazy, with her talk of blood. Now my doubts are gone.

"There are several steps to this," I say, letting my training take over. "The first thing you must do is accept yourself just the way you are. Until you love yourself, there is no hope for change."

"Doctor, haven't you heard me? How can I accept myself when I can't forgive myself? I am a hateful, evil creature. I am totally out of control. I break commandments to survive."

"Cast out everything you've been taught. Everything you know is wrong. Recognize you have always done the best you could with the information you had at the time. Say this: 'I, Ruby, love and forgive myself unconditionally.'"

Sobs shake her, but they make no noise and no tears. She tries to repeat the affirmation. She breaks down on the third word. She covers her face with her hands.

"Ruby, I love and forgive you unconditionally," I say. I feel this is true, but it hurts me to say it, because once she believes me, the balance will start to tip, and she will be her own person. She will reclaim the power she never knew she gave away. I sigh. "I love you, Ruby."

"How can you? I don't believe you! I'm awful, worse than Papa!"

"Ruby, I love you. I *love* you. No matter what you've been, no matter what you've done, no matter what's been done to you. I love you."

She rises and comes around the table, to stand between me and the light, a large dark silhouette. "You lie. No one could love me." She leans closer. I wonder if she sees better in the dark than I. Her clothes smell of rot, but her own scent is musk and apricots. I look up toward her eyes, knowing my love is naked in my face. "You love me," she whispers. Then, louder, "You must be crazy."

"Throw the beliefs away, Ruby, or we'll never get this done."

"What?" She gasps.

"Throw away your beliefs. You are not evil. You are not horrible. You are a perfect being. Say it. 'I, Ruby, am perfect the way I am.'"

"I, Ruby . . ." She stumbles away, bumping the table. She staggers toward the wall and puts her face against it.

"Say it."

She says it, sarcastically. She turns to face me.

I smile at her. "You have to say it as though you believe it. We can't go any further until you convince me you believe it. 'I, Ruby, am perfect the way I am. I, Ruby, love and forgive myself unconditionally.' Say it. And feel it."

She speaks in the night, sometimes loudly, sometimes very softly. The moon rises above the house and out of sight, leaving light and shadows behind. Ruby alternates between fighting me and fighting everything she has ever learned. She paces. She screams at me. Once she stalks toward me and lays her hand against my throat, lifting her lip to show me her teeth. Her canines are longer than usual, but I forget to be afraid. The candles melt down to puddles of pleasant-smelling wax.

At last she stands in the center of the floor, her feet planted firmly, her hands on her hips. "I, Ruby, am perfect the way I am. I love myself unconditionally. I forgive myself—I forgive myself completely!"

At last I believe her.

"Listen," I say. My voice is hoarse. "I hear you believe that now, but once in a while, your resolution may falter. When that happens, there is a source of strength you can call on. Address it however you please. Some call it God. I think of it as my second self. When you need help, ask for it. It will be there for you."

"I don't believe you! Are you a doctor or a priest?"

"I'm a midwife. You asked me to help you give birth to a new self, Ruby. I'm doing my job. This is one of the steps in the procedure. Posit a force you can draw on for strength." My head falls forward. The excitement and challenge of the work no longer sustain me; I am too tired.

"Well, all right. If I can believe I'm a perfect being, I suppose I can believe in The Force." She sits on the floor at my feet. She touches my knee. The candles have dwindled to weak blue flames. "Doctor," she murmurs, "I'm hungry."

"Is it a physical hunger? Consult your body."

She sits a moment in silence, her head lowered. "Yes," she says at last.

"If it is a physical hunger, you should take care of it." The words are coming out of me by rote. "Think of what you most want to eat. Don't settle for anything else." I shake my head, trying to wake up. I cannot believe what I just said. "The secret now is to eat slowly. Pause often and ask yourself if you are satisfed. When you are satisfied, stop eating. Know there will always be food. You don't have to eat it all now. You can have more tomorrow, or whenever you want it."

She sits still a long moment, staring up at me. I glance out the window. False dawn lights the line between sea and sky.

Ruby rises to her feet. She comes to me, gently lifts my chin. Her lips are warm against my neck; her breath smells of ripe fruit. I close my eyes.

I wonder if I will be awake when she stops.

DOC JOHNSON

by F. Paul Wilson

"I THINK YOU'D BETTER TAKE THE CALL ON OH-ONE," Jessie said, poking her head into the consultation room.

I glanced up from the latest issue of *Cardiology* and looked at my wife. It was Monday morning and I had a grand total of three patients scheduled.

"Why?" I said.

"Because I said so."

That's what I get for hiring my wife as my nurse-receptionist, but I had to keep overhead down until I built up a decent practice and could afford a stranger . . . someone I could reprimand without paying for it later at home. I had to admit, though, that Jessie was doing a damn fine job so far. She wasn't letting the pregnancy slow her down a bit.

"Who is it?"

Jessie shrugged. "Not sure. Says she's never been here before but says her husband needs a doctor real bad."

"Got it," I said. Never turn down a patient in need. Especially one who might be able to pay.

I picked up the phone. "Hello. Dr. Reid."

"Oh, Doctor," said a woman's voice. "My husband's awful sick. Can you come see him?"

"A *house call*?" After all, I was a board-eligible internist. House calls were for GPs and family practitioners, not specialists. "What's wrong with your husband, Mrs. . . . ?"

"Mosely—Martha Mosely. My husband, Joseph, he's . . . he's just not right. Sometimes he says he wants a doctor and sometimes he says he doesn't. He says he wants one now."

"Can you be a little more specific?" If this Mosely fellow was going to end up in the hospital, I'd rather have him transported there first and *then* see him.

"I wish I could, Doctor, but I can't."

"Who's his regular doctor?"

"Doc Johnson."

Ah-ha! "And why aren't you calling him?"

"Joe won't let me. He says he doesn't ever want to see Doc Johnson again. He only wants you."

I hesitated. I didn't want to get in the house-call habit, but as the new kid in town, I couldn't afford to pass up a chance to score some points.

"All right," I said. "Give me the address and I'll be out after dinner."

He doesn't ever want to see Doc Johnson again

I thought about that as I drove out to the Mosely house. An odd thing to say. Most people in Greystone Bay swore by Johnson. You'd think he walked on

water the way some of them talked. And that wasn't
making it any easier for me to get started in
Greystone Bay. I'd been living—quite literally—off
the crumbs he left behind. Joseph Mosely appeared to
be a crumb. And so I was on my way to gather him up.

I turned south off Port Boulevard onto New Hope
Road, watching the houses change from post–World
War II tract homes to smaller, older homes on bigger
lots. The January wind slapped at the car as I drove.

This was my first winter in Greystone Bay and it
was *cold*. The natives like to say that the nearness of
the ocean tends to moderate the severity of the
weather. Maybe that is true. According to the ther-
mometer, it doesn't seem to get quite as cold here as it
does inland, but I think the extra moisture in the air
from the ocean sends the cold straight through the
clothing and deep into the bone.

But the cold was locked outside the car and I was
warm within. I had a bellyful of Jessie's tuna casse-
role, the Skylark's heater-defrost system was blowing
hard and warm, snow blanketed the lawns and was
banked on the curbs, but the asphalt was clean and
dry. It was a beautiful, crystalline winter night for a
drive. Too bad Jessie wasn't with me. Too bad this
wasn't a pleasure drive. People attach such rosy
nostalgia to the house call, but in this end of the
twentieth century, the house is a *lousy* place to
practice medicine.

I slowed the car as the numbers on the mailboxes
told me I was nearing the Mosely place. There it was:
620 New Hope Road. As I pulled into the driveway,
my headlamps lit up the house and grounds. I stopped
the car halfway through the turn and groaned.

The Mosely house was a mess.

Every neighborhood has one. You know the type of

house I mean. You drive along a street lined with immaculately kept homes, all with freshly painted siding and manicured lawns, all picture perfect . . . except for one. There's always one house that has a front yard where even the weeds won't grow; the Christmas lights are still attached to the eaves even though it is now June; if the neighborhood is lucky, there will be only one rusting auto in the front yard, and the house's only previous coat of paint will have merely peeled away, exposing much of the original color of the siding; if the neighborhood is especially cursed, there will be two or more automobile hulks in various stages of refurbishing in the front, and the occupant will have started to paint the derelict home a hot pink or a particularly noisome shade of green and then quit halfway through.

The Mosely house was New Hope Road's derelict.

I turned off my engine and, black bag in hand, stepped out into the cold. No path had been dug through the snow anywhere I could see but I found a narrow path where it had been packed down by other feet before me. It led across the front lawn. At least I think it was a lawn. The glow from a nearby streetlight picked out odd bumps and rises all over the front yard. I could only guess as to what lay beneath. A blanket of snow covers a multitude of sins.

I got a closer look at the house as I carefully picked my way toward it. The front porch was an open affair and its overhang was tilted at a crazy angle. The paint on the front of the house was particularly worn and dirty on the porch up to a level of about two feet. It looked to me like a dog had spent a lot of time there but I saw no paw prints and heard no barking. The light from within barely filtered through the window shades.

The front door opened before I could knock. A thin, fiftyish woman wearing an old blue housedress and a stretched-out brown cardigan sweater stood there with her hand on the knob.

"I'm terribly sorry, Doctor," she said in a mousy voice, "but Joe's decided he don't want to see a doctor tonight."

"What?" I said, my voice hoarse with shock. "You mean to tell me I came—"

"Oh, let him in, Martha!" said a rough voice from somewhere behind her. "Long as he's here, we might as well get a look at him."

"Yes, Joe," she said, and let me in.

The air within was hot, dry, and sour-smelling. I wondered how many years it had been since they'd had the windows open. A wood stove sat in a corner to my left. What little light there was in the room came from candles and kerosene lamps.

Joseph Mosely sat in a rocker facing me. He was the same age as his wife but thinner. His skin was stretched tight across his high forehead and cheekbones. He had a full head of lank hair and a three-day stubble of beard. There was something familiar about him. As I watched, he sipped from a four-ounce tumbler clutched in his right hand; a half-empty bottle of local-brand gin sat on a small table next to him. He was staring at me. I've seen prosthetic eyes of porcelain and glass show more warmth and human feeling than Joe Mosely's.

"If that was your idea of a joke, Mr. Mosely—"

"Don't bother trying to intimidate me, Dr. Charles Reid. It's a waste of breath. Take the man's coat, Martha."

"Yes, Joe."

Sighing resignedly, I shrugged out of my jacket and

turned to hand it to her. I stopped and stared at her face. A large black and purple hematoma, a good inch and a half across, bloomed on her right cheek. Due to the way the light had been falling, I hadn't noticed it when she opened the door. But now . . . I knew from the look of it that it wasn't more than a couple of hours old.

"Better get the ice back on that bruise," he said to her from his rocker. "And careful you don't slip on the kitchen floor and hurt yourself again."

"Yes, Joe." She hung my coat on a hook next to the front door.

Clenching my teeth against the challenge that leaped into my throat, I handed her my coat and turned to her husband.

"What seems to be the problem, Mr. Mosely?"

He put the glass down. "This." He rolled up his right sleeve and showed me a healing laceration on the underside of his forearm. It ran up the arm from the wrist for about five inches or so and looked to be about ten days to two weeks old. Three silk sutures were still in place.

My anger flared. "You brought me all the way out here for a suture removal?"

"*I* didn't bring you anywhere. You brought yourself. And besides"—he kicked up his left foot; it looked deformed under the dirty sock—"I'm disabled."

"All right," I said, cooling with effort. "How'd you cut yourself?"

"Whittling."

I felt like asking him if he'd been using a machete, but restrained myself. "They sew it up at Bay Memorial?"

"Nope."

"Then who?"

There was a pause and I looked at him. His eyes were even colder and flatter than before. "Doc Johnson."

"Why'd he leave these three sutures in?"

"He didn't. I took the rest out myself. He won't ever get near me again! Ever!" He half rose from the rocker. "I wouldn't take my *dog* to him if she was still alive!"

"Hey! Take it easy." He calmed down with another sip of gin. "So why did *you* leave the last three sutures in?"

He looked at the wound, then away. "Because there's something wrong with it."

I inspected it more closely. It looked fine. The wound edges had knitted nicely. Dr. Johnson had done a good closure. There was no redness or swelling to indicate infection.

"Looks okay to me." I opened my bag, got out an alcohol swab, and dabbed the wound. Then I took out scissors and forceps and removed those last three sutures. "There. Good as new."

"There's *still* something wrong with it!" He pulled his arm away to reach for the gin glass; he drained it, then slammed it down. "There's something in there."

I almost laughed. "Pardon me?"

"Something's *in* there! I can feel it move every now and then. The first time it moved was when I started taking the sutures out. There! Look!" He stiffened and pointed to the wound. "It's moving now!"

I looked and saw nothing the least bit out of the ordinary. But I thought I knew what was bothering him.

"Here," I said, taking his left hand and laying the

fingers over the underside of his forearm. "Press them there. Now, open and close your hand, making a fist. There . . . feel the tendons moving under the skin? You've probably got a little scar tissue building up in the deeper layers next to a tendon sheath and it's—"

"Something's *in* there, I tell you! Doc Johnson put it there when he sewed me up!"

I stood up. "That's ridiculous!"

"It's true! I wouldn't make up something like that!"

"Did you watch him sew you up?"

"Yes."

"Did you see him put anything in the wound?"

"No. But he's sneaky. I know he put something in there!"

"You'd better lay off the gin," I said as I closed my bag. "You're having delusions."

"I shoulda known," he said bitterly, reaching for his bottle. "You doctors think you've got all the answers."

I took my coat off the hook and pulled it on. "What's that supposed to mean? And haven't you had enough of that for one night?"

"*Damn* you!" Eyes ablaze with fury, he hurled the glass across the room and leaped out of the rocker. "Who the hell do you think you are to tell me when I've had enough!"

He limped toward me and then I remembered why he looked familiar. The limp triggered it: I had seen him dozens of times in the Port Boulevard shopping area, usually coming or going in and out of the liquor store. He had lied to me—he wasn't disabled enough to warrant a house call.

"You're drunk," I said, reaching for the doorknob. "Sleep it off."

Suddenly he stopped his advance and grinned, maliciously. "Oh, I'll sleep, all right. But will *you*? Better pray nothing goes bad with this arm here, or you'll have another malpractice case on your hands. Like the one in Boston."

My stomach wrenched into a tight ball. "How do you know about that?" I hoped I didn't look as sick as I felt.

"Checked into you. When I heard that we had this brand-new doctor in town, fresh from a big medical center in Boston, I asked myself why a young, hotshot specialist would want to practice in the Bay. So I did some digging. I'm real good at digging. 'Specially on doctors. They got these high an' mighty ways with how they dole out pills and advice like they're better'n the rest of us. Dr. Tanner was like that. That office you're in used to be his. I dug up some *good* dirt on Tanner but he disappeared before I could rub his face in it."

"Good night," I said. I stepped out on the porch and pulled the door closed behind me.

There was nothing else to say. I thought I had left that malpractice nightmare behind me in Boston. The sudden realization that it had followed me here threatened all the hopes I'd had of finding peace in Greystone Bay. And to hear it from the grinning lips of someone like Joe Mosely made me almost physically ill.

I barely remember the trip home. I seemed to be driving through the past, through interrogatories and depositions and sweating testimonies. I didn't really come back to the present until I parked the car and walked toward the duplex we were renting.

Jessie was standing on the front steps, wrapped in

her parka with her arms folded across her chest,
looking up at the stars under a full moon. Suddenly I
felt calm. It was the way I had found her when we first
met—standing on a rooftop gazing up at the night
sky, looking for Jupiter. She owned two telescopes
that she used regularly, but she's told me countless
times that a true amateur astronomer never tires of
naked-eye stargazing.

She smiled as she saw me walk up. "How was the
house call?"

I put on an annoyed expression. "Unnecessary." I
wouldn't tell her about tonight. At least one of us
should rest easy. I patted her growing belly. "How we
doing in there?"

"You mean the Tap Dance Kid? Active as ever."
She turned back to the stars and frowned.

"What's the matter?" I said.

"I don't know. Something weird about the stars out
here."

I looked up. They looked all right to me, except that
there was a hell of a lot more of them than I'd ever
seen in Boston.

Jessie slipped an arm around me and seemed to
read my expression without looking at me.

"Yeah. I said *weird*. They don't look right. I could
get out a star map and I know everything would look
fine. But something's just not right up there. The
perspective's somehow different. Only another star-
gazer would notice. Something's wrong."

I had heard that expression too many times tonight.

"The baby wants to go in," I said. "He's cold."

"*She*'s cold."

"Anything you say."

*   *   *

I had trouble sleeping that night. I kept reliving the malpractice case and how I wound up scapegoat for a couple of department heads at the medical center. After all, I was only a resident and they had national reputations. I was sure they were sleeping well tonight while I lay here awake.

I kept seeing the plaintiff attorney's hungry face, hearing his voice as he tore me apart. I'm a good doctor, a caring one who knows internal medicine inside and out, but you wouldn't have thought so after that lawyer was through with me. He got a third of the settlement and I got the word that I shouldn't apply for a position on the staff of the medical center when my residency was up. I suppose the big shots didn't want me around as a reminder of the case.

Jessie wanted me to fight them for an appointment but I knew better. Every hospital staff application has a question that reads: "Have you ever been denied staff privileges at any other hospital?" If you answer *Yes*, they want to know all the particulars. If you say *No* and later they find out otherwise, your ass is grass.

Discretion is the better part of valor, I always say. I knew they would turn me down, and I didn't want to answer "Yes" to that question for the rest of my life, so I packed up and left when my residency was over. The medical center reciprocated by giving me good recommendations.

Jessie says I'm too scared of making waves. Jessie's probably right. She usually is. I know I couldn't have made it through the trial without her. She stuck by me all the way.

She's right about the waves, though. All I want to do is live in peace and quiet and practice the medicine I've been trained for. That's all. I don't need a Porsche

or a mansion. Just Jessie and our kids and enough to
live comfortably. That's all I want. That's all I've ever
wanted.

Wednesday afternoon, two days after the Mosely
house call, I was standing outside Doc Johnson's
house, ringing his bell.

"Stop by the house this afternoon," he had said on
the phone a few hours ago. "Let's get acquainted."

I had been in town seven months now and this was
the first time he had spoken to me beyond a nod and a
"Good morning" while passing in the hall at Bay
Memorial. I couldn't use the excuse that my office was
too busy for me to get away, so I accepted. Besides, I
was curious as to why he wanted to see me.

I saw Joe Mosely on my way over. He was coming
out of the liquor store and he spotted me waiting at
the light. He looked terrible. I wasn't sure if it was just
the daylight or if he was actually thinner than the
other night. His cheeks looked more sunken, his eyes
more feverish. But his smile hadn't changed. The way
he grinned at me had tied my stomach into a knot that
was just now beginning to unravel.

I tried not to think of him as I waited for someone
to answer my ring. I inspected my surroundings. The
Johnson house was as solid as they come, with walls
built of the heavy grey native granite that rimmed the
shore in these parts. There was little mortar visible.
Someone had taken great pains to mate each stone
nook and cranny against its neighbor. The resultant
pattern was like the flip side of one of those thousand-
piece Springbok jigsaw puzzles that Jessie liked to
diddle with. From the front steps here high on North
Hill I had a clear view of the beach and the ocean, all
the way down to Blind Point and beyond.

I wouldn't mind geting used to this, I thought.

I thought about Doc Johnson, too. I'd heard that he was a widower with no children, that his family came over here with Greystone Bay's original settlers back in the seventeenth century. Doctors apparently came and went pretty regularly around the Bay, but "the Doc"—that's what the natives called him—was as constant as the moon, always available, always willing to come out to the house if you were too sick to go to him. If you were a regular patient of the Doc's he never let you down. They talked like he'd always been here and always would be. His practice seemed to encompass the whole town. That was impossible, of course. No one man could care for twenty thousand people. But to hear folks talk—and to listen to the grumbling of the few other struggling doctors in town—that was the way it was.

The handle rattled and Doc Johnson opened the door himself. He was a portly man in his sixties with a full, friendly, florid face and lots of white hair combed straight back. He was wearing a white shirt, open at the collar, white duck pants, and a blue blazer with a gold emblem on the breast pocket. He looked more like a yacht club commodore than a doctor.

"Charles!" he said, shaking my hand. "So good of you to come! Come in out of the chill and I'll make you a drink!"

It wasn't as chilly as it had been the past few days but I was glad to step into the warmth of his home. He fixed me an excellent vodka gimlet with a dash of Cointreau and showed me around the house, which one of his ancestors had built a couple of centuries ago. We made small talk during the tour until we ended up in his study before a fire. He was a gracious, amiable host and I took an immediate liking to him.

"Let's talk shop a minute," he said to me after we settled into chairs and I refused a refill on the gimlet. "I like to feel out a new doctor in town on his philosophy of medicine." His eyes penetrated mine. "Do you have one?"

I thought about that. Since starting med school I'd been so involved in learning whatever there was to know about medicine that I hadn't given much consideration to a philosophical approach. I was tempted to say, *Keeping my head above water,* but thought better of it. I decided to go Hippocratic.

"I guess I'd start with 'Above all else do no harm.'"

He smiled. "An excellent start. But how would triage fit into your philosophy, Horatio?"

"Horatio?"

"I'm an avid reader. You will forgive me a literary reference once in a while, won't you? That was to *Hamlet.* A strained reference, I'll grant you, but *Hamlet* nonetheless."

"Of course. But triage . . . ?"

"Under certain circumstances we have to choose those who will get care and those who won't. In disasters, for instance: We must ignore those whom we judge to be beyond help in order to aid those who are salvageable."

"Of course. That's an accepted part of emergency care."

"But aren't you doing harm by withholding care?"

"Not if a patient is terminal. Not if the outcome will remain unchanged no matter what you do."

"Which means we must place great faith in our judgment, then, correct?"

I nodded. "Yes, I suppose so." What was he getting at?

"And what if one must amputate a gangrenous limb

in order to preserve the health of the rest of the body? Isn't that doing harm of sorts to the diseased limb?"

I said, "I suppose you could look at it that way, but if the health of the good tissue is threatened by the infected limb, and you can't cure the infection, then the limb's got to go."

"Precisely. It's another form of triage: the diseased limb must be lopped off and discarded. Sometimes I find that triage must be of a more active sort where radical decisions must be made. Medicine is full of life-and-death decisions, don't you think?"

I nodded once more. This was a baffling conversation.

"I understand you had the pleasure of meeting the estimable Joseph Mosely the other night."

The abrupt change of subject left me reeling for a second.

"I don't know if I'd call it a pleasure," I said.

"There'd be something seriously wrong with you if you did. A despicable excuse for a human being. Truly a hollow man, if you'll excuse the Yeats reference—or is that Eliot? No matter. It fits Joe Mosely well enough: no heart, no soul. An alcoholic who abused his children mercilessly. I patched up enough cuts and contusions on his battered boys, and I fear he battered his only daughter in a far more loathsome way. They all ran away as soon as they were able. So now he abuses poor Martha when the mood suits him, and that is too often. Last summer I had to strap up three broken ribs on that poor woman. But she won't press charges against him. Love's funny, isn't it? Did you notice his mangled foot? That happened when he was working at the shoe factory. Talk is that he stuck his foot in that machine on purpose, only he stuck it in farther than he intended and did too good a job of injuring himself. Anyway, he got a nice settlement out of it, which is what he wanted, but he drank it up in no time.

"And did you notice the lack of electricity? The power company caught him tampering with the meter and cut him off. I've heard he's blackmailing a few people in town. And he steals anything that's not nailed down. That cut on his arm I sewed up? That was the first time in all these years I'd ever had a chance to actually treat him. He tried to tell me he did it whittling. Ha! Never yet seen a right-handed man cut himself in the right arm with a knife. No, he did that breaking into a house on Accardo Street. Did it on storm window glass. Read in the *Gazette* how they found lots of blood at the scene and were checking ERs in the area to see if anybody had been sewn up. That was why he came to me. I tell you, he will make the world a bright place by departing it."

"You didn't report him to the police?"

"No," he said levelly. "And I don't intend to. The courts won't give him his due. And calling the police is not my way of handling the likes of Joe Mosely."

I had to say it. "Joe Mosely says you put something in the laceration when you sewed it up."

I watched Doc Johnson's face darken. "I hope you will consider the source and not repeat that."

"Of course not," I said. "I only mentioned it now because you were the accused."

"Good." He cleared his throat. "There's some things you should know about the Bay. We like it quiet here. We don't like idle chatter. You'll find that things have a way of working themselves out in their own way. You don't get outsiders involved if you can help it."

"Like me?"

"That's up to you. You can be an insider if you want to be. 'Newcomer' and 'insider' aren't mutually exclusive terms in Greystone Bay. A town dies if it doesn't get *some* new blood. But discretion is all-important. As a doctor in town you may occasionally see something out of the ordinary. You could take it as it comes and deal with it, and leave it at that, and that would bring you closer to the inside. Or you could talk about it a lot or maybe even submit a paper on it to something like the *New England Journal of Medicine*, and that would push you out. *Far* out. Soon you'd have to pack up and move away." He stood up and patted my shoulder. "I like you, Charles. This town needs more doctors. I'd like to see you make it here."

"I'd like to stay here."

"Good! I do my own sort of triage on incoming doctors. If I think they'll work out, I send them my overflow." He sighed. "And believe me, I'm getting ready to increase my overflow. I'd like to slow down a bit. Not as young as I used to be."

"I'd appreciate that," I said.

He gave me a calculating look. "Okay. We'll see. But first—" He glanced out the window. "Well, here it comes!" He motioned me over to the big bay window. "Look out there!"

I stepped to his side and looked out at the Atlantic —or rather, where the Atlantic had been. The horizon was gone, lost in a fogbank that was even now rolling into the bay itself.

Doc Johnson pointed south. "If you watch, you'll see Blind Pew disappear."

"Excuse me?"

He laughed. "Another reference, my boy. I've called

Blind Point 'Blind Pew' ever since I read *Treasure Island* when I was ten. You remember Blind Pew, don't you?"

N. C. Wyeth's moonlit painting of the character suddenly flashed before my eyes. That painting had always given me the chills. "Of course. But where's the fog coming from?"

"The Gulf Stream. For reasons known only to itself, it swings in here a couple of times a winter. The warm air from the stream hits the cold air on the land and then we have fog. Oh, my, do we have *fog*!"

As I watched, I saw lacy fingers of mist begin to rise from the snow in the front yard.

"Yes, sir!" he said, rubbing his hands together and smiling. "This one's going to be a beauty!"

Mrs. Mosely called me Friday night.

"You've got to come out and see Joe," she said.

"No, thank you," I told her. "Once was quite enough."

"I think he's dying!"

"Then get him over to Memorial."

"He won't let me call an ambulance. He won't let me near him!"

"Then I'm sorry—"

"*Please*, Dr. Reid!" Her voice broke into a wail. "If not for him, then for me! I'm frightened!"

Something in her voice got to me. And I remembered that bruise on her cheek. "Okay," I said reluctantly. "I'll be over in a half hour."

I knew I'd regret it.

The fog was still menacingly thick, and worse at night than during the day. At least you could pick out shadows in daylight. At night the headlights bounced off the fog instead of penetrating it. It was like driving through cotton.

When I finally got to the Mosely place, the air seemed cooler and the fog appeared to be thinning. Somewhere above, moonlight struggled to get through. Maybe that predicted cold front from the west was finally moving in.

Martha Mosely opened the door for me. "Thank you for coming, Dr. Reid. I don't know what to do! He won't let me touch him or go near him! I'm at my wit's end!"

"Where is he?"

"In bed." She led me to a room in the back and stood at the door clutching her hands between her breasts as I entered.

By the light of the room's single flickering candle I could see Joe Mosely lying naked on the bed, stretched out like a corpse. In fact, for a moment I thought he was dead—he looked emaciated and his breathing was so shallow that I couldn't see his chest move. Then he turned his head a few degrees in my direction.

"So, it's you." His lips barely moved. The eyes were the only things alive in his face.

"Yeah. Me. What can I do for you?"

"First, you can close the door—with that woman on the other side." Before I could answer, I heard the door close behind me. I was alone in the room with Mosely. "And second, you can keep your distance."

"What's the matter? Anything hurt?"

"No pain. But I'm a dead man. It's Doc Johnson's doing. I told you he put something in that cut."

His words were disturbing enough, but his completely emotionless tone made them even more chilling. It was as if whatever emotions he possessed had been drained away along with his vitality.

"You need to be hospitalized."

"No use. I'm already gone. But let me tell you about Doc Johnson. He did this to me. He's got his own ways and he follows his own rules. I've tailed him up onto South Hill a few times but I always lost him. Don't know what he goes there for, but it can't be for no good."

I took out my stethoscope as he raved quietly. When he saw it, his voice rose in pitch.

"Don't come near me. Just keep away."

"Don't be ridiculous. I'm here. I might as well see if I can do anything for you." I put the earpieces in my ears and went down on one knee beside the bed.

"Don't. Keep back."

I pressed the diaphragm over his heart to listen—

—and felt his chest wall give way like a stale soda cracker.

My left hand disappeared up to the wrist inside his chest cavity. And it was *cold* in there! I yanked it out and hurled myself away from the bed, not stopping until I came up against the bedroom wall.

"Now you've done it," he said in that passionless voice.

As I watched, yellow mist began to stream out of the opening in his chest. It slid over his chest and down to the sheet under him, and from there down to the floor, like the mist from dry ice when you put it in water.

I looked at Mosely's face and saw the light go out of his eyes. He was gone.

A wind began blowing outside, whistling under the doors and banging the shutters. I glanced out the

window on the far side of the room and saw the fog
begin to swirl and tear apart. Suddenly there came a
crash from the front room. I pulled myself up and
opened the bedroom door. A freezing wind hit me in
the face with the force of a gale, tearing the door from
my grip and swirling into the room. I saw Martha
Mosely get up from the sofa and struggle to close the
front door against the rage of the wind.

The bedroom window shattered under the sudden
impact and now the wind howled through the house.

The yellow mist from Mosely's chest cavity caught
the wind and rode it out the window, slipping along
the floor and up the wall and over the sill in streaks
that gleamed in the growing moonlight.

Then the mist was gone and the fog was gone and I
was alone in the room with the wind and Joe Mosely's
empty shell.

And then Mosely's shell began to crumble, caving
in on itself piece by piece, almost in slow motion like
a miniature special-effects building in a low-budget
disaster movie, fracturing into countless tiny pieces
which in turn disintegrated into a gray dustlike powder. This too was caught by the wind and carried out
into the night.

Joe Mosely was gone, leaving behind not so much
as a depression in the bedcovers.

The front door finally closed behind Martha's efforts and I heard the bolt slide home. She walked up to
the bedroom door but did not step inside.

"Joe's gone, isn't he?" she said in a low voice.

I couldn't speak. I opened my mouth but no words
would come out. I simply nodded as I stood there
trembling.

She stepped into the room then and looked at the
bed. She looked at the broken window, then at me.

With a sigh she sat on the edge of the bed and ran her hand over the spot where her husband had lain.

My home phone rang at eight o'clock the next morning. It didn't disturb my sleep. I had been awake all night. Part of the time I'd spent lying rigid in bed; most had been spent here in the kitchen with all the lights on, waiting for the sun.

It was an awful wait. When I wasn't reliving the scene in the Mosely bedroom I was hearing voices. If it wasn't Joe Mosely telling me that Doc Johnson had put something in his wound, it was Doc Johnson himself talking about making life-and-death decisions, talking about triage with literary references.

I hadn't told Jessie a thing about it. She'd think I was ready for a straightjacket. And if by some chance she *did* believe it, she'd want to pack up and get out of town. But where to? There was the baby to think about.

I had spent the time since dawn going over my options. And when the phone rang, I had no doubt as to who was calling.

"I understand Joe Mosely is gone," Doc Johnson said without preamble.

I said, "Yes."

. . . *a hollow man* . . .

"Any idea where?"

"Out the window," I said. My voice sounded half dead to me. "Beyond that, I don't know."

. . . *calling the police is not my way of handling the likes of Joe Mosely* . . .

"Seen anything lately worth writing to any of the medical journals about?"

"Not a thing."

. . . the diseased limb has to be lopped off and discarded . . .

"Just another day in Greystone Bay," Doc Johnson said.

"Oh, I hope not." I could not hide the tremor in my voice.

. . . sometimes triage has to be of a more active sort where radical decisions must be made . . .

He chuckled. "Charles, my boy, I think you'll do all right here. As a matter of fact, I'd like to refer a couple of patients to your office today. They've got complicated problems that require more attention than I can give them at this time. I'll assure them that they can trust you implicitly. Can you take them on?"

I paused. Even though my mind was made up, I took a deep breath and held it, waiting for some argument to come out of the blue and swing me the other way. Finally, I could hold my breath no longer.

"Yes," I said. "Thank you."

"Charles, I think you're going to do just fine in Greystone Bay!"

AT THE BENTNAIL INN

by Robert E. Vardeman

"BE CAREFUL, LARRY!" CRIED ANNA WEXLER. "YOU'RE driving too fast."

"It's this damned road," Larry Wexler grumbled. "Winds all over and the fog. Damn the damn fog. Can't see a damn thing."

"Stop swearing," Anna said sharply. She settled back on her side of the car and stared straight ahead into the white veil of fog, hands folded primly in her lap. "You know I don't like it when you swear."

Wexler said something too low for the woman to hear. She turned, a strand of neatly coiffured auburn hair falling from its place. "What did you say?" she demanded, her voice brittle.

"You wouldn't want me to repeat it. Not if you don't want me swearing." He cast a quick look at his wife, fuming. The road had been made by some demented highway engineer, each curve designed to ensure that he'd lose control in the fog, no matter how slowly he went. And for what?

Larry Wexler snorted and hunched over the wheel, trying to concentrate but finding that his anger mounted too much. His wife wanted this vacation. Such a nice little harbor city, she'd said. So quaint.

Greystone Bay.

He couldn't have cared less. His business was in ruin, the creditors circling like vultures, their beaks clacking at the idea of ripping apart his lifework—his life. His oldest daughter had run away from home twice in the past year. And now Anna wanted to "get away from it all" and take a second honeymoon.

As if six days in an out-of-the-way spot would mend all that had gone wrong in their fourteen-year marriage.

"There," Anna said suddenly, jarring him from his trance. "There's Plummer's Run."

"There's a damned cemetery," he murmured, but he guided the car expertly along the narrow lane, the fog lifting as if in silent tribute to those laid in the ground. Droplets of moisture on granite tombstones caught the headlights and reflected it back as if the eyes of the dead opened.

"There's Point Street. Head down it," she said, her voice completely neutral. She reached forward and touched the AAA tour book on the dashboard. "The Bentnail Inn will be off on the right. There!"

Larry cursed again as he missed the rough cobblestone lane. The side of the car scraped a building ancient before the Civil War and broke the door handle. He stopped and peered out the window. Opening the door might be a problem. But he didn't think he could convince his wife to turn around, go find a nice Holiday Inn near a service station, and spend a civilized night.

"This is it. Bentnail Lane. The bed and breakfast is at the end."

"In the middle of the bay," he said. The fog had again pulled misty white fingers across the small town, making every new doorway and alley a surprise.

Larry Wexler found the Bentnail Inn's sign outlined by the twin headlight beams. It didn't do much to bolster his sagging spirits. The sign had been assaulted by saltwater and storms until the lettering all but vanished. Only the rusted and bent nail driven through the center of the rotting wood gave any hint about the dilapidated building's identity.

"I suppose we can leave the car here," said Anna, craning her neck and peering into the fog. "I don't see a parking lot."

He said nothing. He gingerly opened the door. The outer handle fell off and sent clattering echoes down the silent lane. He kicked the offending handle under the car. He wanted nothing more to do with it. He wanted nothing more to do with any of this second honeymoon or the sickening "quaintness" Anna found so desirable.

"I'll see if there's anyone inside," Anna said. "You'd better get the bags. I don't think there's a bellhop." She stood erect, shoulders back, chin up, and went through the fog like the Queen of England preparing to knight a hero.

Wexler pulled their luggage from the trunk and dropped the heavier bag—Anna's—to the ground to close the trunk lid. As he reached up, a tiny, almost imperceptible scratching noise made him spin about.

For an instant, out of the corner of his eye, he

caught sight of a man dressed in rags, scrabbling in the gutter to find a discarded cigarette butt. But as quick as Larry was in turning, the apparition proved faster and faded into the fog.

"Damned bums are everywhere," he grumbled. "Even in a jerkwater place like this." He hefted the luggage and wrestled it into the lobby, where he dropped it and stared.

The outside hadn't hinted at such a fine hostelry. Anna and an older woman stood at the oak counter, working through the tedious details of registration. "Where's the phone?" he asked.

"Don't have one," the graying woman answered. "No need. Not in Greystone Bay. Who'd want to call out?" She smiled in a way reminding him of his grandmother. "And who'd *ever* want to call in?"

"You got a point," Wexler said.

"He only wants to call his lawyer. I swear, Larry, you spend too much time with her." Anna straightened her shoulders even more until she looked like a toy soldier.

"The company's going broke. I want to save it and Hill's damned good at what she does."

"Larry," his wife said primly. "This is not the time or place to discuss such matters."

"You'll have the room, top of the stairs, second on the right. A nice view of the bay," the clerk said. She seemed oblivious to the currents flowing around her. "It's a special room, one just filled with history."

"Great," Larry said sarcastically. "Let's hope it has a firm mattress, too."

He started up the stairs, then paused. In the shadows above moved a form, an amorphous shape that fleetingly came into light and vanished. Larry blinked. It looked for the world like the bum out in the street.

"Is there a back way?" he asked, eyes fixed on the stairs.

"This is it. Not much in the way of fire regulations when the inn was built back in 1893."

He hurried up the steep, narrow wood steps and stopped in the hallway littered with maple stands with marble tops and a dozen different varieties of artificial flowers. Of the bum he saw nothing. He looked at the floor, thinking he'd find wet tracks. The only damp footprints he found were those behind him —his own.

He walked along the hall, listening intently. As far as he could tell, he and Anna would be alone in the Bentnail Inn. For a second honeymoon, that would be nice. For a man whose business and life were both unraveling, it might be hell.

He opened the door and peered into the small room dominated by a huge brass bed. He edged around the bed and dropped the suitcases by a head-tall wardrobe. A small sound attracted his attention. He looked back into the hall and caught sight of the bum in a mirror mounted on one wall. He spun out of the room to face the man and found only empty, echoing hallway.

Puzzled, he went back to the lobby, where Anna still talked with the other woman.

"Where did that scroungy hobo vanish to?" he demanded.

"What are you talking about?" asked Anna.

"You must have seen him. About five foot seven, bent over, tattered rags for clothes. He was upstairs in the hall. He didn't have time to duck into any of the rooms—I'd have heard the door shutting. He had to come by you."

Larry saw the expressions on the women's faces and fell silent. He had no desire to create a scene. Shaking his head, he said, "Must be too tired from driving through the fog."

"Nothing a night's rest won't cure," the clerk said. "And I'll see that you get a good breakfast." She smiled and touched Anna's hand. "In bed."

Anna returned the smile but her face lost all warmth when she turned to her husband. She took him firmly by the arm and led him upstairs to their room. Once inside, she closed the door.

"What was all that about?" she demanded. "Are you trying to prove you're crazy? Is that what your lawyer told you to do to avoid bankruptcy?"

"Anna," he said tiredly. "I *saw* this bum. Out in the street, then in the hall. Twice."

She sniffed derisively and poked about the room, getting her clothing from the suitcases and into the wardrobe, examining the spotless adjoining bath, pointedly ignoring Wexler.

He lay back watching her, his thoughts diffuse and disconnected. Wexler tried to sort through his troubles, both marital and business, and found himself slipping off to sleep, the soft lapping of Greystone Bay providing a soothing counterpoint to his breathing.

. . . the water, the water rising around him, buoying him, letting him drift, drift to . . .

He jerked upright, eyes wide and heart pounding. He looked around the room, not recognizing it at first.

"Larry, what's wrong?" asked Anna, returning from the bathroom. "You look a fright."

"I . . ." He paused to get his thoughts into a semblance of order. "A dream, I guess. I was out on the bay, swimming or just floating. But it was different somehow and I went into a . . . a different place. Not this world."

Anna looked unimpressed. "It's the stress. You're letting it get to you." Her words stung like a whip, an accusation she had made in a dozen different ways over the past months. Larry wanted to shout, to cry out that he hadn't created their problems, that Anna ought to accept some of the blame.

But he couldn't. A part of his mind refused to release the taunting memory of that other . . . place.

He lay back down, eyes staring at the ornate patterns on the plastered ceiling. The patterns began to blur, to shift and move away. Wexler snuggled down in the softness of the comforter, tried to follow the infinite plaster curlicues and listen to the distant tide working its way to land. Again, he slipped into a dream-filled sleep.

. . . He swam in the frothy surf, working his way to land, sighting the ancient buildings and—almost —recognizing them. This had to be Greystone Bay. A part of him said that it was, while a more rational fraction of his mind worried over the dream state so obviously affecting him.

He pulled himself onto the sandy beach and shook himself like a wet dog, sending water droplets flying in all directions. Bright sun caught the drops and turned them into miniature rainbows.

And he instantly found the pot of gold at their ends. Strewn over the beach were thousands of gold coins. With a whoop of joy, he dropped to his knees and scooped up a handful. At first, his eyes refused to focus on the wealth he'd found.

The coins hardened as he held them and the edges sharpened.

"Kruggerands! Maple Leafs! Coronas! This is a fortune in gold!" he cried. On hands and knees Larry Wexler began pulling the riches in, stuffing the gold coins into his pockets until they weighed him down heavily.

"I can save my business. I can get out of hock and pay off the bank and the loan shark and—" He looked up when he came to the slim, tanned legs blocking his way. Slowly, he tipped his head back, taking in the full picture of the lovely blonde woman standing in front of him.

Legs too slim and tanned and perfect to be true blended smoothly into flaring hips sheathed in skin-tight red silk jogging shorts. A flat, bare midriff, also tanned to perfection, drew him ever upward. Breasts, full and firm and lush, hid behind a halter top which had been designed with him in mind. Larry licked his lips unconsciously as he saw—almost—the woman's breasts through the peekaboo mesh fabric.

But it was her face that truly captivated him. Never had he seen a woman more beautiful. If an angel had descended from heaven, for all its divinity, it would have seemed ugly in comparison.

When she spoke, silver bells rang. "Please, Larry, let me help you."

"What?"

"The gold. You *do* want it taken back to the house, don't you?"

"House?" He tried to shake off the feeling that he ought to know who this gorgeous woman was, where the gold had come from, that he had been here all his life.

"Oh, silly," she said, picking up the nearest coins. As she bent, he stared at her. She turned dancing green eyes on him. "Unless you don't really want to go back. Unless you want to do something else here."

"On the beach?" He looked around. No one was in sight. He tried to push out of his mind the worry about such a warm sun beating down in the middle of February. Then he found more to think about.

She came to him, softness and strength, loving and urgency.

His arms pulled the woman close and . . . Larry yelled as hard floor smashed against his legs and arm. He thrashed about and finally pulled himself upright.

Anna peered myopically at him. "You fell out," she accused. "Get back into bed and go to sleep."

He shook himself, trying to regain a sense of place. It had seemed so real to him, the gold, the sunny beach, the lovely woman.

"What a dream," he said, standing. His foot batted against something hard but he ignored it. He dropped into bed beside his wife. This time he slept dreamlessly.

When Larry awoke, it was to the sound of eating. He pried open one eye and peered out. Anna worked her way through the large breakfast the clerk had promised. He moaned and tried to pull the covers over his head. He only succeeded in getting himself tangled. With great reluctance, he sat up.

"Save some for me," he told her.

"Good," Anna said. "But almost all gone."

"To hell with it," he said. He ate two pieces of thick toast smeared with the best homemade jam he'd tasted in years, then carried the remains to the hall and placed the tray beside the door. He paused, hearing faint sounds. Trying not to appear obvious, he looked around but saw nothing.

He closed the door, waited and listened. Again he heard small noises. He jerked open the door. Eating the scraps of food from the breakfast tray was the bum he'd seen too many times before.

"You!" Larry cried. He grabbed for the man's collar. Greasy cloth ripped and let the bum escape. "Come back here, dammit!"

"What's wrong, Larry?" asked Anna, crowding past him and into the hall.

"The bum I told you about. He was eating our garbage."

She shot him a strange look. "I don't see anyone. And even if this bum of yours was finishing off our breakfast, so what? You aren't into collecting garbage, as you call it, are you?"

"Go on, be sarcastic. I'm going to find him. The landlady should at least know he's prowling around."

"Sometimes you worry me, Larry."

He was torn between going back into the room with his wife and seeking out the bum. Being clad only in his underwear decided him. He went back in and dressed.

"I'll find him," he told Anna. "You wait and see."

"What is it with you, Larry? This isn't supposed to be a big-game hunt. You're not the local police, though heaven knows this man doesn't seem to have done anything but take a few crumbs from a tray."

"You don't even believe he exists, do you?"

She looked at him, head tilted slightly. In a low voice she said, "No, I don't."

Larry slammed out of the room and took the steep steps to the lobby two at a time. The grey-haired woman stood behind the counter. He didn't bother with her. Rushing into the street, he looked up and down Bentnail Lane. Tendrils of fog lingered, obscuring his view. He started walking, as much to work off his frustration as to find the bum.

He slowed when he came to the piers. The dock area seemed familiar; it took several seconds for him to remember it from his dream. But the reality was so different. Oil spills stained the pilings, and a heavy, catch-in-the-throat fish odor pervaded the area. No pure golden sand dotted the beach. Only refuse strewn as far as he could see in the fog met his eyes.

He walked and thought. The pieces of gold on the beach? What of them? He saw only flotsam washed ashore during the night.

And the woman? Of her he saw no trace. But the buildings had the same aspect. The dream had revealed them as cleaner, more livable. Greystone Bay struck him as virtually unlivable as it was. But the dream would had been perfect!

"Perfect," he muttered to himself, eyes misting with tears as he remembered what he'd had and then lost. "Only a dream, it was only a dream."

But it had seemed more than that. Much more. No dream had such texture, such *reality*.

A feeling of being watched turned him cautious. Slowly, he turned and looked into every noisome shadow, every spot where someone might hide. From behind rusted oil drums he saw darkness moving in darkness. Quicker than a tiger, he pounced. He stumbled as he grabbed hold of a thin, sinewy arm but recovered in time to pull the man to the ground.

"Got you!" he cried, holding the bum in a schoolboy pin, his knees on the man's shoulders. Eyes wide with fear stared up at him.

"You found the way!" the bum accused.

Larry blinked in confusion. This wasn't what he'd expected the man to say when finally confronted.

"You found the way!"

"What the hell are you talking about?"

"I can see it in your face," the bum said. "I can. I know you've been *there*."

Larry shifted his weight to one side, letting the man sit up. Something deep inside him told of extreme importance in finding out what this derelict meant.

"Tell me everything," he ordered.

"You know it. You came here. You stayed in *that* room, at the Bentnail Inn. There's no other reason. You want to go *there*."

"We stayed in the room because it was available. My wife and I are on our second honeymoon." The words rang hollow and burned like acid on his tongue. He saw that he hadn't convinced the bum.

"You went *there* and saw it all. You've tasted paradise and want more. I can tell." A stricken look came over the man's face. "I went *there* once and I was fool enough to return. I shouldn't have. I should have stayed *there*."

"I had a dream," Larry said. "Is that what you're talking about?" Then it struck him as ridiculous. "But you couldn't know what was in my dream."

"Paradise," the derelict said firmly. "You found everything you've ever wanted there. And it can be like that forever." The bum leaned forward and put his face in his hands. "I was *there* but I came back and now I've lost it! I've got to go back. I've got to!"

Crazy, he thought. The man is a stark, staring crazy.

"Uh, what do you mean?" he asked, trying to calm a man who might become violent.

"You saw the place. What did you find? Wealth? It's

there for the taking. Beauty? I could paint the land-scapes and people forever!"

"You're an artist?"

"Michel Dupree."

Larry rocked back on his heels and sat heavily on the ground. He knew of Dupree's work—and how the artist had vanished over two years ago. No one had seen him since he left his loft in Tribeca in New York City. Larry was no art connoisseur, but Anna had claimed that Dupree's work was among the finest being produced in America. He had stopped her from paying an exorbitant sum at auction for a small watercolor the artist had done.

"You've been in Greystone Bay since you left New York?" he asked.

Eyes sharp with cunning fixed on him. "We're both looking for it. That bed has something to do with opening the way. Unfinished dreams. I don't know what or why, but it no longer works for me. But it does for you."

"You sneak in and sleep in that particular bed?" He was perplexed.

"That's the only way. The only way *there*."

"Just sleeping in the bed opens the way? Why didn't my wife mention it? Why didn't I see her *there*?" He shook himself. He was talking like Dupree.

"Your wife's not got much of an imagination, has she? That might be part of it. I can't say. All I know is that I must go back. It's every artist's dream."

"Being famous and rich?"

"Creating, damn you!" shouted Dupree. "That's all there is to life. *There* I can create art no one has ever before seen!"

"And riches? Like the gold I found along the

beach?" Larry had almost believed. The flare of insanity in Dupree convinced him that he had been pulled into a madman's fantasy.

"If that's what you want. Or beautiful women. Or men. Anything. Success? It can be yours. *There*."

"How have you been living? No one's seen your work in years."

Dupree shrugged. "Odds and ends about this miserable sinkhole."

"Stealing crumbs off breakfast trays?" he suggested.

"Dammit, yes! To return, I'll do anything. But I dare not leave. If . . . if I do, I might lose my chance. Nothing can stand between me and *there*!"

Larry stood and brushed the dirty sand from his pants. Dupree might have been committed and escaped. If not, he ought to be locked away where he wouldn't hurt anyone. Then he laughed ruefully. Greystone Bay was as good a place as any for a social misfit like that. Who could he hurt in this town that would matter?

"If you find the way, tell me, please!" the artist pleaded.

"Yes, yes, I will," he said. Both knew he lied.

Larry wandered the narrow streets of the town, seeing little of the quaint shops and small plaques commemorating this and that from a time long past. He walked and considered and decided that Michel Dupree had deluded himself.

Paradise? He shook his head as he turned back toward the Bentnail Inn. This world was more like hell. Only that could exist. Not paradise. Never.

He went up the steep, narrow staircase and entered the room.

"Anna?" he called. His wife had gone out. That

might be just as well. He didn't feel like facing her again, hearing her accusations, her put-downs about their life together and how he had run the business into the ground.

He threw himself on the bed, a pillow slipping out from under his head. He reached over to pick it up off the floor when a glint of gold caught his eye. Curious, he fumbled under the bed and found a gold coin. His mind recoiled. When he had awakened from the dream, he remembered having kicked something under the bed.

It was an Austrian Corona, just like the one he had picked up off the beach before encountering the blonde.

His hand began to shake and he went cold all over.

"Dupree's not crazy," he said. "This proves it."

He sat on the edge of the bed, trying to control his shaking and order his rampaging thoughts.

"Sleep, if I go to sleep," he said aloud, the words echoing in the room. "I can get to sleep, find more gold, bring it back, and save my business." He smiled wickedly. "Maybe divorce Anna. That's what she wants." Ideas of dalliance with the sun-tanned blonde on the beach floated across the surface of his mind.

"Why save the business? Why come back? Maybe Dupree was right. Stay there. Stay *there*!"

He lay down and tried to sleep, to get caught up in the dream that would transport him back to the world of success and perfection and all the things he desired most. But the harder he tried, the more awake he became.

After almost an hour of tossing and turning futilely, he rummaged through his suitcase and found the bottle of sleeping pills. He took two and quickly swallowed them without water. Stiff as a board he lay on the bed, waiting for sleep.

Slowly, he relaxed and felt the familiar lethargy of sleep overtaking him. Eagerly he sought it. The world faded into darkness for Larry Wexler, then returned, brighter, better, perfect.

Smiling, he sat up on the beach strewn with the gold coins. The gorgeous blonde waved to him and started running to greet him. He reached out for her, stumbled and fell—was pushed!

"At last, at last, I'm here!" Michael Dupree cried.

Larry looked up to see the artist. Somehow, Dupree had crowded through with him.

He started to complain, then smiled. There was no need to be angry. Paradise could be shared. He need never see Dupree again, unless he wanted.

He shrieked as the perfection around him began to fade, to turn grey and amorphous and frightening.

"Goodbye," Dupree said, smiling, his arm around the blonde, who had transformed into a slim-hipped, dark-haired Latin beauty. "There can be only one guiding genius *here*. Paradise can*not* be shared."

The artist's mocking laughter brought Larry upright in bed, cold sweat pouring down his face and body. In panic, he looked around—and saw only the tiny room at the Bentnail Inn.

He clutched the single gold coin so tightly in his hand that it drew blood around the milling.

"No," he cried, "no, I won't give it up. Not like this."

He tried to go back to sleep, to again find the way into that other, better world. He tried and failed repeatedly.

On nights cloaked in fog, a solitary figure can be seen—barely—along the streets of Greystone Bay. He lives off refuse and never strays far from the Bentnail Inn as he seeks the single dream that will take him back to a world he possessed for a brief instant, then foolishly lost.

OCCUPANT

by Kim Antieau

PETER STOPPED UNPACKING FOR A MOMENT TO GAZE down at Greystone Bay. The line where the ocean and the town met was blurred, as if the foundations of the dark New England homes were made from seawater. The morning fog shifted to the east as he watched, and the town appeared to move slightly, draping itself around the bay like some scaly prehistoric creature.

Peter turned from the window and took his typewriter out of its case. He placed it on the table near the window and then ran his fingers across the keyboard. Here in the Bay, he would finally be able to write uninterrupted. He wouldn't be bothered by Mary or the phone or his former colleagues at the newspaper. He had left all that three thousand miles away.

As he glanced out the window again, he felt a rush

of freedom. The fog had burned off and now the sun was out. He wanted to explore. He practically skipped outside and looked up and down the street. The other homes on his block were close together, yet each of the two- and three-story houses seemed like fortresses, with curtains drawn and gates closed. Steam rose from huge empty stone porches. His rented house looked puny in comparison.

He stepped through his wrought-iron gate and swung it closed behind him. The hinges creaked loudly in the silence and he glanced about uncomfortably, feeling as he had as a child when he made too much noise in the library. He grinned and went to the row of mailboxes at the curb. He shouldn't complain; he wanted a place where neighbors stayed to themselves, and had spent a week in a rented car driving up and down the coast looking for a town like Greystone Bay—one with few civic organizations or tourist attractions.

As he opened his mailbox and looked inside, he heard the echoes of children laughing. He closed the empty box and quickly walked down the deserted street toward town.

On the waterfront, Peter went into a diner with few people inside. An older woman dressed in a pink uniform came from behind the counter and held out a menu to him.

"No, thank you," he said, sliding into a booth next to the window. "I'd just like some coffee with honey, please."

"Honey?" she said. "I'm not sure we have any. I'll check in the back."

A minute later she returned with coffee and a tiny plastic bear filled with honey.

"Thank you," Peter said.

The waitress nodded and walked away. He was grateful she wasn't the talky type. He wanted to get to know the locals eventually, but for now he didn't want any distracting relationships.

Peter sighed pleasurably and leaned back in his chair. He had dreamed of living in a place near the ocean where he could spend all of his time writing. Now he had found it. He looked at the men who sat at the counter drinking coffee and talking quietly among themselves. Their faces were dark and lined, as if they had each spent a lifetime running against the wind. He wondered if any of them had pursued their dreams. He took a newspaper from the stack on the jukebox behind his table and opened it up. It was a typical small-town paper, he decided as he scanned the pages, filled with tacky local ads and gossipy news items. His dream fifteen years ago had been to work on a newspaper and win a Pulitzer. Things—people —always seemed to be in his way. Now all that had changed.

He sipped his coffee and gazed out at the bay. He was certain he was going to like this town.

Later in the morning, Peter found a grocery store within walking distance of his house. At the checkout he asked the clerk, "Is the weather always like this?"

The man nodded blankly and handed him his change.

"Thanks," Peter said, picking up his bag. "Nice talking with you."

Once home, he sat at the typewriter and stared out at the ocean. Several fishing trawlers were coming into the bay; some moved sideways as they fought the wind and waves. Mary liked fishing, he remembered.

She had tried to get him to go with her on several occasions. "You don't have to fish," she would say. "Just keep me company." He never went.

He tapped his typewriter keys and shrugged her memory away. Mary was a part of the past now, too.

Peter prepared several manuscripts to send out. As he put them in the mailbox, the mailman drove up. He let his truck idle while he whistled tunelessly and opened boxes.

"Any mail for me? Peter Gibson?" Peter asked.

The mailman looked up, squinted, and glanced at the house.

"Nope," he said.

"That's funny," Peter said. "I thought some of my mail would have been forwarded by now. I left a week ago."

"Sometimes that takes a while," the mailman said, reaching into Peter's mailbox and taking out his manuscripts. He put the flag down and started the truck forward again.

Peter watched him drive away. He should have heard from at least one of the editors by now. Several of his stories had been out for months. He shrugged. No news was better than rejection slips, he supposed, and looked up and down the street. It was Saturday afternoon, yet no one was outside washing a car or playing ball or screaming at children to behave. Nothing except silence. He walked toward the house. Perhaps it was the fog. Who would want to wash a car or play ball in the fog?

That night he dreamed of Mary. When he awakened to the sound of wind blowing against the house, he couldn't remember much, only that Mary had stood at his door knocking soundlessly. Peter got out of bed and padded into the darkened living room.

Outside, the trees looked like bloated figures bending to the harvest. Grey clouds skirted the full face of the moon. Where moonlight shone on the bay, Peter glimpsed ships with canvas sails inflated by the wind. An instant later, clouds covered the moon and the ships disappeared.

Peter sat at his desk and watched the black trees sway back and forth. Why had he dreamed of Mary? Although he left her a week ago, he stopped loving her long before. Mary knew something was wrong, but when she suggested counseling a year ago, he refused. Instead he sat at his typewriter knocking out short stories between assignments at the newspaper, biding his time and waiting for the right moment to change his life. The night he left, Mary sat on the bed crying quietly while she watched him pack.

"You never even tried," she told him. "You never even put your name on the mailbox."

"I didn't promise to stay," he said.

Poor Mary. He had not meant to hurt her, really; he had just—forgotten her.

He looked out his front window. Several windows in his neighbors' houses glowed golden, as if lit from the inside by candles. Perhaps the electricity had gone out because of the storm. He turned on the desk lamp. The darkness seemed solid. Only his typewriter was illuminated. He switched on the machine. As long as he could see to type, he had all the light he needed.

A week passed and still Peter received no mail. When he went to the post office and questioned the postmaster, the man smiled and shrugged. "These things happen," he said. Peter wrote to his former post office in California to make certain they had his correct change of address.

He spent most of his time writing. Sometimes he

walked to the wharf restaurant and had lunch. The same waitress always served him. Each day she treated him as though she had never seen him before. The clerk at the store was the same way. Peter told himself they needed time to warm up to him. It was a small town, after all, and he was a stranger.

At the end of the week, he put out another manuscript. The mail truck pulled up.

"Good day," the mailman said.

Peter grinned, glad the man had noticed him.

"Any mail for me today?" Peter asked.

The mailman squinted and looked out at the ocean. The horizon was covered with clouds.

"Damn fog," the mailman said. He opened Peter's box and took out his manuscript. "No mail for you," he finally said.

"I can't understand it," Peter said. "Isn't there at least something addressed to 'occupant'?" He smiled.

"Nope," the mailman said. The truck jerked forward.

Peter went into his house and tried to think of someone to whom he could write. If he sent letters, perhaps someone would answer them. He typed notes to his former editor and one of the reporters at the paper. He hadn't written to either of his brothers, Dave and Mark, for years. They spoke on the phone occasionally during the holidays, but that was it. After his parents died ten years earlier, he lost touch with them. Now he felt awkward typing out letters to them. What could he say? He knew so little about their lives.

Some time later, he sealed the letters and went outside in the dark to put them in the mailbox. He paused before going inside again. The fog made the streetlights glow unnaturally. Everything was indistinct; lines wavered. He could barely tell where his neighbors' houses began and the darkness ended. He put the flag up. He hoped someone would write soon.

When Peter awakened the next morning, he felt edgy. He sat at his typewriter and wrote as usual, but he couldn't concentrate. He watched for the mail truck. After it came and left, he ran outside, opened the box, and put his hand inside. It was empty. Why wasn't there an advertisement at least? What about his magazine subscriptions? Didn't he owe someone money somewhere? He went back to his typewriter and wrote to his magazine editors, his banks, old school friends. Someone would have to answer.

Several days passed and still there was no mail. Whenever Peter left his house, he felt eyes watching him through curtained windows. He wondered if they waited until he was away to come out of their homes. Downtown Greystone Bay moved about like any other town, except Peter felt like he wasn't there. The stupid waitress still had to be asked to bring honey for his coffee. And the clerk called him Mr. Morgan or Mr. Jones, even after he had taken a check from Peter and looked right at his name.

The fog was everywhere, clinging to Peter like a damp shirt. Sometimes it cleared, and he went down to the bay and walked along the tidemark. Even the gulls appeared indifferent, hardly acknowledging him when he tossed stones at them.

One afternoon he went to the post office.

"What is happening with my mail? I can't believe it could take this long to get to me," he told the postmaster.

The man smiled at him. "Mr. Gibbons—"

"Gibson!" Peter cried. "How can you expect to get my mail to me when you can't even remember my name!"

"Mr. Gibson, I assure you, if you were getting any mail we would deliver it," the man said. "You probably have a pile of it in the Colorado post office—"

"California!" Peter cried. He strode out of the post office and into the fog.

He suddenly longed for the noisy city room. Everyone there had at least known his name.

Hadn't they?

He tried to remember what they had called him. He breathed deeply. It was stupid to get so upset, he told himself. The mail would come tomorrow.

The mail didn't come, then or the next day. One morning Peter woke up feeling ill. He coughed and shivered and walked around the house with a comforter pulled about his shoulders. He wished he had gotten a phone. Then he could at least call his editors and see why none of his stories had come back.

"That's it," he whispered as he shook off the comforter. "I'll get a phone." He needed to speak with someone from the outside. He pulled on a sweater and laughed. The sound was strange to his ears. "From the outside," he murmured. "I'm talking about this town as if it were a prison."

He stepped out into bright sunshine. He looked up and down his street, almost expecting to see California adobe or Spanish colonial houses, but the brick Greystone Bay homes remained, looking less somber in the sun. Some of the curtains were open. Peter walked briskly down the sidewalk. The flags were up on the mailboxes. The mailman was running late today.

At the phone store, they told Peter it would be two weeks before they could install a phone. He gave them a deposit, arranged for a date and time, and walked outside again.

The fog had rolled in. Shivering, Peter hurried to the wharf restaurant.

"What would you like?" the waitress asked him as he sat down.

"Coffee with honey, please," he said.

"Honey? Gosh, I'll see if we have any," she said, turning away.

"Yes! Honey!" he called after her. "You had it yesterday!"

Several people turned to look at him. He picked up the paper and tried to read, but the words blurred. He wondered if he had a cold or the flu. He put his hand on his forehead; his skin was damp.

The waitress brought coffee and the little plastic bear of honey and then left without a word. Peter stared after her. He had to talk to someone who knew him.

"Mary," he whispered. He hurried to the pay phone by the rest rooms. A white "out of order" sign hung from the receiver. Peter slapped two quarters on the counter and left the restaurant.

Outside, the fog moved all around him, thick and white. He walked slowly. Buildings seemed to come and go as the fog swirled about the town. Peter tried a phone near the post office. It was out of order, too. He went from street corner to street corner, and each phone was out of order, as if everywhere the fog had been, the lines had gone down.

On the west side of town, Peter found a telephone that worked. He fumbled in his pocket for change and came up with only forty-five cents. He would have to call collect.

He stepped inside the booth and pushed 0 and then the number. "Collect from Peter," he told the operator. The phone began ringing at the other end. Peter

glanced around anxiously. He could see nothing beyond the fog. He stared at the silver push-button
squares. "Come on," he said, "answer the phone."

"Hello," a man said.

"Collect from Peter," the operator said. "Will you
accept?"

"Peter? Just a minute," he said. "Mary! There's a
collect call from a Peter."

Peter heard Mary's voice in the background. "Peter
who?" she asked.

Peter slammed down the receiver. What a nasty
trick, pretending she didn't know him! He kicked the
phone booth. She certainly hadn't wasted any time
finding someone else.

"Calm down, Peter," he told himself. "This is
stupid. Call Mark. Your own brother will remember
you."

He took the number from his wallet and pushed the
buttons slowly. The phone began ringing.

He heard his brother's voice. "Hello?"

"Will you accept a collect call from Peter Gibson?"

"Peter!" his brother said. "Well, sure, I'll accept.
How are you doing, old boy? I haven't talked to you in
two years!"

"Mark," Peter sighed, leaning into the phone. "You
can't imagine how good it is to hear your voice. I'm
stuck out in the middle of this nasty little town
working up a deep depression."

"Where are you? You didn't let us know you'd
moved," Mark said.

"I wrote you last week," Peter said. "Didn't you get
it? I'm in Greystone Bay."

"Greystone, eh?" Mark said. "No wonder you're
depressed. I've been through there; it isn't the friend-
liest of places. It's not far from here, you know.

Maybe two hundred miles. You should come up for Thanksgiving."

"That would be great," Peter said. "I hadn't realized we were that near to each other."

"Well, you have been somewhat of a stranger for a number of years, now, haven't you? We can fix that, though. I've got to run. Kathy's waiting. We've got tickets to the theater. But do keep in touch. The kids would like to see their other uncle."

"I will," Peter said, smiling, hugging the phone to his shoulder.

"I'm glad you called," Mark said. "See you soon, Dave."

Mark hung up. Peter stared at the receiver. "Peter," he whispered. "I'm Peter."

He opened the door and went outside. The sun had set and it was nearly dark. Or light. He couldn't tell through the fog. He looked around until he had his bearings and then he started home.

It was Greystone, he decided. It drained him. Or had this all started long before, when he began spending most of his time alone? He shook his head. He was being ridiculous. There were people out there who knew him, and he would hear from one of them soon. He looked down at his arms. He could hardly see them for the fog. He peered more closely at them. It was almost as if he could see right through them. His heart raced. He looked down at his chest. Was he seeing the ground through his chest? He closed his eyes. No. He was imagining all of it. He was fine, he was whole. He had just been out of touch for too long. Besides, he had a cold and his thought processes weren't functioning properly. He hurried up his road. His legs. He could barely see his legs. He wanted to scream or run. Something was not right. How could he run without legs? The fog twisted around him. The mailbox. That's it. This had all started because of the mail, but there would be mail in the box today. There had to be. Then he would be all right.

He ran. He stumbled once and his fingers touched the cobblestone. The stone was hard and slippery. He could feel it, but he couldn't see his own fingers or arms. He ran and ran. Suddenly, the shadows of the mailboxes loomed up at him, looking like the tines of a giant fork.

His hand trembled on the lip of his box as he pulled it open.

It was empty.

He opened his mouth to scream, and no sound came out.

The mail truck pulled up to the row of boxes. A child ran in front of the truck, chasing a bright red ball. Someone washing a car called to the child and waved at the mailman. He waved back. He opened the boxes one at a time and put mail inside.

When he opened Peter Gibson's box, a wisp of fog floated up into the clear blue sky and then disappeared.

"Damn fog," the mailman murmured.

He slipped a piece of mail marked "occupant" into the box and then he drove away.

PRAYERWINGS

by Thomas Sullivan

"HERE!" SHE SAID.

She had a voice that went all gossamer at moments of delight, but when you looked at her, you looked at her eyes. Great blue eyes that took you round and round with mischief before letting you in. She was a woman who waited a long time for things—the right future, the right man, the right moment—and now they had all come with a rush, and she had Michael beside her and her trousseau in the trunk of the LeBaron and a postcard town that teased the sea in its lap in her lap as they looked down from the stark northern cliffs and read the roadside sign.

She couldn't be wrong about her choices. Not after being so patient. It had to be the right town, too. There was gossamer in her voice as she repeated:

"Here . . . this is where I want to honeymoon. In Greystone Bay."

His broad, smooth brow was too strong to pucker. It just sort of whitened. What he saw was a satyr of a town, half beast, half civilized. There were avenues neatly dicing pleasant neighborhoods and larger enterprises housed in the red brick of native clay, but at this distance they looked more like outposts on the corpse of a different Greystone Bay. Many corpses. There was the one of quaint cottages, picturesque but weathered and melancholy, and another of frame mansions, and again skeins of lately encroaching vegetation where the earth had curiously begun to buckle and warp as if to evict still older dwellings and fences. These last stuck out at nightmarish angles. A large mill of some kind—or was it a prison?—had burned and sat scowling through charred rows of monotonous windows above the south end. And then there were the moldering hovels centralized and closer to the beach, dust returning to dust, perhaps the historical root of a village that had never been able to reconcile change. The overall effect of Greystone Bay was of a saurian creature shedding its skin, green and glittering here, dead and decaying there. Only, he couldn't tell whether it had crawled out of the sea to die or was trying to flee back into it.

"You sure?" he asked.

"It's perfect." Gossamer.

"What do I know? I'm just a sex-starved manufacturer's rep who trashed his accounts to get married and go find a bedroom with a lock on the door."

Smiling pertly, she pulled the seat belt across his lap and clicked it home. She was glad she had made him wait. It may have been old-fashioned, but it had shown he really loved her, and now she had the right man at the right moment in the right place.

"Passion-restraint system," she said about the seat belt. "And you didn't trash your accounts. And I intend to make it worth your wait tonight."

"Tonight? We've still got three hours of daylight. If we don't find a bed quick, I'm going to give this burg an X rating right on the corner of Horizontal and Main."

"Patience, dear boy." She ran bone-white fingers through his black, swept-back hair. "Let's check in somewhere and then take a walk by the ocean."

"You want water? We'll sprint around a hot tub."

"There!" she exclaimed.

"A hot tub?"

"A room to rent. Stop."

He stopped.

"Oh, Michael, look at it. They don't make houses like that anymore."

"Not since building codes."

"It's exactly right for a wedding night. Let's take the room."

He yanked his sunglasses off, blinked down the road. "Probably a Holiday Inn up there with a bridal suite right on the ocean."

"Please, Michael, this is important . . . I want to make love to you in that house."

"Hot damn."

The LeBaron shot into the drive of something rambling and Victorian. Bright yellow clapboards and white trim gave it a confectionery appearance. Leaded cames and stained glass dignified it. The woman—Mrs. Lorcaster—who came slowly to the door as if from realms beyond a mere house was the same: leaded with creases, dignified as glass, but with a bright, confectionery smile.

"Twenty a night and breakfast," she told them. "I'll get you towels and soap. Please watch out for the cat, she likes to sleep on the footstool in the spare room."

Spare room. Except for the parlor and the kitchen where the old widow trafficked, all the rooms were vestigial.

"Where can we see something historical?" Sue asked of their hostess as soon as the suitcases were settled in.

The confectionery smile sagged then and introspection came into the old lady's eyes, as if to say that she herself was history. But she waved seaward and perhaps a little southward to where the charred monolith scowled. And that was where they went and found . . .

The cemetery.

Like the town it had its divisions, neighborhoods bounded by ages, time zones. The architecture ranged from gleaming granite to chalky limestone thawing into the elements. The landscape mirrored these extremes—new grass, old grass, virile shrubs, sucked-dry brambles—as if the newer cadavers were still pumping out life while the suppurated ones had exhausted it. The only exception was the thing in the very center of the oldest part.

It was an arboretum and its perimeter was thick and lush. Behind it was yet another, green to the point of blackness, and so closely hemmed as to belie rational planting. The barren, unscratchable ground that surrounded it seemed to have loaned its nutrients to some protean cavern that fed the surface there.

Sue peered through the branches. "Now, who do you suppose is in that one?"

"A sex fiend who died of rust."

She slid away from his caress. "Is that a gate or a cage?"

He followed her closer to the frail wire structure that rose within.

"It's a trellis," he said.

"For what?"

"For all that ivy."

She tried to follow it with her eyes, a fragile viridescence, palpitating, radiating, disappearing in a greener than green wall, reappearing where open sky should have been.

"It's a cage," she affirmed. "And why are there two gates?"

He stepped in front of her now, staring in. There was a wire annex separating the gates. "Don't know. But that other is definitely a framework for the ivy." He put his hand on the latch.

"Sign says that's a no-no."

It lay at the foot of a juniper, a carved tablet, streaked and barely legible:

PRIVATE BURIAL PLOT
NO TRESPASSING

"I don't see any grave markers in there." He was thinking that the place was probably a bower for Friday night's passionate teenagers. "Let's take a look."

He unlatched the first gate.

Despite the openness of the wire mesh, something intangible seemed to be released. It wafted by them, an atmosphere—pungent, hermetic, hot. They passed through into a slightly altered realm whose subtle diminutions suggested the aberrations of a fairy tale. There was the low ceiling of the cage beyond the second gate, for instance, like a child's playhouse, and the tiny perfection of each leaf, shimmering a green greener than the chloroplasts any earthbound botany could account for.

She leaned over, a wisp of hair touching his bicep. "There's a tombstone."

He brought his cheek close to hers, slid his right hand around her waist. There was a stone, deep in the shadows of the place. He laced the fingers of his left hand in the mesh just above the second latch.

"Oww-w!" he cried, jerking them free again. "Damn ivy has thorns."

But now the vibration set up by his contact with the wire seemed to free the stuff in a great, green undulation. Silent energy tore around the cage, light and air punched through, and the leaves began to dance apart like . . .

"Butterflies," she murmured.

Butterflies. Palpitating in a silent frenzy that gave the illusion of roaring flight. Around and around they went, emerald motes flowing together now in a sunshot ether, and revealing in the dappled luminescence of their dementia the inscription on the stone:

REGINALD DEAKEN
1771–1809

What travesty would imprison butterflies?

It was beautiful but somehow grotesque, and she threw him a quick, fearful glance. "You're not going in?"

"Why not?"

He had the second latch disengaged. Already one of the smaller insects was shivering through the crack.

"Because . . . they'll all get out."

"So what?"

"Maybe they're not supposed to get out."

Behind them the outer gate rang shut and a pipestem man, bug-eyed and bewhiskered, hurtled past to push the inner one tightly closed. The butterfly wriggling through was caught by a single wing and held pulsing against the latch.

The pipestem man rocked and scrutinized the cage, hands poised inches from the mesh, as he ranted: "Damn you . . . damn, damn, damn!"

"Who the hell are you?" from Michael.

He whirled around. "I could have you arrested for this. Desecrating a grave—" The butterfly lost its wing, fluttering to the ground. "There's a sign out there"—he caught himself up, eyeing the powdery green thing semicircling toward his shoe—"for those who don't have the sense to leave memorials alone."

"We're sorry," Sue intervened. "We didn't mean any disrespect."

Michael resisted the pull on his sleeve, sizing his adversary up and down.

"Leave!" commanded the pipestem, and advancing a step he precisely crushed the crippled butterfly.

"Now, that's really respectful!" Michael scoffed, but Susie had him around and in transit.

"Something's wrong with him," she whispered. "Look at his clothes."

He started to turn back, and that was when he tripped over a small wooden bucket the pipestem man had apparently set down. Whatever was in it stayed in it. But not the smell of something nightmarish.

"What in hell is that?" he grimaced.

"Let's go," she pleaded.

He let her lead him away, back through the segregated neighborhoods of Greystone Bay's dead, back to the LeBaron parked facing the ocean.

"Didn't you see what he was wearing?" she asked when they had turned up Port Boulevard.

"A straightjacket."

"It was broadcloth. And he had breeches on. Like some kind of colonial sailor."

"Standard uniform for butterfly zookeepers in these parts."

"It's a weird way to beautify a grave, but I'll give him a nine for effort."

"Whatever is in that bucket is a minus six."

"It smelled like a dead cat."

"Butterfly food. You can't skimp with those carnivores."

"Or on brides. Do I have to cook on the honeymoon?"

They ate at the Red Foxe Inn on the north cliffs —crab and lobster hors d'oeuvres, prime rib, mulled ruby port. And then they went back to their Victorian lodgings in anticipation of a very un-Victorian dessert.

The right man, the right place, the right moment.

You waited and you savored, she thought. You made them right. He had wanted her so badly when they got into the room, spinning her around, landing on her mouth with his, grasping her with hands that seemed to shape her as they explored. The tongue and the fingers and the crushing pleasure of his body had almost melted her beyond resistance. But she did resist. Because it wasn't the right way to come to him. Not the first time.

She made him shower and shave, and while he waited in bed she took a bath.

It was the right bath, a Cleopatra bath with the frangipani oil and the sandalwood perfume she had packed in her suitcase. Then came the right outfit: a lavender corset from Frederick's of Hollywood, sheer nylons, an insignificant bikini you could have laced a shoe with if it didn't have too many eyes. Michael would be all eyes. When he saw how ripe she was and how bold she could be, he would burst into flames like Christmas wrap in a fireplace.

She stroked perfume under her breasts, inside her thighs. Tugged the bikini up tight. Then she opened the door and sauntered toward the bed, nylons hissing promises of friction.

He was facing her, the light from the bathroom behind her. She stopped, put her hands on her hips, shifting her weight seductively.

He just lay there.

Stunned the poor boy, she thought, and taking another two steps, she arched her hips forward a little. "Well . . . ?"

And then she saw that his eyes were closed.

It was not the right thing to happen, not a funny ploy at all. But he wouldn't play it for long. Not if he peeked a little and saw her practically begging for it. She put her knee on his chest.

"Well, I guess I'd better put my pajamas on before I catch cold standing here almost naked." She rocked her knee. No reaction. "Michael?" He couldn't actually be asleep. She hadn't taken *that* long.

But he was.

She straddled him. Ran her fingers down his neck below his ears. Jiggled her bottom. And that was when she understood that it was something more than sleep.

"Oh, my God, Michael—"

She grabbed a robe and ran to the stairs, calling for Mrs. Lorcaster.

The old lady was still in the kitchen, brewing tea. She looked whiter and even more wrinkled in the lights, but her eyes had the steady vigor of one who had known crises before.

"I can't wake him up, he just lies there," Sue babbled, and it would have been a funny wedding-night complaint if her hands and voice weren't shaking. She followed the widow back up to the bedroom, lagging a little at the door.

"Is he diabetic?" Mrs. Lorcaster snapped, staring down at him from a few feet away.

"No," Sue whispered.

"He's never talked about this happening before?"

"No."

"Has he been drinking?"

". . . a glass of wine. Not enough to—"

"Where?"

"At the Red Foxe Inn."

"You ate there?"

"We ate the same thing. I feel fine. We had seafood appetizers—"

"Some people are allergic to crab or oysters."

"Not Michael."

The widow softened. "He doesn't look ill, my dear. Your wedding night may be ruined, but you'll have many years to make that up. I'll call a doctor. Can you think of anything else you did or ate that I can tell him about? It might help. Was he feeling well all day, for instance?"

"He was fine. Eager for this. We just drove down to the end of town you showed us, and we stopped by a cemetery where there was a cage full of butterflies—"

The old lady stiffened. Susie felt it rather than saw it. When she looked up, the rheumy grey eyes were as steady as ever.

"You went to Deaken's grave?" came the prompting.

"Yes . . . I guess so. But we didn't go all the way in."

"The butterflies were out?"

"Out?"

"You saw them?"

"They were in the cage. We didn't go in . . . just to the second gate."

"I'll call Dr. Plummer."

He came within minutes, a tall, elegant man, almost as old as the widow Lorcaster, and he took Michael's pulse and blood pressure, checked his pupils, and listened to the story about the cemetery with a look of defeat. Afterward he asked the questions he must ask—had Michael ever fainted? was he on medications? did anyone in his family suffer seizures?—and then he began scrutinizing Michael's arms and hands with a lens.

"You're sure he never came in contact with the butterflies?" he pressed her gently.

"We didn't go in. One of them got out, but that odd little man I told you about stepped on it."

"How did it get out?"

"Michael started to open the gate. We thought it was ivy at first, and he touched the screen and . . ." She lit up. *"He said the ivy had thorns!"*

The doctor was already examining her husband's fingers. It was only a moment before he seemed to find what he wanted. When he looked at her next it was with real command.

"I'm not going to gloss this over," he said. "Your husband is in a coma. He may come out of it in a few days, he may not. But he mustn't be moved, and he mustn't have disturbances around him. I strongly suggest you wait before you notify any relatives. I know this is difficult, but if you want to give him the best chance, you must keep people away from him. I'll bring in what's necessary to maintain him here, and Mrs. Lorcaster, I believe, will handle the care. If at the end of a week he doesn't show signs of coming out of it, you can do as you wish."

Her eyes flashed. "What do you mean, 'do as I wish'?"

"Mrs. McDonald, there is no treatment for this. Either he'll survive or he won't. A week will make it clear."

"Are you trying to tell me the butterflies poisoned him?"

"They did something to him."

She tried to laugh, but it was harsh and short "You know that for a fact? Without a blood test or . . . or hospitalization?"

"There is no blood test. Only the circumstances and the coma. Unfortunately, the move to Bay Memorial would surely kill him. I'm sorry. I feel quite helpless. And I'm afraid I'm the only physician who has had experience with this. The insect is unique to the area."

She was stunned and outraged. She accused him of incompetence, of folklore delusions. She said she would move Michael anyway, call his whole family tree and half the doctors in the state. They would come en masse to carry her and her husband out of this vile cancer on the sea. He listened sadly, repeated that no one else would recognize what had happened and that they would kill Michael with searching. She would end up with an inconclusive autopsy report for consolation. And then he showed her his credentials. She stayed stunned and outraged. But in the end she let them take control. Because she was also very, very frightened.

"The odd little man you spoke of is Coddy," Mrs. Lorcaster explained much later. Susie had calmed down some and they sat together in the bedroom where Michael lay. "He's a direct descendant of Reginald Deaken, whose grave you visited. The Deakens go back to the founding of Greystone Bay. Coddy is peculiar."

She said it as though the last two statements were linked.

"Does he breed lethal butterflies?" Sue asked caustically.

"He . . . discovered them. Encouraged them, I suppose."

"Why?" Passion went into the question now. "Why doesn't someone just kill them?"

Abruptly the wrinkles galvanized. "The old families cannot be meddled with if they stay within their places. The butterflies were in the cage on Reginald Deaken's grave, after all, and they don't appear often, and you were trespassing."

"But where do they come from? How come nobody knows about them? How do you know nobody knows about them?"

"This isn't the quaint, little coastal town you took it for, my dear. Greystone Bay was born of the *un*ordinary. It will always stand apart. There is no way I can convey that to a tourist or even to those with no roots here, but the earth itself seems to recycle the taints of the past, and unspeakable things come from the damned. God knows, Greystone Bay has had its share of the damned. Reginald Deaken, for one."

You couldn't expect an enlightened viewpoint from an old lady in an old house in an old town, Sue thought cynically. Yet here she sat on her wedding night with her husband in a coma, having touched a cage full of butterflies on a gravesite. She took up Michael's hand for perhaps the tenth time, locating the tiny fistula the doctor had found.

"And what was he damned for?" she asked about Reginald Deaken.

"That's another thing we don't do here. We never speak of the sins of the old families. To cast the first stone is to invite judgment. Whatever else we've been, we've had to be forgiving. Survival required it."

"Then I'll have to ask Coddy directly."

"Not likely you'll find him if he doesn't want to be found."

"Well. I know where his ancestor is."

"You're going back there?"

"I have to."

"Do you think that's wise?"

"I think . . . survival requires it."

The fog was just one more insidious development of the past twelve hours. It remained at dawn, an opaque white sheet after the blanket of night had been stripped away, and it made the search for Coddy that much more difficult. She tried the phone book, coming up with five descendants with the Deaken name. Two hung up on her; a third waited until she mentioned the gravesite; number four listened patiently, playing dumb; number five didn't answer. She groped out in search of the fifth address, but all the directions she elicited seemed dependent on landmarks shrouded in fog. And when she finally did locate the weathered cottage on the south shore, it was as impenetrable as the dawn to her knock.

Fog. Coddy's cerements. Mrs. Lorcaster had warned her he would be hard to confront.

So she went to the cemetery.

Whatever had been green on her wedding day was now black, and the whites of the newest tombstones were grey. She picked her way through, straining to see the ground and generally moving uphill to where the silhouettes of other markers stood in ordinal rows against the ghost-light. The arboretum was easily the darkest and most conspiratorial cluster. Now that it was in sight, she dreaded what she was about to do.

The latch was wet and cold. She turned it slowly, measuring out her courage and a warning of her arrival. *Attention, things . . . are you there?*

They were always there.

She passed into the annex, went to the second gate. There was nothing clinging to the cage wall that she could distinguish. The few feet of earth she could make out clearly looked bare. For a long while she stared into the mist, seeking telltale shadows, movement. Where did they go in fog? What did they do at night? They couldn't possibly fly, she thought. Those powdery emerald wings would have to dry in sunlight first. But they might be crawling around. They might be clustered in some shadow overhead. She had the second gate open now. They might drop on her . . . One step, two. The earth felt different. Softer, spongier. The fog seemed to be staining her shoes. She quickened her pace to the tombstone, not sure what she expected to find. There was a tiny key light in her purse, which she retrieved and directed inch by inch down the marker. But nothing save the name and dates appeared, no worn lettering, no plaque with cryptic eulogy. The sins of this crazy Deaken family were not to be hinted at here. Still, their dynasty had caused or at the least allowed her tragedy to happen by the very existence of this grave—certainly they understood better than any others what had happened. The key light shone at the bottom of the stone now, and that was when she saw that the fog really had stained her shoes. Only it wasn't the fog. It was the powder she had stirred with each step. Because her shoes were emerald green.

The ground was covered with wings.

Just wings. The butterflies were gone. She knew already *where* they had gone, but she didn't want to think about it. Not here. Not now. Nausea iced her brow and plummeted like a pile driver into her stomach. She thought she tasted oranges beneath the dryness in her mouth. *I'm safe,* she kept telling herself. *The butterflies are gone, I've got to finish looking.* She backed off the grave, stumbled behind it. Something else was there. A pile of rotting wood and peat. Some of the timbers were still clinging together, and the key light traced a graceful arc to the single word *Pilgrim*. That was all she could stand before unconsciousness threatened to pull her down. Because the butterflies were not really gone, and she thought she understood now what Mrs. Lorcaster had meant about them not appearing often. The vile little things had mated and gone underground to lay their eggs. With atavistic fervor they had swarmed back to their origins, which, she had no doubt, lay in the putrid grave of Reginald Deaken.

It came out of the fog at the corner of Port Boulevard and Red Sky Road, a sprawling frame house with huge windows tiered in even rows. She saw the books through the glass before she read the sign: *Greystone Bay Library.* That was where she wanted to go. The past in a building. Greystone Bay's past.

She parked on a crescent drive and passed through the foyer into an irregularly shaped room watched over by the obligatory spinster type. The woman behind the desk wore no jewelry, was clad to the chin in silk, and offered a raptorial gaze over teacup lenses. The look said, "Speak!" But Sue McDonald was not about to be bullied anymore, and she stopped in the middle of the floor to slowly survey the shelves. *History* was an interior wall between *Biography* and *Reference.* It took her less than ten minutes to acquit it; Greystone Bay was not a matter of record in its own domain. Or else it had fallen between the cracks.

She tried the microfiche, the clipping file, the card catalog, even the *Reader's Guide.*

"May I help you?" The frost-pinched voice of the librarian came just as her patience was unraveling.

"This bloody little town hasn't got any help," Sue rattled acidly, "only dirty little mysteries."

The matron went all smooth then, as if she had just understood something. "Yes," she said, "lots of them."

It backed Sue down some, this unruffled acknowledgment, and in a moment she was dumping on her, telling her everything from how much she loved Michael to Dr. Plummer's unscientific handling of his coma and the whole crazy episode with Coddy. The librarian's eyes remained steady until she mentioned Coddy, and then they closed for a few seconds—a mind swallowing an unpleasant fact—and when they opened again the fact remained indigestible there.

"You're too young to be married," she said.

"Thank you very much," Sue replied wearily, and swung away.

"I can tell you that Dr. Plummer is the only man to have dealt with this before."

She stopped, gave the librarian three quarters of her profile and all of her attention.

"When he says your husband will die if he's moved, believe it."

"Am I too young to be a widow?"

The librarian never blanched. "You're too young to understand that the past doesn't always die for the present. Newness doesn't fill the cup. It dilutes it. Greystone Bay is a different brew, and you can't march in here and expect the same high-technology world you left to be waiting for you."

Sue searched her openly. "What's the matter with you people? You've got TVs, cars. You know there have to be sensible reasons for things."

"The Deakens go back to the founding. Reginald Deaken committed a crime for which he was stoned and buried apart from the rest of the community." She was looking at the emerald stains on Sue's shoes now. "His grave is a festering thing. No one from the old town would question it. But if you want a more rational explanation, you'll have to pretend coincidence brought the Prayerwings to that site and that Coddy bound them to it. Their breeding cycle would bring them back there now anyway, I suspect. The cage just protects the rest of us."

"Prayerwings? The butterflies? You're telling me this whole thing is supernatural?"

"Oh, I think it's very natural. At least in Greystone Bay. But it's not very scientific. To a lot of folk around here science seems like a pompous ass. We'll be happy indeed when it broadens its understanding to include us."

"I don't believe this. You're all looney-tunes and you're acting like it's the rest of the world—" She broke down, and the older woman put a hand on her shoulder. Sue shrugged it off gently but firmly. "What was Reginald Deaken's crime?"

"We don't speak about each other's sins here in Greystone Bay."

She sounded like Mrs. Lorcaster now. "Is it against the rules to kill butterflies, too?"

"It's against the rules to trespass graves."

Just like Mrs. Lorcaster. "Oh, yes. You don't 'meddle with the old families.'"

Silence.

"Well, one of the old families has meddled with mine before it got started, and I intend to do something about it!"

She drove recklessly through the fog, daring the town to get in her way, in a hurry to reach Michael, frustrated that there was so much helplessness. You asked librarians about the past, taxi drivers about the present, but whom did you ask about the future?

He had moved. She came into the bedroom and he was curled up in a fetal position, and that was good. Except that he was clasping his stomach, his lips were drawn back, and he was drooling blood and spittle.

"Michael, Michael . . ." she tremoloed, stroking, kissing, hugging.

There were little noises coming out of him.

"Call an ambulance from the nearest hospital!" she demanded of Mrs. Lorcaster.

"Dr. Plummer was here—"

"Call an ambulance!"

"He said your husband is coming out of it. He said he's going to be all right."

"He saw him like this?"

A quick, firm nod. "He said for you to call him."

Outrage and fear counterpointed through her blood once more. *The doctor said* . . . But what if he did know what he was talking about?

He answered his phone on the first ring.

"Dr. Plummer," she began, fighting to keep raw anger out of her voice. "You saw him. He's knotted in half and spitting blood—"

"Your husband is nearly conscious, Mrs. McDonald."

"He's in agony!"

"He'll survive the agony. The important thing is he's no longer in a paralytic coma. I've never seen anyone come out of it this fast."

He sounded so positive. She wanted to believe. "You're sure?"

"As sure as I can be, having seen only a half dozen cases."

"Why can't you give him something?"

"It would be risky. A muscle relaxant might deepen the coma. Anything palliative might interfere."

"Interfere with what?"

"With fighting it."

It. He didn't know what *it* was. Could she trust him?

"Mrs. McDonald, when he does come out of this he's going to have to take it easy for a while. He may not want to, and it will be up to you to restrain him."

"You're so damn upbeat . . . he's bleeding inside—"

"Mrs. McDonald?"

"I'm listening," she affirmed with an effort.

"No swimming or exercise, and no sexual relations for two weeks."

She began to laugh slowly, overwhelmed by the insanity of what was happening.

"I know you're newlyweds, but you'll have the rest of your lives—"

"Anything else, Doctor? Any spells or incantations, or should I catch a toad by the light of the full moon?"

There was a dignified pause, and he resumed with pseudo-calm: "Let me know if the coma should deepen, and don't be alarmed by his struggles. In fact, I strongly recommend you don't watch them."

"How much do I owe you, Doctor?"

"Nothing, Mrs. McDonald. Nothing at all."

You asked librarians about the past, taxi drivers about the present, and *doctors* about the future. But not this one.

She went back upstairs to Michael. He was pale as snow and sweating. *Dear God, what was the matter with that doctor?*

"Let me watch him, my dear," Mrs. Lorcaster said behind her. "You'll just be upset if you stay."

"That's my husband," Susie began, pointing to emphasize what her voice could not, ". . . that's my husband, and nobody else much cares what he's going through." She caught her breath, swallowed hard. "Any more than they care about a psychopathic family that breeds lethal insects."

"It's because nothing can be done about those things. You're the only one we can help."

"You want to help me?" She engulfed the woman with teary eyes. "Then tell me what Reginald Deaken did, for starters."

"It wouldn't do you any good to know."

"Then tell me what Coddy wants with those butterflies, or are they called Prayerwings?"

"Prayerwings to some. *Prey*erwings to others. The original name was He-Flies. And I don't think Coddy wants anything to do with them. He feels mandated to tend them the way his family has always tended them since Reginald's time."

"Why?"

"Because the town stoned a Deaken to death. The He-Flies were retribution for a time. Somewhere along the line a compromise was struck. Whatever remains unsettled of Reginald Deaken continues its cycle, but the townspeople are safe as long as they stay away from the gravesite."

"That's pure folklore."

"You asked for an explanation. There's nothing more to know, my dear."

"Oh, yes." She looked at her husband on the bed. "There's plenty more. I went back there. They're gone. They dropped their wings or something and crawled underground." Rheumy grey eyes refused to waver in front of her. ". . . and Coddy with that bucket, what was he doing?"

"Feeding them, I imagine."

"It stunk."

"The He-Flies are carnivorous and voracious. It was probably meat."

And now Susie blanched, because she saw the connection. "Michael . . . that thing was trying to eat Michael—"

"No."

"The little beasts really are carnivorous."

"They eat carrion mostly."

"Like Reginald Deaken's corpse?" Her tone was near hysteria.

"You ought to lie down, Mrs. McDonald—"

"And then they mate and go back under . . ." She really did feel faint, dropping onto the footstool, narrowly avoiding the cat. "What was that thing with *Pilgrim* written on it?"

"It was a longboat from a packet ship, *The Pilgrim*. She foundered and sank in a storm. Reginald Deaken and one of the helmsmen—who was also the ship's chaplain—escaped in it."

"Then why is it in the cemetery?"

"Because it was considered an unholy thing."

"You mean he did whatever he did in it."

No reply.

"These . . . He-Flies, what do they turn into when they lose their wings?"

"They don't turn into anything."

"Then . . ."

"They devour each other. The wings are left."

"They're cannibalistic?"

No reply.

Nausea rose like a warm fountain in Sue's throat. *Oh, God . . .* she thought, choking it down. *Reginald Deaken ate the chaplain!*

Mrs. Lorcaster's denials echoed after her, but Sue McDonald was in motion as mindlessly and relentlessly as He-Flies in a mating frenzy. The insidious fog still blanketed everything, and the LeBaron's grille tore through it like teeth through cotton candy. She stopped at the Shell station on Port Boulevard to buy a can of gas, and then she went on to the cemetery.

She had a headache from the smell of gas as well as the tension now, and the can knelled off her knee as she struggled up the hill. Both gates were open just as she had left them. She passed through, icily aware of the change in texture beneath her feet, trying not to notice the darkening as puffs of emerald powder commingled with the fog. And then she unscrewed the cap and the silvery stuff sloshed over the mound. The act exhilarated her somehow as she raked the edge of the can down the grave and poured the remainder along the furrow. Then she stood back and lit the match.

It seemed to leap out of her hand, fire jabbing like a pointing finger into the earth, and then the whole blasphemy exploded with a sigh and a snap. The heat drove her back against the wreck of the long-boat. Flame swayed seductively above the tombstone, licking the top of the cage and threatening the cloistering trees. Bits of cindered wings climbed higher still, ascending through the gaps like pleading souls from purgatory. *Prayerwings*, flashed through her mind.

She was thoroughly mesmerized by the time he got there. He scampered through, too alarmed to pause for breath, and it wasn't until he insinuated his sweating, bewhiskered face into hers that she actually saw him.

"You're going to pay for this!" he screamed hoarsely. "You're going to pay and pay and—"

"They're dead!" she shot back, frightened but resolute. "Those little obscenities of yours are dead. I've sent them to the hell where they belong!"

He blinked at her as if she was the one who was crazy.

"I know all about you, and I know all about your cannibal ancestor," she rambled on. "I know all about these abominations, and I've put an end to them at last."

He was a mix of anger and uncertainty now. "What abominations?"

"The maggots you think crawled out of his soul!"

A very bitter smile ate across his face, triumph flaring from his eyes. And it disturbed her enough to start her moving away from him.

"A cannibal? Maggots, you say? You know everything, do you?" He was nodding, backing her up. "Who told you this?"

"Lots of people."

"Lots? I doubt that. The few that could, know better. More likely you've pieced it together, and that's why you've got it so wrong."

"It's too late, Coddy." She waved at the banking flames. "You know it is."

He followed the gesture, suddenly calm. "The He-Flies will be back," he said.

"It's a gasoline fire. If the flames or the heat don't reach them, the fuel soaking down will. The larvae will die."

"What larvae?"

"They didn't all eat each other. The survivors must have mated with the females."

"What females?"

That stunned her. *He*-Flies.

"They only come in one sex," he said. "And only one survives the feasting. And you didn't get him."

As if inhaled, the burning grave suddenly went out, fog slipping back as opaque as ever. She groped for the cage door.

"And the crime they stoned my long-departed ancestor for wasn't cannibalism," Coddy continued, turning with her. "It was sodomy."

The LeBaron was the only thing that anchored her. She held on to the wheel to keep from being hurled off into space, and every now and then she felt her own tremors resonating through the steering column. There seemed to be no shock absorbers anymore —figuratively or literally—none at all. The car jolted along, hitting potholes and clipping the curb as she swerved in at the boardinghouse. Hermaphroditic butterflies. Sodomy. They wanted her to believe that Michael had not been bitten, that the thing had tried to put its larvae into him. What kind of blasphemies were they trying to manufacture? Reginald Deaken had not metamorphosed into an obscene insect any more than . . . than— But she no longer wanted to understand it, because her sanity itself was at issue. What mattered was to awaken Michael and get away from Greystone Bay.

Michael.

He lay twisted on the bed. The paleness was unreal.

"I want you out of here," she said to Mrs. Lorcaster. "We'll be gone from your house the minute he can walk, but until then I want you to leave us alone."

Indignation sparked and died in the old grey eyes. Leaded cames reset the creases and she became Victorian again, but without the confectionery smile as she left the room.

Sue caressed her husband then. Sleeping Beauty. Snow White with whiskers. She prayed and soothed and called to him. He came out of it gradually, unbending, taking on color. And when he opened his eyes, it was because it was the right moment, and she was the right woman. And everything was going to be right from now on. Forever.

Laughing tearfully, she murmured his name over and over in a voice gone gossamer.

"What's the matter?" he managed, strength still at bay in his voice.

"Nothing, anymore."

"Oh, do I feel hung over. What have you been doing in there?"

The bathroom, he meant. He didn't know any of what had happened. He thought it was still their wedding night. She wondered suddenly if she should tell him. If he knew—if he believed her—he would certainly do something rash. Then they would never get out of here.

"You've been asleep for twenty-four hours. Some stud."

"Twenty-four hours? What are you talking about?"

"You ate a bad hors d'oeuvre at the Red Foxe, I guess. Doctor's been here. Said you had to sleep it off."

"You're kidding." He sat up stiffly. Glanced at the date on his watch. "You're not kidding. I'll never live this down. Hey, you look a little washed out yourself. You okay?"

"I'll have to work on my allure."

"I didn't say you weren't alluring."

He slid a hand around her waist, pulled her on top of him as he fell back.

"Michael, the doctor said you should rest."

"What the hell have I been doing? Can the doctor." Right.

And how was she going to stall him off for two weeks without telling him more than she had? He was out of the coma; she was out of the nightmare. She could be rid of quack Dr. Plummer and his shaman medicine for good now. She could take faith and a cure in strong arms.

"Are you sure you feel all right? The doctor said you might not want to take it easy, that I'd have to restrain you."

"I'm fine," he said, bringing one knee up between her thighs.

He certainly was. "Michael, why don't we pack and go to a hotel up the coast? This place has gone sour for me."

"Now?"

"Why not?"

"Because you've got too many excuses. I'm beginning to think you drugged me last night to save yourself from carnal knowledge."

She gave him all the mischief in her enormous blue eyes then. "Michael, if you'll take me out of here now, this instant, when we get to the next place, I'll do it and do it and do it until you can't walk straight."

They were on the road in thirteen minutes, out of Greystone Bay in twenty. And when they got to the next place they did it . . .

and did it . . .

and did it.

It was six months before he got the franchise assignment. A businessman in Greystone Bay wanted to open a Honda dealership. He repped Honda.

"Michael McDonald," he said, introducing himself.

The prospective dealer shook his hand and by lunchtime he had signed an agreement and purchase order.

"Do you come through often, Mike?" he asked over a seafood bisque at the Red Foxe.

"Not often, but I honeymooned here."

"Really."

"Sort of. My wife hates the place because I got sick, and it kind of spoiled things. Not the town's fault, but I didn't even tell her I was coming back. It's beautiful here, I think. She won't even talk about it."

"My apologies to your wife. Do you have any children?"

"One on the way, thanks to the rest of the honeymoon. Actually, more than one. Doctor says we've got at least two in there, kicking like boys."

"That's nice."

It was nice, he thought. He was going to be a father, and that filled him with pride and prowess. Seeing Greystone Bay again as he had on their wedding day, he had a sudden longing to know his children now. After lunch, he drove past Mrs. Lorcaster's Victorian house, up Port Boulevard, and finally to the old cemetery they had visited. There he parked the LeBaron and climbed the hill to the arboretum. There was no "ivy" this time. He passed through the gates. Something had scorched the tombstone, he noted, and felt compelled to go behind it to where a lot of rotting timbers lay.

It was silly, trying to recapture a day that had turned out all wrong. Nevertheless, it had been the beginning for them. Marriage. Parenthood. Twins, at least, the doctor had said! Talk about prowess. A stud like him might even sire triplets! He couldn't wait to see what they looked like. And again by compulsion he reached down and lifted one of the blackened timber ends. There were two big membranes there, bulging moist and translucent out of a hollow. Inside, wriggling against the skin of each womb, were count- less emerald-green bodies. He watched for a moment, feeling an odd pride and prowess, and then he ginger- ly replaced the timber. Maybe even quads, he thought about his children. He couldn't wait to see how many.

AN OVERRULING PASSION

by Galad Elflandsson

I| HE SAT IN THE LOUNGE OF THE ATLANTIC VIEW HOTEL, nervously checking the time every two or three minutes on a very expensive diamonds-and-white-gold watch he wore on his wrist, beneath the French cuff of a cream-colored dress shirt, secured with a diamonds-and-white-gold cuff link that matched his watch. His three-piece suit was custom-tailored, immaculate, a slightly darker shade of cream, as was the tie that seemed to flow down from the diamond collar studs of the shirt. And he sat in the lounge of the Atlantic View Hotel, nursing a Scotch and soda, in an agony of doubt—and even fear—that she would not respond to his letter; that his trip from New York City would be a pointless exercise in futility.

The lounge was fashionably dark, amber-paned carriage lamps casting a comfortable, warm glow over

123

the walnut-framed booths of brown leather, the brass-wreathed bar along the far wall, the tables with their complements of captain's chairs. A log fire snapped and crackled on a raised slate hearth to his right, and from where he sat in his corner booth he could see the lounge in its entirety, note the entrance of anyone, or the exit of the half dozen patrons who sat over glistening balloon glasses of brandy, sipped at foaming steins of imported beer.

One couple leaned toward each other no more than five feet from where he sat, their conversation and muted laughter causing him actual pain. The woman was tall, auburn-haired, and slender, her bare arms like gold in the firelight and her fingers manicured and elegant where she stroked her companion's face, plucked at the waist of her black evening gown; he, in turn, wore an evening suit and a blindingly white shirt with a ruffled front. His face was a mirror of adoration as he gazed at his wife . . . girlfriend . . . whoever she might be, he was utterly devoted to her . . . very much so . . . as he himself was utterly devoted to Cassandra . . . whom he had begged to meet him at eight o'clock . . . and now, as he glanced at his watch, was forty-three minutes late . . .

The note she had left had been very brief —"Forgive me, but I must leave you"—and he had read it with an ache in his heart that, in the stasis of Time wherein the words struck home, had become unbearable. Released from the shock of their meaning, his mind had searched almost frantically for some reason, a cause for her desertion . . . yet they all had been so trivial . . . he could not begin to believe she would leave him for any of them. And then his thoughts had turned to where she might have gone . . . remembering the days before their marriage

. . . brief allusions to the place of her birth . . . a small New England town where she had grown up . . . Greystone Bay . . .

His letter had been addressed to her care of the postmaster, a small rectangular packet of desperation with "Please forward to the proper address" written neatly, but desperately, in the lower right-hand corner of the envelope. A day later, in the lavender shadows of an early summer twilight, he had followed the letter, hoping she had received it . . . read his entreaties . . . and would meet him as he had requested. He had arrived late last night, checked into the Atlantic View, and risen at dawn to seek the post office . . .

"Yes, sir, the Boones still live here in Greystone Bay," the postmaster had said. "And I forwarded your letter, just as you requested on the front of the envelope . . ."

And now he sat in the lounge of the Atlantic View Hotel, nervously, nursing a Scotch and soda . . . watching two lovers . . . waiting for Cassandra . . . who was forty-four minutes late . . .

She must have come back here, he thought/prayed. *She must have received my letter . . . and knows I'm waiting for her . . .*

He stared blindly into his Scotch, gripped the highball glass tightly in his fingers as the firelight danced in the dissolving cubes of ice . . . that seemed to be the cruel end of his hopes . . . as footsteps whispered over the thick carpet of the lounge . . . approached him . . . came to a standstill before his booth . . .

"Mr. Rawdon? Mr. Michael Rawdon . . . ?"

At the sound of his name he looked up, found a tall white-haired man regarding him through piercing

dark eyes that seemed to glare from beneath heavy
white brows. He nodded in acknowledgment, blinking stupidly.

"I am here in response to your letter to Cassandra
Boone," said the stranger.

II | RAWDON CONTINUED TO STARE AT THE NEWCOMER IN
dull surprise, unconsciously taking note of his angular
face, emotionless save for the almost feral light in his
eyes, and the way his light linen suit—though well
tailored—nevertheless seemed to be far too large for
his gaunt frame.

For God's sakes say something, Rawdon, he told
himself. *Don't just sit here gawking at him like an
idiot . . .*

"Who are you?" he said out loud, but his voice was
hoarse, sounding strained in his own ears. "What are
you doing here . . . and where is my wife . . . ?"

The man studied him closely for some moments
and Rawdon swore silently as he felt his face coloring
beneath the other's scrutiny. He repeated his questions, but received no answer; instead, the stranger
signed to the young man behind the bar and, in one
fluid motion, sat himself across from Rawdon. The
bartender brought a snifter of brandy at once, setting
it before Rawdon's unlooked-for companion hastily,
before retreating back to his station behind the bar.
Still, the stranger continued to ignore Rawdon's questions, warming the glass between his pale stiletto
fingers and then sipping the contents delicately. At
length, he looked up and addressed Rawdon directly.

"As I said a moment ago, Mr. Rawdon, I am here in

response to your letter to Cassandra," he said softly. "She is well, but was unable to meet you. I have come in her place, and you may speak to me with every assurance that the import of your words will reach her ears."

Michael gulped at his Scotch convulsively, regretted it instantly as the still-fiery liquor made his head swim.

"Who are you?" he demanded a third time. "What right do you have—?"

"I have every right in the world, Mr. Rawdon," snapped the stranger impatiently. "I am Gerald Boone, Cassandra's father . . ."

III | ". . . WHY ARE YOU HERE?" MICHAEL SAID, WISHING he could keep the desperation from creeping into his voice. "Why didn't Cassie come herself?"

He saw the look of distaste on Gerald Boone's face at his diminution of her name, thought to see the dark eyes flash with disgust and anger, as if his daughter had been made low and common by its use.

"Cassandra did not wish to meet you . . . alone . . ." Boone said meaningfully. "She allowed me to see the letter you wrote, asked if I would act on her behalf in this matter. By coming here I have done so, Mr. Rawdon."

"I don't understand," Michael said quickly, trying to disguise the trembling in his voice. "What *matter* are you talking about?"

His right hand went reflexively to his neck and throat—a nervous habit he had taken up in the last year or so—massaging the skin with glass-cool fingers

as his collar suddenly became tight and constricting.
Boone seemed to enjoy his discomfort, a slow smile
touching at the corners of his mouth.

"The matter of your marriage with my daughter,
Mr. Rawdon," he said carelessly. "I advised Cassandra against it—quite vehemently, I might add, and
for a variety of reasons—and she has come to realize
my reservations were well founded. In short, Mr.
Rawdon, my daughter is not happy—"

"That's ridiculous!" Michael cried, too loudly it
seemed, for the lovers at the table nearby turned their
heads curiously for a moment. He went on in a hoarse
whisper, "Cassandra and I have been very happy
together."

Boone's hint of a smile disappeared, his mouth
becoming hard and tight-lipped . . . again . . . with
disgust.

"She is my daughter, Mr. Rawdon—"

"I didn't even know you were alive until a few
minutes ago!"

"Don't interrupt me again, young man!" Boone
hissed. "I say she is my daughter, and as such,
Cassandra keeps no secrets between us. She is not
happy in her arrangement with you . . ."

Gratefully, Rawdon felt a spark of anger flare inside
him, something with which to combat the maddening
calm of the man before him, the cold dispassion with
which he dared to inform him of the shortcomings of
his relationship with his own wife.

"I don't believe you, Mr. Boone," he said fiercely.
"I won't believe you until I hear it from Cassie herself.
I'm the senior partner in a very successful law firm,
and Cassie and I live more than comfortably; she can
have anything she wants materially. If she's been

unhappy I haven't heard of it . . . and even if what you say is true, I'm certainly not going to discuss it with anyone but her!"

"Are you calling me a liar, Mr. Rawdon?" Boone asked dangerously. He leaned across the table and Michael saw his hand tightening around the fragile stem of his glass.

"No, sir, I am not," Michael responded with inner satisfaction as having broken through Boone's composure. "What I'm saying is that you, perhaps, have misunderstood your daughter's words, or read into them a reflection of your own personal feelings with regard to our marriage."

"That is impossible."

"Nothing is impossible, Mr. Boone," Michael said, smiling to himself. As it had happened so many times before, his training as a lawyer again was serving him well outside a courtroom . . . and the man who claimed to be Cassandra's father now was looking at him thoughtfully, with even a small hint of grudging respect in his strange eyes.

"Perhaps you are right, Mr. Rawdon," Gerald Boone said quietly. "And it may well be I have misjudged you. In any case, Cassandra charged me with making the decision as to whether or not the two of you should meet in person. I now think such a meeting would be advantageous for all concerned."

"You're much too kind, Mr. Boone," Michael said coldly. "When, if I may presume to ask, can I see my wife?"

Boone drained the rest of his glass in one swallow. "I shall send a car for you, Mr. Rawdon," he said. "Tomorrow evening . . . at eight o'clock . . . Thank you for the brandy."

And then he left the booth and walked out of the lounge without a backward glance.

IV| MICHAEL RAWDON DID NOT SLEEP WELL THAT NIGHT, as he had not slept well the previous night, or the one before that . . . when he had come home from the office . . . found Cassandra's note on her pillow. His accommodations at the Atlantic View were comfortable, but he was not; the double bed was firm and far too large for him without Cassandra sharing it. He roamed the twilight world between sleep and wakefulness, reaching out for her, finding no one. When the sun finally labored over the eastern horizon, heaving itself up from the ocean to cut through the ground mist that had covered Greystone Bay in the course of the night, he was standing at one of the windows of his room, his light brown hair a spiky tangled halo around the haunted misery of his face. Only once in his fourteen-month marriage to Cassandra Boone had he been away from her—three days and nights on a case in upstate New York—and the nights had been the same . . . interminable . . . aching nightmares of loneliness. He showered and shaved, dressed in a lightweight suit of charcoal grey with darker pinstripes, and went downstairs for a breakfast he did not want.

The restaurant on the ground floor was empty; though it would not have taken many more diners to fill it to capacity, to Michael it seemed a yawning desolation of white linen, less than brilliant silver, and filmed glass. He sat at a table by the windows, dividing his time among coffee, a copy of *The New York Times* he had purchased at the desk in the lobby, and short, almost furtive glances at the shimmering sun-gilded expanse of the bay as it curved away into the last wisps of morning fog at its northern end. A young woman in a starched white uniform with an old coffee stain over her left breast eventually brought him breakfast.

"Here you are, sir," she said, smiling. "Scrambled eggs, sausages, home-fried potatoes, and whole-wheat toast."

She was nineteen or twenty, pretty in a pale washed-out sort of way—not at all like the rich dark beauty of his wife—perhaps up from one of the Boston universities for the summer. Michael looked up at her dazedly, then down at the steaming plates she had placed before him.

"I ordered my eggs sunny-side up, miss," he said quietly. "With bacon and *white* toast. I'm afraid I don't eat any of this . . ."

The waitress cocked her head to one side, looked puzzled, her empty serving tray poised in midair.

"Sir, I brought you . . . exactly what you ordered," she said hesitantly. "I've got it right here, on your bill . . ." She put her tray on his table and began to fumble through the pocket of her apron, pulling a ragged receipt book out for his inspection. "You see . . . right here on top . . . two eggs scrambled, sau—"

"I did not order this food, young lady," Michael snapped. "Perhaps *you* intended to eat this breakfast, but I certainly did not . . ."

"Sir, I asked if you wanted whole-wheat toast and you said you never ate anything but," she said unhappily. "I mean . . . I . . . I could've gotten your order wrong . . . I'll bring you another plate . . . but . . ."

Michael stood up impatiently, throwing the newspaper down on his chair. "Never mind," he snarled angrily. "I'll go somewhere where the waitresses know how to take an order properly."

He stalked past her, out into the lobby of the hotel, through the front doors where they opened onto the Harbor Road. He stood there, trembling with rage, while a voice whispered inside his head:

Why did you do that? You've never treated anyone like that before . . . not even the clumsy fool who once spilled wine all over Cassie's dress . . .

Rawdon walked the splintered weather-worn planks of the boardwalk beside the bay, blinded by the rising sun as it glittered on the water, turned the small arc of dingy sand into a field of sparkling diamonds. Though it was quite warm, the town's share of summer tourists would not be arriving for at least another week and he had the beach to himself, wandering aimlessly . . . dazzled by the sun . . . feeling his brain baking in a feverish heat as images of himself and Cassandra superimposed themselves upon the deepening blue canvas of the sky . . . and his fingers itched with the memory of how her skin felt beneath his touch . . . when they held hands . . . walking . . . made love on the silk playground of their bed . . . high above New York City . . . with the flashing neon pulse of its night life shooting through their windows . . .

The day following the discovery of her note—after that first horrible night of being without her—had been torture, a mindless treadmill journey from dawn to dusk, going through the motions of case preparation and making notations on file briefs for his junior partners. His personal secretary had given him a dozen puzzled looks through the course of the day; he had overheard the office receptionist commenting on his strange behavior; Paul Jennings had gone so far as to ask him if he was feeling all right, had shrugged carelessly when told to mind his own business. The second night, after writing his letter, had been even worse . . .

And what little he saw of Greystone Bay did nothing to lessen the sense of impending disaster that followed him through its odd conglomeration of old clapboard houses, the shoddy rows of low-rental brick buildings, the stately but decaying Victorian mansions, and the modern glass-and-steel structures in the town's business district. When the sun went down over the hills to the west, bloodying the sky and the water and everything in between, he was a tired, disheveled wreck . . . dragging himself back to the hotel . . . his room . . . where the bathroom mirror mocked him with his own reflection and his perspiration-soaked suit seemed an unbearable weight . . .

At eight o'clock he was standing in front of the Atlantic View, looking fresh after a second shower and changing into a Harris tweed jacket and tan slacks . . . but inside he was in pain, his guts writhing with doubt and nervousness. When Gerald Boone's long black Lincoln pulled up to the curb, the driver had to open the door for him.

V | WOMBED IN PLUSH GREY VELOUR BEHIND THE TINTED windows of the car, Michael Rawdon was whisked into the deepening shadows of the night, the bay falling away behind him as the Lincoln turned left somewhere along Harbor Road and coiled swiftly

upward into the hills to the west . . . twisting almost
silently toward the last smears of dirty crimson on the
horizon . . . the driver a silent black ghost in livery
. . . bearing the silent ghost of Michael Rawdon on his
journey along the River of the Dead and Dying.

He is Charon the boatman, Michael thought dazedly, reaching into his jacket pocket for coins with
which to pay his passage. *And this is the asphalt river
Styx . . . oh, Cassie, why did you leave me . . . you
knew I would be lost . . .*

Without her, he felt like the severed limb of a
soldier, with only minutes of survival left before the
instinct of Life passed out of him and he became a
dead purposeless chunk of bleeding flesh. In the
rearview mirror he saw the face of the chauffeur
—bland and featureless, uncaring of his passenger
and the urgency of bringing the limb back to its
owner . . . of rejoining it to the world of the living.
Michael's doubt and fear were replaced by an over-
whelming lassitude of mind and body . . .

He was half asleep and meshed in nightmare when
the Lincoln made one last turn onto a semicircular
drive, slowing as it pulled up before the *porte cochère*
of a large house drenched in shadow. The driver let
him out of the car, led him up a short flight of carved
stone stairs to the doors of the house, where a second
black-liveried ghost took him in hand, ushered him
inside with many lukewarm smiles and words of
welcome. The master awaited him in the library, he
learned from the animate skeleton in its black shroud,
but first there was the matter of reuniting him with
Miss Cassandra . . . his wife . . . Cassie . . .

She sat quietly in the parlor—a Victorian splendor
of old brocades and cranberry glass—and as the
double doors closed behind him he saw the vein in her

white throat pulsing to the rhythm of a tall gilt clock on the mantelpiece. The night had turned chill and a small fire crackled on the grate below, flickering its light across the midnight wonder of her long hair, the gentle curves outlined in the clinging silk of her black gown. When he entered the room, and stood as one turned to stone on the borders of the rose-colored carpet that covered the floor, she started up from the divan and regarded him curiously, her long white fingers clutching at a wisp of yellowed linen held between them.

"Michael . . ." she whispered softly, and her lips trembled as she said his name, a hint of tears glimmering in the wide darkness of her eyes.

"Why, Cassie . . . ?" he replied hoarsely. "How could you go like that . . . with no explanation at all . . . ?"

She moved toward him slowly, a half dozen paces, before she stopped and her bare arms stretched out to him imploringly, as if to beg forgiveness.

"I . . . I had no choice, Michael," she said brokenly, and now the tears in her eyes spilled outward over her cheeks. "He called to me . . . I had to go . . . come here . . ."

"Who called to you?"

"My father, Michael," she said. "My father called me . . ."

"And you just came here?" he demanded. "Without a word to me . . . nothing at all . . . to explain . . . make it easier to deal with . . . ?"

"Michael, you don't understand!" she cried desperately. "He's my father—"

"And I'm your husband, Cassie!" he said, hating himself as she cringed under the lash of his words. "Doesn't that count for anything? Didn't it count when you wrote seven words on a blank piece of paper? What would've happened if I hadn't remembered the name of this place? My God, Cassie, it was torture! Were you going t'leave me to that . . . ?"

"No," she sobbed. "No, Michael. He would've written to you, told you where I was . . . I didn't want to leave that way, you must believe that. It was horrible for me, too . . . but I couldn't say anything more in my note, and I had to come when he called to me . . ."

The clock ticked and the fire snapped through the silence that fell between them; ten feet of Turkish carpet yawned as an impassable gulf as they gazed into each other's eyes—she pleading for understanding where there was none to be found for him, he knowing only the ache to feel her arms around him, the length of her body pressed closely to his own.

"Come back with me, Cassie," he said weakly. "Come back with me now . . . just walk out the door with me . . . back to New York. We were happy, Cassie, weren't we? What he said wasn't true . . . ?"

"Of course we were happy, Michael! I love you . . . and I know you love me. I've never known anyone so kind or gentle as you, someone who cared about me even though—"

"Then come with me now," he said. "Come back to everything we share and—"

"Michael, please!" she cried. "I can't do that . . . not yet . . . I . . . I have a responsibility to him, Michael, you must accept that, trust me enough to know I wouldn't have done what I did if there was any other way . . ."

Rawdon felt himself growing dizzy, put out one hand to the frame of a tall wingback chair to steady himself. There was a surrealistic quality to their conversation that made him light-headed and nauseous with the thought that she simply might begin to fade from the room . . . dissolve into the carpet and leave him alone . . . again . . .

"He won't let me go, Michael," she whispered. "Not until you've proven yourself to him, convinced him that I made the right choice . . ."

"Cassie . . ."

She flung herself forward at last, hurled herself across the rose-colored chasm and fell into his arms.

"Just hold me, Michael. I've missed you so much, just hold me . . . for a little while . . . and then you must talk to him again . . ."

VI | THE LIBRARY WAS DEEP WITHIN THE HOUSE, WINDOW-less and dark but for the light of another small fire and a pair of candles in hurricane lamps on the massive oak desk in its center. Gerald Boone sat behind that desk, a thing made from shards of firelight and shadow, eyes burning fiercely beneath the overhang of his fire-stained white brows. Michael faced him across the desk, dwarfed by the massive wooden chair on which he sat, faint in the pervasive atmosphere given off by the ranks of leather-bound books lining the walls.

"You have seen Cassandra, Mr. Rawdon?" inquired Boone. "You have spoken with her?"

"I have," Michael replied. "I asked her to return to New York with me at once—"

"And, of course, she informed you it was impossible; that she no more could accede to your request than either of us swim the Atlantic Ocean in a single day."

"That's correct," Michael said, striving to keep his voice cold and steady. "She told me I must first prove to your satisfaction that I am a proper mate for her; that I meet the standards you have set for one who would be your son-in-law."

Boone nodded, as if Michael had recited a lesson prerequisite to anything further between them, and filled two glasses from an ancient bottle of cognac at his right hand. After passing one of the glasses to Michael, he sat back in his chair and gazed down into its rich amber translucence.

"I had thought her to be the one wayward offspring of her mother," Boone reflected quietly. "She is my youngest daughter, you know, the last of seven children—three male and four female—but the only one ever to go against my wishes . . . which she did when she married you, Mr. Rawdon. I have told you I was less than pleased when I learned of your union. My opinion, since then, has scarcely altered. You must do that yourself . . . now . . . before I will allow my daughter to return to New York with you."

The supreme assurance and arrogance of the man refueled the anger Michael had felt during their meeting the night before. He leaned forward in his chair, ignoring the slightly sickening sensation that the mustiness of the library engendered in the sudden movement.

"Your daughter is a grown woman, Mr. Boone," he informed him. "She has a right to make her own decisions and live her life as she sees fit . . . without interference from you!"

Again, Boone nodded, this time with the faint smile touching on the corners of his lips.

"You are quite right, Mr. Rawdon," he said complacently, "but Cassandra *has* made a decision of her own accord—to respond to my summons, as is befitting a dutiful daughter—even as she made the decision to marry you against my wishes. Now, if you would have her, the decision is yours and yours alone—either hear that which I require of you and, in provision of same, earn my respect and my daughter . . . or go your miserable way and leave her to someone more worthy . . ."

Michael met the unwavering stare of Boone's luminous eyes, read the mocking challenge in their depths, saw it again on the widening smile of his lips. He leaned back in his chair, sipping cognac, without letting his eyes break their contact with Boone's taunting stare, and felt rage coupled with longing for Cassandra rush through his body. Finally, he lowered his glass and said:

"What do I have t'do . . . ?"

VII| THE BLACK CAR RUSHED DOWN THROUGH THE HILLS, bearing Michael in its velour-lined belly, back to the town where he would have to make his choice, once and for all.

You have twenty-four hours, Mr. Rawdon, Boone had told him. *My man will take you back to Greystone Bay, leave you wherever you please. Thereafter you shall be on your own. If you are equal to the task I have set you, you must contrive your own return to this house; elsewise, you will never again set eyes upon my daughter . . .*

For the first few minutes in the car, Michael had thought himself safe, miraculously escaped from the insanity of Gerald Boone and his ultimatum, the pervasive darkness of the ancient house; but then he thought of Cassandra, and as the lights of the town sprang up again around him, he realized he had no more escaped the snare set for him than a man who, for a price, had been given the power to decree life or death for his loved ones. The Lincoln slowed for a traffic light, crawled through the ground mist that seemed to encroach upon the town every night; the windows became wet with light rain, and the salty tang of the bay crept into the car for all its womblike warmth and quiet. When a bank of garish neon lights winked at him through the darkness, he knew his decision already had been made; that the insanity had followed him, and he was part of it. Reaching toward the panel of glass separating him from the driver, he rapped on it to gain his attention, slid one section of the glass aside, and said:

"Stop, driver. You can let me out here."

He saw the man grin into his rearview mirror as the throbbing of the engine sank to a low rumbling purr, and the car came to a halt opposite the neons.

"Have a pleasant evening, sir," said the driver with a smile. "The master asked me t'wish you good luck—"

I'll bet he did, Michael thought bitterly.

"—But if you wasn't intendin' t'come back, please don't be foolish enough t'think any action against him'd result in anything but trouble for yerself . . . and Miss Cassandra . . ."

Michael paused as he got out of the car.

"You can thank him for me for his kind advice," he said softly, "and tell him to go to hell."

The driver nodded, still smiling, and said, "I'll do that, sir," waiting only so long as it took Rawdon to get out of the car before gunning the engine. Michael watched it disappear into the rain and mist, taillights like two grinning crimson eyes; then he crossed the street slowly, hesitated before the door of the tavern . . . took a deep breath that did nothing to still the sudden trembling in his legs . . . and went inside.

Rock music blared from speakers mounted on the ceiling, roared through the haze of cigarette smoke, the babble of shouted conversations, the wet steamy warmth generated by dozens of dancing, drinking patrons. Michael cringed, no more than ten or twelve years older than the tavern's youngest customers, yet feeling totally out of place, wrenched from the sedate, unhurried pace of his normal life.

But nothing's normal anymore, he told himself. *Nothing will be normal ever again unless I get Cassie back . . .*

He shouldered his way through the press of people before the door, squirmed his way to the rough-hewn wooden bar where he shouted at a barmaid's inquisitive stare for a Scotch and soda, paid for it, stood in a corner where he wished for someplace to sit while he tried to imagine what he must do, and how he would do it. His eyes roved restlessly over the faces surrounding him, that yawned in and out of focus as they moved past him, drew nearer and then floated away. His Scotch tasted thin and smoky, unable to quell the nervousness in his stomach, the trembling of his legs . . . and then all the noise seemed to fade away . . . the dense crowd before him parting like the Red

Sea . . . giving him an unobstructed view of the opposite corner of the room . . . a table . . . where three
young women sat over tall glasses, their heads bent
toward each other as they laughingly conversed . . .

And one of them was nineteen or twenty years old,
pretty in a pale washed-out sort of way—not at all
like the rich dark beauty of his wife—perhaps up
from one of the Boston universities for the summer.
Even without the starched white uniform of the hotel,
Michael recognized her at once and—without even
thinking he had, perhaps, found the object of his
quest—began to move forward . . . past the walls of
human bodies to either side of him . . . until he stood
before her table . . . waiting patiently for her to take
notice of him. Finally she looked up, recognized him
as quickly as he had recognized her, and her face
became stonelike with annoyance.

"What d'*you* want?" she said disdainfully, though
he could sense an underlying curiosity in her. He
shifted his drink into his left hand, put on his most
convincing look of quiet contrition.

"I've been looking for you," he said slowly, "hoping
I would find you . . ."

"Don't you think—?" she began angrily.

"Please," he interrupted. "I want to apologize . . .
for my behavior this morning. I had no right to treat
you the way I did. I was upset . . . and probably didn't
even know what I had ordered . . ."

Her very pale blue eyes lost their glint of anger and
indignation, her manner already softening under his
careful attempt to convey regret, heartfelt remorse
for his treatment of her. As if on cue, her companions rose from their seats and left the table with
knowing smiles on their faces; Michael extended his

right hand cautiously as he took one of the vacated chairs.

"My name is Alan Michaels," he said, "and if you'll forgive me, I'd like t'buy you a drink . . . show you how very sorry I am for having been so rude . . ."

VIII HE DROVE SILENTLY THROUGH THE NIGHT, MIND and body racing far ahead of the rain-washed ribbon of highway in his headlights, nerves tingling with her nearness, dancing to the slap/hiss of the windshield wipers on rain-spattered glass. They were in Rhode Island, nearing the Connecticut border on their way back to New York City . . . with Greystone Bay . . . that dark house . . . Gerald Boone . . . all of that behind them . . . forever . . . just himself and Cassie . . . going home . . .

"I'm sorry, Michael," she whispered softly beside him. "I'm so sorry . . ."

He shook his head violently, barely able to control his excitement at the sound of her voice.

"Don't be sorry, Cassie," he said earnestly. "I'm not . . . not at all . . . We're together again and that's the only thing that matters."

He loosened his tie, undid the top button of his shirt, and massaged his neck where the collar had chafed it throughout the night.

"But what you did—!"

"It doesn't matter, Cassie," he said quickly. "Nothing matters but you and me. Let's just forget all of this ever happened. I left her in the car, told her I had checked out of the hotel but they were holding my bags for me . . . and she waited until I got back . . .

and her apartment was somewhere along the way back t'your father's house so she didn't realize we were going there until it was too late . . ."

He glanced at her for a moment, saw the sheen of tears on her cheeks, felt his heart ache and burn with wanting her.

"It's over now, Cassie . . . we can start all over again . . . with no more doubts, no more interference. He gave us his blessing, Cassandra. Your father blessed us—"

"I know, Michael," she sobbed. "I know . . . but I tried to make him understand that you couldn't do what he demanded of you, that it was against everything—"

"You're the only thing that matters to me, Cassie. Everything . . . everyone else means nothing. I love you, and even the thought of living without you was more than I could take . . ."

He reached for her hand as they slashed through the rain into Connecticut, still hours away from the city . . . their apartment . . . the soft silk comfort of their bed . . . and as he twined his fingers in hers, joined his flesh to her flesh, the electricity of her skin shattered what was left of his patience, jolted into the marrow of his bones, set his entire body to trembling with desire. His foot came off the accelerator, went slowly to the brake pedal as the car decelerated toward the gravel shoulder of the highway . . . slowed . . . came to a stop . . . in darkness he turned to her . . .

"She's going to die, Michael," he heard her say.

"I love you, Cassie."

"Most of them die," she said brokenly.

"But not us, Cassie," he whispered joyfully, cupping her face in his hands. "Not us . . . we'll go on forever . . ."

He drew her head down to where his collar stood away from his neck, and as her teeth sank lovingly into his flesh, he sighed:

"I gave your father what he wanted . . ."

THE SUPRAMARKET

by Leanne Frahm

SALLY JUMPED OUT OF THE CAR, BRUSHING INSTINCTIVELY at nonexistent wrinkles in her print polyester button-through. She glanced back at Helen, still unbuckling her seat belt. "Come on," she said impatiently. "If we get in now we'll beat the rush."

Helen looked round the parking lot that seemed to stretch, from her position, to infinity. It looked three-quarters full already. "*Beat* the rush?" she murmured, but Sally wasn't listening, was popping her keys in her shoulder bag.

They walked up the gentle rise toward the looming, almost organic, shape of the supramarket, its immensity dwarfing the precise plantings of shrubs and trees that tried but failed to soften the harsh grey bitumen of the lot, or hide the development of homes south of the road into Greystone Bay. As usual, Sally was striding ahead. Helen idled along behind, watching Sally's erect back, admiring the confidence that she radiated. She wondered again why she felt none of Sally's exuberance.

Sally swung round suddenly; Helen was sure her eyes would be flashing beneath the cloudy film of sunglasses. "*Do* hurry up," she said. "You've got to get the hang of it. I've told you before, the first lesson is to be *quick*."

Helen shrugged slightly, her lips clamped in a polite smile. Sally ran back and seized her arm, pulling her along. "Honestly," she continued as Helen half ran to keep up with her, "it's just as well you moved into our neighborhood. All those years of shopping at little supermarkets in that tiny town, wasting god knows *how* much money on their prices. You'd think you'd be *glad* to be able to shop at a marvelous supramarket like this at last."

Helen winced inwardly. I should be more grateful, she thought. Sally's been so kind, bringing me to the shopping center and the famous supramarket, getting me used to its complexity—the thought was accompanied by an image of a cutaway nautilus shell that revealed its intricate coiling maze . . . But each visit, instead of accustoming her to it, seemed to make her more reluctant next time . . .

A blast of cold air leaped out at them as the electronic doors parted, driving off the bite of salt air from the Atlantic. Helen shivered, and took an involuntary step backward.

"Wow!" exclaimed Sally. "Doesn't it feel cold after the heat!" She glanced back at Helen. "Come on," she said again. "The doors'll stay open all day if you just stand there."

Helen blushed hotly. How silly, she thought, to feel so uncomfortable about the supermarket—no, the *supra*market. But I hate shopping here. There; an admission at last. But why? Perhaps I'm developing claustrophobia or agoraphobia or something. Maybe I need to see a doctor . . . She gave Sally a bright smile and resolutely caught up with her in a few quick strides.

They made their way to the rows of turnstiles, battling, despite Sally's hopes, through oblivious crowds and a wave of Muzak. Helen stopped halfway through one. It only goes one way, she thought, examining the gleaming silver tubing. You can't get out. How curious I never wondered about that before. A sudden shove in her back sent her forward. "Sorry," muttered the large woman behind her. She stood to one side as the big woman hurried to the rows and rows of shopping carts. Sally was already there, yanking one loose from its neighbor, cursing its obstinacy under her breath. Helen walked slowly over, feeling the unaccountable reluctance deepen.

The carts looked somehow different today, like animals crouching in a huge pen, waiting patiently to be unleashed and guided into the fray, like lions in a Roman circus. It was dimmer here; the bright lights of the supramarket were focused on the shelves and the passageways between them, as if this were the wings and the aisles the stage. Helen felt suddenly nervous —stage fright, perhaps, she thought wryly, determined to laugh at her fantasies.

She grasped the shining handlebar of the cart and pulled. It sprang out at her without resistance, catching her by surprise. She had expected to have to wrestle with it as Sally had done. It seemed almost *eager* to begin. She turned it round. Sally was already onstage, walking steadily along the first long aisle, bathed in the brilliance of the lights. Her head jerked purposefully from side to side, seeking her purchases. Helen swallowed, and plunged after her.

Soap, tissues, shampoo—she reached automatically for the items, checking her mental list. Sally was just in front now. They swerved around a half-laden cart and into the next aisle—batteries, ballpoints. A turn again.

"Look!" said Sally excitedly. "Dog food's on special!" She darted off toward the bin as if the towering pyramid of tins might suddenly vanish, and began piling them into her cart. Helen passed her, reached for a packet of birdseed. She had no dog. A thought struck her, and the air seemed abruptly colder. Did *Sally* have a dog? Helen didn't seem to remember one . . .

Sally caught up with her, flushed and smiling. "Right!" she said, her voice infectious in its eagerness. "What next? Ah—two rows over—toilet paper!" Helen smiled at her own ridiculous suspicions—everybody used *that*. Of course Sally must have a dog. She shook herself and followed Sally, up and down the lengthy corridors, mechanically adding to her cart plastic wrap and aluminum foil and a tin of cat food—another 180-degree turn, picking up a package of cheap biscuits on a specials stand on the way—detergent and rubber gloves . . . She glanced at her cart. A tin of cat food?

She stopped, and the cart of a woman behind her caught her heel painfully. The woman veered around her, darting a defiant look from a pursed face, and swept on. Helen barely noticed. She stared at the cat food. Pilchards in aspic. I don't have a cat, she thought. Picking it up gingerly, she turned to the nearest shelf, her face numb. She pushed it in among the ranks of Vinyl Magic, carefully rearranged the plastic bottles to hide its squat rotundity.

"Come on," called Sally impatiently, already at the end of the aisle. Helen reddened, and jerked her hand away from the bottles with a guilty start. One toppled to the floor with a dull thud. Hastily she kicked it against the bottom of the shelf and hurried after Sally. That's probably why I hate shopping here, she thought, trying to calm herself. So easy to forget what you're doing and end up with something you don't want.

A bag of flour, a package of dried apricots, a bottle of dried parsley flakes; she checked each one even more carefully than before. Such a lot of walking for so few things. The bottom of her cart was barely covered; Sally's was half full already. She noticed that a woman ahead of them had parked her cart across the aisles, blocking it while she browsed through the gravy mixes. Helen slowed down, preparing to wait, but Sally continued.

"Excuse *me*," she said loudly, nudging the offending cart with her own. The woman affected not to hear, her head tilted, her face wearing an expression of intense concentration.

"I said 'Excuse *me*'!" Sally repeated, thrusting her cart forward violently. The other woman's cart swung round, hitting her on the hip. She glared at Sally and wrenched the cart to one side. Sally grinned triumphantly and sped on. Helen recalled her thoughts about the animals in the arena and flushed, averting her face as she passed the woman more slowly. A pain was beginning to send questing tendrils behind her eyes. It's so bright, she thought, blinking. Too bright. And so loud. An amplifier-enlarged voice broke through the Muzak and grated above the noises of the supramarket, strengthening the grip of the headache tentacles. She grasped the slippery cart handle more firmly and pushed on.

Canned mushrooms and corn—the headache was throbbing in unison with the squeal and clashing of carts. Sally was a bright floral blur ahead of her, arms gathering in groceries at an astonishing rate. Soup packets—Helen hardly noticed the flavors, a chicken and something, a tomato . . . She made a determined effort and caught up with Sally at the dairy products.

"Sally," she began, tugging at the other woman's arm. Sally turned, her arms full of packaged cheeses, her eyes shiny and inquiring. Helen felt shaky with embarrassment. She reached for a carton of cottage cheese to cover the trembling of her hands. "Sally," she started again.

"The 'use by' date, dummy," cried Sally. She dropped her cheeses into her cart and pulled the tub from Helen's hand. "Always check the 'use by' date. They put the oldest ones at the front!" She scrabbled through the tubs of cottage cheese and turned to Helen, her hands balancing what seemed an incredible array of cartons. "How many do you want?" she said proudly.

The lid had jarred loose from the uppermost tub, and runny curds of cottage cheese dripped over the others to the floor. Sally didn't seem to notice, just stared at her expectantly. Helen shut her eyes, opened them hurriedly as she felt herself begin to sway. Her head pounded.

"Sally," she whispered, "I don't think I can take any more of . . ." A woman's nasal voice blared unintelligibly from the loudspeaker, cutting her words off. "What?" mouthed Sally, cocking her head up at the loudspeaker. Before Helen could repeat herself, Sally had dumped the cottage cheese into her cart.

"Toothpaste!" she cried. "They're having a special on toothpaste! It's right back at the start. Come on!" She whirled her cart and disappeared into a crowd of shoppers who seemed to be traveling in the same direction.

Helen stood rooted to the floor. It was suddenly deathly quiet. Even the Muzak had stopped. The bright lights bounced off the white refrigerator units at her, haloing the rows and rows of identical boxes and cartons and packets that stared impassively down at her. Her feet ached; she felt she'd been walking forever. Abstractedly, she watched the cottage cheese ooze over the contents of her cart. Just a couple of minutes, she decided. I'll give Sally a couple of minutes, then I'll go without her.

A sound of padding and a cart squeal broke the silence. Helen turned. Far off, a woman was shuffling down the same aisle toward her. As she moved closer, Helen could see that she was a young woman, her hair blond-streaked and stringy, her dress a faded floral shift, her feet grubby in battered thongs. A little girl in a torn playsuit sat in the carrier seat of the cart, facing her mother's flat chest. The cart was heaped with expensive delicacies and imported tins. The woman stared to the left as she came along, her eyes never faltering from the shelves of groceries. The child screwed up her face as they neared Helen and began to wail. Helen noticed dried tear-tracks on the toddler's cheeks already. Then the young woman brought up her hand and slapped the little girl across the shoulder without taking her gaze from the shelves.

Dismayed, Helen hesitated, wondering if she should say something, but the moment had passed;

the child was silent. Helen saw a look of terror on the tiny soiled face and shuddered. Then, with a sickening shock, she realized the child's terrified expression was directed not at the woman, but at the rows of towering shelves that surrounded them. The woman passed on as if in a trance.

Helen's unease, her headache, her coldness, all crystallized into a dread so profound that her breath caught in her throat. She glanced wildly round. Where was Sally? How long had she been gone? The shelves seemed to curve toward her. The lights seemed brighter, as if to obscure the shadows that seemed to glide just beyond the edge of her vision. The cart handle seemed to pulse under her sweat-filmed palms . . .

A uniformed assistant came into the aisle, holding a pricing gun limply at her side. A wave of relief flooded over Helen as she stared at the girl across the acres of freezer chests that sent misty wisps of condensation trailing upward. She pushed her cart toward the girl.

"Excuse me," she said. The girl turned slowly toward her, her face blank. "I seem to have lost my friend," said Helen, forcing gaiety into her voice. "Have you seen a . . ." Her words trailed into silence. How could she describe Sally adequately, just an anonymous shopper, in a print dress, with a cart? She realized the girl was still staring at her, her mouth slightly open, her eyes opaque. She hasn't heard a word, thought Helen in horror. The gun came up, and the girl began marking prices on packets of butter without looking at them, her face still turned to Helen. Only the mechanical click of the pricing gun punctured the silence. Helen backed slowly away from her, tugging at her cart.

"There you are!" Sally's bright voice sounded over a sudden tumult. At once the passages were filled with shoppers and Sally was struggling determinedly through them toward her. She waved a handful of toothpaste boxes. "Did you miss out?" she said as she came abreast of Helen. More boxes littered the mound of groceries piled high in her cart.

Helen stared at her wordlessly. A conviction grew in her mind, lapping across her consciousness like turgid floodwaters. This was not Sally. Sally had been taken—Sally, the ideal customer—absorbed into the supramarket she served so well. And in her place, some product of the supramarket, some artificiality kept deep in the recesses of the freezers, behind the pizza subs and the hamburger patties, something to be turned loose with frosted hair and rime-encrusted arms, a siren to lure more shoppers into the caverns of the supramarket.

"Where were you?" she whispered, her voice papery dry. Sally looked puzzled, innocent. "At the toothpaste," she said. "Didn't you hear me say I was going?"

Helen let go of her cart and turned blindly away. "I'm going," she said. "I'm going outside. I'll wait for you there."

Sally's tone was scandalized. "You can't go without your cart!" she called after her. Helen ignored her. She dashed toward the dizzyingly long row of check-out counters. All were full. Queues of women stood in line, their carts thrust in front of them like pagan offerings. She was suddenly conscious of the loud tapping sound her shoes made as she hurried toward the queues. Women turned to look at her, some indifferently, some suspiciously. She paused, indecisive.

The turnstiles wouldn't let her out—they were made that way deliberately. She couldn't push past all

those women. She couldn't wait in line without a cart.
For one wild moment she considered leaping the
fence that caged the shopping carts—but the thought
made her burn with embarrassment.

"See," came a voice behind her shoulder. "I *said*
you couldn't go without your cart." She turned. Sally
was there with her cart as well as her own. She offered
Helen the handle, her smile as sweet as a Sara Lee
dessert, her eyes like chips of ice. The handle where
she had held it was icy cold to Helen's nerveless
fingers.

"Are you sure you have everything?" Sally went on.
Helen nodded mutely. She sensed the shadows closing
in. She saw Sally smile again, revealing snow-white
teeth and a frosty breath. "That's good," Sally said. "I
knew you'd learn. The supramarket *loves* a satisfied
customer."

JENDICK'S SWAMP

by Joseph Payne Brennan

AT THE TIME, CHRIS KELLINGTON WAS ONLY A CONSTABLE in Greystone Bay; he didn't have much to do. Occasionally he was called out by a farmer whose fences had been damaged by a neighbor's cows. Now and then there were minor thefts—pumpkins lifted from somebody's back lot, a few tools taken from the town truck.

Sometimes he stopped at my place for a chat. If I was hunched at my typewriter, hammering away, he'd merely remark on the weather and stroll off. If I was puttering around, he'd stay and talk.

One afternoon, after I'd finished my writing chores, he came in and sat down. No matter what the weather was, he'd head for a worn and somewhat rickety kitchen chair near my old wood-burning stove. He'd

157

prop his feet on the edge of the woodbox and lean back.

It was late August, warm and sultry. I broke out some chilled apple cider.

Chris sipped appreciatively. "Best cider I've had all summer!" After some routine remarks, he looked up with a quizzical expression. "Kirk, any chance you remember the Jendicks?"

I had to ponder a minute. "I remember some rumors. A sort of inbred, run-down family. Squatters, kind of. Built a big house on a knoll in the middle of a quicksand bog. Lived by hunting mostly. A wild bunch best avoided. Died out many years ago."

Kellington nodded. "You've summed it up fairly well. Wasn't a bog, though; it was the marshes on the other side of North Hill. A treacherous-enough place, no matter what you call it. I was in there only once and I was glad when I'd sloshed my way out. I didn't sink in any quicksand but probably I was close to it. It's pretty certain that a number of hunters went in there and never returned."

"What brought the Jendicks and their quicksand swamp to mind?" I asked.

He set down his cider glass. "Funny thing. About a week ago some New York character named Lawton was visiting the Clarksons in the Bay—cousins, I think. He considered himself a hunter. Brought along a brand-new sporting rifle. Well, he wandered around the back end of North Hill without any luck and was about to give up when he spotted a deer. Spooked it but caught sight again and kept following. Tracked it into the marshes. The deer got clean away; before long Lawton was lost. Trudged around for hours getting soaked up to his beltline and finally glimpsed a house standing on a knoll—he called it a hill. Said the house was a wreck, rotted and moldy-looking, and he naturally assumed it was uninhabited. Well, he climbed up the knoll to rest and dry off a bit, if that was possible. While he was sitting there, he had a strange feeling that he was being watched. The Clarksons quoted him as saying: 'I had the worst sense of impending danger I've ever experienced.' Stood up and turned around and there were two eyes glaring at him from one of the dark window apertures. Eyes like those of a wild animal. But he swears he saw the shadowy form of a man.''

Kellington shrugged. "That's about it. He rushed away, back into the swamp, and never turned around. Found his way out by sheer luck. Doesn't know whether he was followed or not. By the time I got the story secondhand from the Clarksons, Lawton had left for New York.''

I refilled the cider glasses. "Makes a spooky little anecdote. I imagine a tramp had settled down in the old Jendick house and didn't welcome visitors.''

Chris frowned. "Well—maybe. But I've got a nagging urge to check it out.''

"What's to check, Chris? A squatter in an abandoned house surrounded by a swamp where scarcely anybody ventures? Sure, you can get yourself half drowned going in there but what's accomplished? You evict some half-witted derelict and like as not he takes up quarters in somebody's barn and causes real trouble.''

"I'd make sure he cleared right out of town. Aside from that, I guess maybe I have a hankering to get a look at that old Jendick house—or what's left of it.''

He rearranged his feet on the woodbox and leaned back. "They were a weird bunch, Kirk. You've heard some rumors, but maybe not all. Seems old Jendick

was part Indian—Pequot, I guess, though I'm not
sure. Anyway, there's a legend that some of the early
tribes worshiped a so-called Spirit of the Swamp. I
think he—it—was named Iththaqua. In exchange for
sacrifices, Iththaqua was supposed to guide his worshipers safely through the labyrinths of the swamp
and eventually grant them other favors as well. I've
heard it said that during a hunt in the swamp, the
Jendicks always tried to catch one creature alive
—even though wounded—in order to sacrifice it to
Iththaqua."

"And in exchange, Iththaqua kept them from getting lost or drowned?" I interposed.

"Something like that. Anyway, there might be some
clue left in the house."

I shook my head. "The Jendicks don't sound like
the kind who kept written records. And even if they
did, any journal would be long gone by now
—weather, rats, roaches."

"You're probably right," he agreed. "But I'd still
like a look in that house before it rots away completely."

I grinned at him. "You always were a stubborn cuss!
Well, let me know when you plan to drown yourself
and I'll tag along. My current yarn's hit a dry plateau
and I need to get away from it for a day or two."

"How about tomorrow, then? Midmorning. Say,
ten. I'll bring a Thermos and sandwiches."

"Fine. I'll be ready."

He turned at the door. "Better wear hip boots!"

The next day was overcast and humid. The hip
boots were hot and highly uncomfortable, but once we
started into the swamp, I was grateful for Chris's
suggestion that I wear them.

The swamp was a world to itself. On the north end

of the marshland, it was shadowy, nearly silent, filled with the smell of still water and dissolving vegetation. Dense stands of hemlock, spruce, and black ash crowded along narrow aisles slippery with sphagnum moss. Tall cinnamon ferns and tangled patches of nettles clustered around the trunks. In some places the remains of fallen and decaying trees had created little hummocks which rose above the level of the surrounding pools. I recognized a few bird sounds but the only bird I glimpsed was a small green heron which glided away over the glistening water.

Although many of the pools were relatively shallow, the old-time quicksand rumors held us to a slow and hesitant advance.

While we paused as Chris adjusted his shoulder pack, I questioned him in regard to the location of the Jendick house.

"I might as well admit," he confessed, "that I'm trusting largely to luck. I do know that the place is supposed to be situated in the middle someplace and that—at one time at least—there was a stand of black-gum trees alongside the knoll the house is set on."

We slogged along in silence most of the time. The footing was treacherous; our attention was concentrated on the terrain immediately ahead. At one point, I slipped and went to my knees in algae-scummed water. The hip boots helped.

The silence became oppressive. Although sun seldom penetrated the overhead screen of tree branches and climbing vines, heat and humidity increased as the morning wore on.

"Does this devil's morass have a name?" I asked, by way of conversation.

Turning, Chris looked at me in surprise. "Jendick's Swamp, of course."

Around noon, chancing on a cleared and relatively dry patch of ground, we stopped and sat down. Coffee and an egg-salad sandwich revived my spirits a bit.

"We'll stumble on the place soon," I predicted with forced optimism.

"Sure," Chris agreed, "if we don't travel in a big circle."

"Didn't you bring a compass?"

"There's one in the pack somewhere. We've been moving north so far. But the trouble is, I'm not positive about the knoll's location. I *think* it's about in the middle, but I can't vouch for it. And I'm not sure of the size of the swamp. It may have shrunk—or spread—drastically over the years. I think we'll swing toward the northwest. That means we veer left. I don't need a compass for that."

We moved on. Conversation dwindled away. The silence seemed all-pervading and somehow ominous. We plodded through an acre or more where close-growing, creeper-laden swamp oaks proved nearly impenetrable. More than once, we waded through pools up to our waists. Our boots, luckily tight at the tops, kept out most of the water.

As I slogged doggedly along behind him, I noticed that Chris was becoming increasingly hesitant. Frowning, he paused frequently while he peered through the moist, matted tangle of trees and twisting vines which surrounded us.

I feared he was lost but I said nothing. The heat and the unaccustomed exercise were taking their toll, however. My legs ached; I was starting to feel dizzy.

I was on the point of suggesting a ten-minute break when Chris stopped and pointed.

"There! To the left, ahead!"

Squinting in the direction he indicated, I saw a line of dark trees which rose slightly above the level of the others around us.

"Look like black gums to me. Let's check!"

Minutes later we pushed our way through under-brush beneath a stand of tall black-gum trees.

Pointing ahead, Chris nodded. "Jendick's house!"

Sprawled on an overgrown knoll before us lay a half-collapsed, ramshackle building which nearly de-fied description. Rooms appeared to have been added at random with no regard for uniformity. A sagging second story stretched over only part of the first. All windowpanes were broken or missing; two window apertures had been boarded up; the others gaped open. Shingles hung askew alongside patches of loose tar paper. A wooden front door, panels split, hung by one rusty hinge. A green mold, abetted by the damp air of the swamp, lay like a slimy glaze of hastily applied paint over the entire house. Shaggy clumps of juniper, burdock, and willow saplings crowded along-side the structure.

There was no sign of life, much less occupancy. Save for the metallic chirr of a cicada, far off in the swamp, unbroken silence prevailed.

Chris spoke first. "A few years more and it'll just sink into the cellar—if there is one. Let's take a closer look."

Moving through a barrier of burdock and juniper shrubs, we walked up to a window aperture and looked into a plank-floored dusty room, empty except for a heap of sticks and straw in one corner plus a scattered litter of rusting cans, cracked bottles, and miscellaneous rags of discarded clothing.

What struck me at once—almost literally—was the

smell. Part of it was merely the musty pungency of mold and rotting wood, but there was something else—a sickening rancid stink which I could not identify but which I found more repellent than any other odor I could remember.

I pulled away from the window. "What is *that*?"

Chris drew back as hastily as I and shook his head. "I guess some critter crawled in there to die. Maybe it's the combination of mold and maggots!"

Treading cautiously, we circled the house. In the rear we stumbled on some discarded remnants of broken furniture, a split cask, and the nearly liquescent remains of a rotting carpet. Whenever we paused to peer into a window, an overpowering reek drove us back.

"The chances of any written record surviving in that reeking shambles is remote," I observed.

"I sure wouldn't bet on it," Chris agreed.

We made our way to the far edge of the knoll, away from the house, and sat down on some dry ground near a juniper bush. Sunlight had glinted through the overcast several times during the morning but now the sky was filled with dark grey clouds again.

Seen from the knoll, the surrounding swamp appeared even more forbidding than when we were actually slogging through it. At a distance, the fetor emanating from inside the house was no longer detectable, but I loathed the mere sight of the sagging mold-covered clapboards.

"After we've rested a few minutes, let's get started out of here," I suggested.

Chris remained silent for a minute or two. Looking out over the swamp, he scrubbed his chin. "Well, it would be sort of a shame, having come this far, to leave without even going inside."

I stared at him as if he had gone insane. "*Inside?* We'd never get that smell out of our clothes—or off our skins!"

He grinned. "Bad, isn't it? But I think after we'd beaten our way back out of the swamp, it would be pretty well worn off."

Knowing Chris, I sighed and stood up. "Let's get it over with, then. My stomach is doing flip-flops already."

As we shoved aside the splintered front door, the one remaining hinge fell out and the door dropped to the ground.

Chris smiled wryly. "Vandalism, that is. I'll bring charges against myself when we get back."

As soon as we stepped inside, the smell overwhelmed us. Hoping Chris would hurry, I tried to take only shallow breaths.

We tramped through a succession of grimy, dust-laden rooms. One contained the frame of an armchair, another a ripped mattress, sprinkled with mold. A rear room, whose floor and walls were saturated with congealed grease, we assumed had served as kitchen.

Glancing up a staircase which appeared on the verge of total collapse, we saw grey daylight filtering through a sagging roof.

"We'll skip the second floor," he said. "If the stairs didn't tumble under our weight, the roof would probably fall on our heads."

I sighed with relief. "That's it, then. Let's get out."

"Well, I guess. Wait—" Crossing back through the kitchen, he called to me. "There's a corner door here."

I heard a door creak as I reluctantly returned to the kitchen. Chris stood in front of an open door in one corner. He pointed downward. "We forgot the cellar."

My stomach tightened at the smell which swept through the open door. It was the same sickening odor which seemed to permeate the entire house—only stronger.

"We forgot the cellar?" I repeated. "Let's *forget* the cellar! We're apt to pass out down there."

But he was already pulling a small flashlight out of his pack. "Pretty awful, isn't it? But I ought to take a look. Stairs look fairly good. You stay here."

He started down. Shaking my head, I followed.

Once at the bottom of the stairs, the rancid reek all but overcame us. By the light of the flash, we saw that the floor of the place was dirt, shiny with spreading snail tracks and grey-green fungus. A cobwebbed open doorway just beyond the bottom of the flight of stairs led into a large room which was obviously the main cellar space.

As we entered, the light picked out a heap of crates and cartons piled in the center of the room. Beyond, near the far wall, stretched a long double row of big vats, interspersed with smaller casks.

The stench here was insufferable.

Chris played his light along the lines of vats. "We'd better look in one of those. There's the source of our sweet aroma."

The first vat was empty, as was the adjacent one, but Chris stood frozen as he directed his light into the third.

"What is it?" I moved to his side, curiosity overcoming my initial hesitation.

The vat was loosely packed with irregular-shaped chunks of bloody-looking grey-white meat immersed in a yellowish liquid which appeared to be some kind of brine.

I stared down at the vat contents for a long half minute before I realized what I was looking at.

When I finally looked up—white-faced, I'm sure —Chris was watching me. He nodded. "I'm pretty sure it's what we think it is."

He flashed his light around the cellar. A two-pronged, long-handled, skewerlike fork hung from an overhead hook.

Taking it down, he probed into the vat.

When he lifted the fork, it held a forearm with the hand still attached. The brine had prevented decay but the flesh looked puffy and discolored.

Chris shook it back into the vat and we went on down the rows.

About a third of the vats and a few of the small casks were partially filled with ghastly chunks and gobbets of human flesh. The last vat at the end of one row was crammed with human bones.

Chris played the light over them and spoke one word which made me shudder. "Gnawed," he said.

"Maybe," I whispered desperately, "they fed —some kind of swamp animal."

Chris shook his head. "No sense kidding ourselves, Kirk. The Jendicks became cannibals at the last. No other explanation."

"But you said the Jendicks died out a long time ago."

"I thought they had. And even strong brine wouldn't preserve flesh year after year—at least I don't believe it would."

I didn't think the time or place was suitable for a discussion on the preservation properties of brine.

"Chris," I urged, "let's get out of this butcher shop! We can talk later!"

"Agreed." He moved toward the doorway.

We were just starting up the stairs when the thing appeared at the top. We both froze, staring upward with shock and disbelief.

It looked human, but barely so. A huge greasy mass of tangled white hair. Wild staring eyes of a rabid animal. Writhing lips around a toothless hole of a mouth. A cadaverlike body, hairy, gaunt, scab-covered. Clothing, a tattered remnant of trousers, ending at the knees. A nightmare shape straight out of Goya.

The thing's voice was a high-pitched, half-coherent scream. "Thought ye the Jendicks been all gone, eh? Old Asa ain't! Come snoopin', hah? Ah'll pickle ye both!"

It had been holding out of sight a massive length of tree limb, or trunk, which it now swung into view. The club looked like an oak sapling torn up by the roots. One huge hairy hand circled the base of it.

As it started down the stairs, Chris gripped my arm. "Back into the other room! Quick!"

As we ran into the brine-vat room, the creature's shrill, mirthless chuckle followed us. "'Twon't do ye no good ta hide! Old Asa c'n see in the dark!"

Chris stuck the flash into my hand. "Shine it in his eyes. Give me a minute."

As he groped somewhere behind me, the murderous thing appeared in the doorway. I directed the light straight into its eyes.

It froze, startled and obviously blinded, for a moment. Abruptly, squealing with rage, it flung itself sideways into the room.

At that moment Chris moved up beside me. As I swung my light, I saw that he was holding the long-handled, skewerlike fork.

"Keep it on him!" he warned me.

I quickly swept the light in a half circle but the thing which called itself Asa Jendick had disappeared in the darkness.

"Crawling," Chris whispered. "Lower the light."

As I did so, both of us heard a slight scraping sound somewhere among the vats. Instinctively, we dropped to a crouch. Something hurtled through the air where our heads had been a second before and crashed against the farther wall. I assumed it was a cask. It seemed to have been hurled with the force and speed of an artillery projectile.

I aimed the flash along the row of vats and casks. Before the cone of light reached the far end of the row, something came rushing toward us from the near end. By the time I swung the light back, it was only feet away. In the circle of light it seemed like an impossible apparition materialized from the darkness and the foul, seething corruption of the cellar itself.

Chris dropped something at my feet. "Backpack. Thirty-two."

Holding the skewer fork at the ready, he sprang in front of me to meet the lunge of the crazed creature.

I heard a tearing impact followed by a scream of rage and pain. Chris stepped backward, nearly tripping over me. "God!" he exclaimed in a shocked voice.

My frantic groping closed on the butt of the .32 automatic at the bottom of the pack. Yanking it out with one hand and aiming the light with the other, I saw what had caused Chris's exclamation.

Asa Jendick's huge hands were tugging at the skewer projecting from his chest. It had been driven into his ribcage up to the handle.

As we watched in disbelief, he managed a fierce final tug. The fork came out. Blood poured out of the wound; when he opened his mouth in another squeal of rage, blood spilled out of that as well.

Holding the skewer in both hands, he lurched toward us. I fired the .32 six times without stopping and at that range I couldn't miss, but he kept on coming.

We sprang aside as he stabbed the air between us with the lethal fork.

He fell to his knees, stood up, still holding the bloody skewer, raised his head, and screamed shrilly: "Iththaqua!"

For just a moment, he seemed to be listening. He dropped, rolled, twitched, lay still.

I held the light on him. Neither of us spoke.

For relief, I looked off into the cellar darkness, away from the last Jendick lying on the fungus-covered floor.

"Kirk!" Chris said suddenly. He stood looking down at the hideous hairy thing.

It appeared to be undergoing some kind of degenerative transformation. The facial skin, matted hair and all, had loosened. As we watched, it slid off, exposing the skull bones. The body skin began to shrivel. Instead of blood, a yellowish ichor began oozing out of the gaping chest wound.

We went on watching, horrified but hypnotized, as the process of decay and dissolution accelerated. Within minutes we stared down at a half-mummified skeleton. Even this, swiftly turning black and desiccated, started to disintegrate.

Chris heard it first and raised his head—a roaring sound in the distance, a sound like a hundred tractors suddenly revved up and rolling fast.

"Let's go!" Grabbing his pack, he ran through the doorway, up the stairs. I bolted behind him.

When we charged out of the ruinous charnel house, through the juniper bushes, across the overgrown knoll, the sky was already black. The roaring sound seemed nearly overhead.

"Swamp's our only hope! Far as we can get!" Chris yelled.

"Tornado?" I yelled back; he didn't answer.

Plunging into the swamp, we ran like madmen. Chris grabbed my arm and pulled me down where dense tangles of shrub and brush surrounded us.

"Too dangerous near trees!" he shouted. "Lie flat!"

A darkness like that of moonless midnight closed on the swamp. The roaring increased, obliterating all else. A mighty wind swept through the swamp. Rain cascaded down. I was aware of toppling trees nearby. Bushes were torn out by the roots and tossed away. I felt that at any moment I would be scooped up by the wind, pitched and pummeled to death.

I lay prone, arms over my head, as the tornadolike torrent of wind, rain, and sound raged on. Suddenly aware of light, I moved an arm and glanced aside at Chris. He was watching the sky. I looked up.

Etched above, against a background of rushing sulfurous cloud masses, was the huge fiery image of a distorted Indian face, a diabolical face, blazing with fury, filled with the evil of the Pit itself.

It hung there, its flaming outline crowding the sky over the swamp. I felt convinced that the glaring eyes in that malevolent face were fixed upon us.

"Iththaqua!" Chris gasped.

Slowly, at first almost imperceptibly, the roaring sound began to abate. As it did so, the lurid countenance towering above us gradually faded. Contours of the burning, hate-twisted face became blurred. The glaring eyes turned blank. At length only the jagged yellow outline of a face remained. Finally even this was swept away in the tumult of racing, gale-driven clouds.

Soaked and shaken, we stood up unsteadily. The sky was still black, and though the wind had dropped noticeably, it remained strong enough to fling wet leaves and other debris into our faces.

Our trip out of the swamp was a suspense story in itself. All trails and landmarks appeared to have been torn away. And the swamp was flooded. Hillocks and ridges we had traversed on our way in were now under water. The heavy rain never slackened. It was a miracle that we both escaped from that mud-laden watery morass without drowning.

By the time we emerged from the swamp, skirted the marshes, and found our way over North Hill and back to my place, we were at the end of our strength.

After I had started a fire in the wood stove and poured two stiff brandies, we sat down in the kitchen.

Chris scarcely spoke until we had finished one glass and poured a second.

"Well, Kirk, I'm feeling half human again, but I'm too dragged out to talk much. I've been thinking that I ought to do a little research. Meanwhile, I'd be grateful if you kept our little adventure to yourself —at least for a time. I'm hoping the town folks think it was just a random tornado centered around the swamp. If they saw the sky image, it will complicate matters. But maybe even that could be explained away as a freak of lightning combined with funny cloud formations."

I gave him my word. Over a week passed before I saw him again.

He sat down in his favorite kitchen chair and propped his feet on the woodbox.

"As I hoped," he told me, "the natives shrugged it off as an early tornado spinning around near the swamp. Not a soul noticed the sky image." He chuckled. "I guess nobody stayed outdoors to watch cloud formations!"

"You've done that research?" I asked.

He nodded. "I found some information about Iththaqua in an old volume at the Hartford library. A collection of local Indian legends. Iththaqua was supposed to be a sort of swamp demon who granted favors to Indians who made sacrifices to him—both animal and human. In return for blood sacrifices, he would protect hunters in the swamp. And—listen to this—in some cases he would grant unheard-of longevity to faithful worshipers!"

I thought back to that repulsive, bullet-riddled body on the floor of the cellar, quickly decaying before our eyes.

"That *was* old Jendick, then?"

"I'm convinced of it. So far as I can figure, he would be nearly a hundred and fifty years old!"

"How do you explain that fiery face looming in the sky above us?"

"In his last extremity, old Jendick called on Iththaqua for help—and Iththaqua responded. Jendick must have been the very last of his worshipers, however, and with Jendick's death, Iththaqua's power immediately started to wane. Iththaqua, you might say, was kept alive by the faith of his followers —and by the blood of their sacrifices, perhaps. When none of his followers remained alive, he himself could no longer exist. The best he could do was to summon up enough final strength for a kind of thunderbolt exit while he glared down at us—boiling with fury but basically impotent."

"What about—what we found in those brine barrels?"

Chris shifted uneasily. "I feel guilty about that. You know, about eight months ago, a tramp was staying in the remains of a shack in woods near the edge of the swamp. Never bothered anybody, so I let him alone. After he suddenly disappeared, I looked in the shack and found quite a cache of new canned goods, crackers, coffee, and so on. Seemed strange to me that he'd leave all that stuff, but I shrugged it off. Now I'm wondering if he wandered into the swamp and ended up as a sacrifice to Iththaqua—and subsequently an occupant of the brine vats!"

He stood up. "I'm also wondering about those hunters of years ago who were supposed to have been caught in quicksand. You'll remember that we didn't see any sign of quicksand, bad as the swamp was in other respects. Maybe those lost hunters were caught by the Jendicks!"

After he left, I regretted that I hadn't asked him what he proposed to do about the pickled human flesh we had found in that charnel-house cellar. I had an answer a month or so later when he stopped by.

"I have an aviator friend at the Hartford airport," he told me. "We took a helicopter ride over the swamp one afternoon. The Jendick house—in fact, the knoll itself—was washed away. The row of black-gum trees has disappeared. Not a stick of wood visible. The chances of recovering any brine-preserved human remains is gone forever. And I can't honestly say I'm sorry!"

I've tramped through the woods and meadows around Greystone Bay many times since my adventure with Chris, but I never again ventured into Jendick's Swamp. In fact, I've been very active in all movements to preserve the marshland as a wildlife preserve. I'm not protecting it against people so much. It's the swamp. It keeps moving south.

FOGWELL

by Steve Rasnic Tem

HE'D NEVER FELT LIKE ONE OF THEM, NOT EVEN FOR A moment.

Willis watched them at night, from his bedroom window. His parents didn't understand why he was always going to bed early. He said it was because he wanted to read, or because he was tired. But he really just wanted to be in his bedroom with the lights out, in protected dark, so he could watch them, see what they were up to.

Not that he could ever really tell. They stayed in the shadows, and whispered a lot. But at least he'd be able to see if they ever decided to climb the wall to the porch roof, and his window. If they ever decided to come after him.

If they ever came after him he could always cry and scream, create what Grandma would call a ruckus, and Mom and Dad would come in to save him from them.

He knew that last part wasn't true. They'd come in, all right, but they'd come in to see what the hell was going on. They'd come in to see what was wrong with Willis this time. Why he was such a baby. Why he couldn't sleep through the night like other boys.

Sometimes Willis thought that Mom and Dad didn't understand because they had lived here so long. Mom and Dad had both been born in Greystone Bay and had lived here all of their lives.

Willis had been born in Chicago, when Mom and Dad were on vacation. Dad had always kidded about that: "Your mama just couldn't wait, I guess." And then he'd laugh, but Willis didn't think it was a real laugh. Willis thought it was one of those laughs people made when they were trying to hide something.

Willis heard a lot of laughs like that in Greystone Bay.

Once he had come home early from the library and heard his mom and dad in their bedroom, talking about it.

"If he'd been born here in the Bay like we'd planned he wouldn't be this way," his dad had said.

"You've no right to blame me. You were the one who wanted to go so far away, you know, even with me pregnant."

"I didn't know you were going to pull a stunt like that. I didn't know if I was even going to get you out of Chicago."

"It was a better hospital, and . . ."

"It was *Chicago*! You didn't want to leave after he was born. Or are you trying to tell me you don't remember that? You wanted to stay in Chicago, and not tell any of the people back here where we were!"

"I was scared, John. I was a lot younger then, and I was scared."

Willis couldn't quite figure out what they were talking about, but he sneaked out of the house after that last part. He was suddenly afraid about them finding him there, home early from the library and everything. So he went off into the woods and stayed awhile, until it was the time he'd told them he'd be home.

Willis liked the woods around the Bay. There wasn't the noise (he couldn't understand how people could live in the city) and there weren't all the faces—pale and staring. There were trees so tall he couldn't see their tops. There was ground that hid stone and pockets of stone, and bold animals.

Sometimes Willis wondered what the animals thought about the people of Greystone Bay. If they wanted to have anything to do with people other than him. The noise people made would bother them, he thought, so he tried to be as quiet as he could.

The animals who lived in the woods outside Greystone Bay surprised him some. The animals he saw in books and on TV had lots of teeth and were wild, and wild meant you couldn't keep them as pets because they'd act nervous and try to get away and maybe even go crazy and try to bite you. Willis knew that wild animals were nothing like the stuffed animals his mom used to make him.

The animals Willis met in the woods didn't show their teeth, although he figured they must have them. The animals Willis met in the woods had pale fur and white eyes and were thinner than what he would have expected wild animals to be. They looked as if most of their guts had been taken out.

But they moved okay, and they didn't act sick.

There was a rabbit in the woods that moved around on its hind feet and stood taller than he would have expected a rabbit to.

There was a cat-thing (he couldn't tell what kind) that made a sound like a whisper and you couldn't always see it move.

There was a deer that leaped in slow motion, and when it landed it shook all over for a few minutes, before leaping again.

Willis was sure that all these things had teeth, but none of them showed their teeth.

Sometimes when he'd run off into the woods these and other animals would come close to him, only a few feet away, and they'd stay with him, watch him, until it was time for him to go home again.

At school he usually didn't have any friends, but sometimes on the playground a few kids would come close to him, only a few feet away, and watch him until it was time to come in from recess.

They didn't show their teeth either, but he knew they had them.

Sometimes at night, when they thought he was asleep, Willis's mom and dad came into his room and stood at the foot of his bed and watched him.

Willis spent most of his time by himself. That part didn't always bother him, at least not so bad. He had other things to fill his time.

He could imagine things. He could imagine things better than the things he saw in Greystone Bay. He could imagine city halls bigger than the town's City Hall. He could imagine hotels far more elegant than the Ocean Arms. He could imagine houses far older, far more ornate. Even though he'd never seen these bigger and better things—he'd never been outside the Bay since he was a few weeks old—he could still imagine them. He had a real talent for imagining but only his sister Elaine and two boys at school—Johnny Williams and Roger Plummer—knew he was so good at imagining. He could see this thing in his head, and he could see that thing in his head, things far more wonderful and strange than what could be found in the "real" world.

Until they showed him the fogwell, and he saw what it could do.

He didn't know if he could call Johnny and Roger his friends, exactly. If they were his friends they were the only ones he had. Not that that bothered him too much—he had the imagining, after all—but maybe it bothered him a little. Sometimes maybe it bothered him a lot.

But Johnny and Roger were *best* friends, and had been ever since Willis could remember. Willis was the *third* friend, the friend of Johnny *and* Roger. Second best. And somehow he knew that's the way it would always be. Whoever he met, he'd be the third one. He'd never be anybody's *best* friend.

But you couldn't say that. You couldn't complain about it, really. Then you might end up with no friends at all, like *he'd* been, most of the time, most of what he could remember.

Willis couldn't figure why that was, unless it was something in *him* that made it be that way. That's the only thing he could figure. Something in him that made him imagine so well, and something in him that made him nobody's best friend. It had to be something like that.

Roger was the short friend, the friend with the dark hair, but with eyes so pale you didn't always notice they even had pupils. Willis had first noticed this future friend standing on the corner near their house —it had seemed he'd stood out there for days, because every time Willis had looked out his bedroom window Roger was there.

Then one day, while Willis was passing by this strange boy on his way to school, Roger had handed him a frog. Just handed it to him, put it right into Willis's hand. Willis had been so surprised he'd taken the frog, accepted it just like it was a natural, everyday thing for somebody to be handing you a frog. The frog had been an albino, all pale and shiny, so pale and bloodless, in fact, that Willis would have sworn it was a dead thing, all the blood drained out of it. But its eyes had moved, round and round inside the bulging sockets, and then its feet had started rubbing back and forth across Willis's forearm, as if it were dreaming of water, swimming along Willis's arm.

Willis had been afraid, at the time, that it might open its mouth all of a sudden, and Willis would have to scream. But the frog didn't, and Willis didn't.

The next day Roger had met Willis out on the playground, and brought his friend Johnny to meet him. Johnny was taller than anyone else in the class, and had very thin blond hair. His hair was so thin and so light that it almost disappeared on real sunny days, so that Johnny looked old, bald and tall and stooped.

Johnny didn't say much, just seemed to always be looking down at you, breathing all the air somewhere over your head. Johnny made little gasping noises when he breathed. It was kind of creepy. Like a fish out of water.

"Hey, Willis! Let's go in the woods! Tell us what *you* see. Tell us some stories about the woods."

That was Roger. He was always trying to get Willis

to go into the woods with them. He was always trying to get Willis to tell new stories about the woods. That would make Willis feel all funny inside. Kind of good, that Roger would invite him, that Roger would want him there. And kind of proud, that they'd see that he had that imagination, and that they'd want to hear some more of his stories. But kind of scared, too, and unsure, because Willis liked to be in the woods by himself. It was *his* place. He didn't want to share it with anybody else.

"C'mon, Willis! We can camp out! You can tell us all about the woods!"

Until there was that one day that Willis finally gave in. Roger and Johnny had been gone most of the summer—Willis never knew where—and he'd had nobody to play with the whole time.

Summers were the worst. You couldn't pretend you had too much schoolwork to do to play with the other kids. You couldn't pretend you didn't need to play with the other kids. And he'd wanted to play with somebody so bad.

So Roger and Johnny finally dropped by the house a couple of days before school was supposed to start that year. Willis had wanted to play so bad, and Roger and Johnny were already walking toward the woods.

Before he knew it Willis was running after them. He had an awful time catching up.

"What do you see, Willis?" That was Johnny, and he always breathed even funnier when he asked questions like that.

Willis just kind of grunted, like it was a joke. They weren't even near the woods yet.

"What do you see, what do you see," Roger chanted, and the two boys raced ahead of him. Willis ran as hard as he could, but they were too far ahead of him. Before he could catch up they had disappeared into the woods.

Willis didn't like it, didn't like it at all. The woods were his place, and now his sometimes friends were in there by themselves. Finding his secret sitting places and his secret lying-down places. Looking at his secret animals.

He stumbled as he ran after them, falling hard on his face. He began to cry. He got up and ran toward the woods, that suddenly seemed too far away, just a dim grey fence of a thing over the hill.

Willis tried to imagine being there, being with his animals, curled up in the dark places, so dark you couldn't see the spiders and lizards and other things he didn't like so much. Just the animals, his animals, because they kind of glowed inside and didn't show their teeth.

Then he was there, standing right inside the woods, the trees suddenly taller than anything he had ever imagined, hurting his head with their tallness, crowding out the sky with their tallness.

And everything was so quiet, quieter even than his whole life.

The trees were like the ones in the Snow White story, or Snow-drop, when she was taken into the woods to be killed on order of the wicked queen, the wicked mother. Or like the trees in "The Sleeping Beauty of the Woods," that grew so tall and wide, interlaced with brambles and thorns. He could see grey running shadows in the distance, weaving their way through the narrow spaces between the trees. He stopped and breathed deeply of the dark air to calm himself. Then he followed.

As Willis hiked deeper and deeper into the woods,

disappointment began to seize him, and the dark air tasted sour on his tongue. They'd gone in so quickly, without hesitating, it appeared as if Johnny and Roger knew their way around here. And all this time, Willis had thought of these woods as his own.

The trees had grown taller to protect Sleeping Beauty, but here they seemed an ever-growing screen to keep Willis out.

Suddenly the sound of Johnny's and Roger's progress through the woods became audible again, and Willis chilled—the sounds seemed so close by.

The luminous deer leaped the spaces between trees. The pale cat-thing rolled in the branches overhead. The tall rabbit remained invisible except for its eyes, which danced and floated in the dark.

Willis closed his eyes, wishing them gone. If he had to share them he'd rather not have them at all. But even with his eyes closed he could feel the patterns they made in the air.

Something tall and silver-gray moved from tree to tree. For a moment, Willis couldn't remember if he had opened his eyes or not. He thought it might be Johnny, playing hide-and-seek with him. He shut his eyes and opened them again—or was it the other way around? Either way, what he saw was the same. Something tall, something silver-grey, moved from tree to tree.

He hated hide-and-seek. Of all the games they played, this one was the worst. Kids you thought might be, might become, your friends suddenly went away, hid somewhere laughing at you while you were looking for them, so afraid that they were gone. They were off playing and having a good time and here you were all by yourself.

Mist had seeped out of the ground here and there,

and here and there Willis thought he could see Roger and Johnny running, hiding.

The woods had grown colder, the bark on the trees ice to the touch. Willis's breath turned to fog. Fog wreathed the trees like phantom boughs.

Willis imagined himself pulling the darkness over him like a cloak. To keep the fog away.

The fog hissed, and dampened his socks. The skin between socks and pant cuffs felt hard, brittle.

The fog hissed again, and there was Roger, a small dark silhouette in the fog. His arm a black branch in the air, beckoning.

Willis wanted to stay out of the fog, but he wanted to play so bad. The fog frightened him, and he was afraid he might get some of it inside. When he stepped into the fog he was careful to keep his mouth shut.

He figured the two grey shapes ahead of him—now and then disappearing, now and then broken into pieces by the fog—were Roger and Johnny. They'd slowed down some, maybe to let him catch up.

Willis was grateful, and didn't want to let them down. He tried to walk faster. The fog would stick to his shirt, his pants, his skin. Like it had glue in it. He had to keep rubbing himself as he walked, just to keep the fog off.

After a long time walking—Willis knew he'd never been this deep inside the woods before—the fog began to separate some. Roger and Johnny stopped. The darkness here was blacker than anything Willis had ever imagined. The trees were so black Willis couldn't tell how tall they were anymore. The sky was so black he couldn't see the stars anymore. He closed his eyes and opened them again, and there was no difference.

The ground was so soft he couldn't feel it. He felt as if he were standing in night air.

"Tell us what you see," Roger whispered, and Willis felt a center of blackness inside him give way, and a place even blacker opened up at the center of the woods, near where Johnny and Roger were standing.

The black center began to breathe, rough and heavy, just the way Johnny breathed. And smoke came out, wispy and thin, like hair—long, pale strands of it—and for some unaccountable reason Willis thought of his mother and wanted to run away, thinking that his mother must have died and she was there in the hole and her body was going to follow her hair and come out of the hole.

Willis could see pieces of the woods behind the smoke, like the smoke had light in it, and finally pieces of ground, low-lying brush, and backlit fallen branches.

And the smoke became fog, long columns then irregular clouds of it. And then there were pale animals coming out of the hole, the well, and drifting off into the darkness through the trees.

A white rabbit turned and stared at Willis before fading back into the night. A pale cat-thing hissed, and leaped into the dark.

Roger Plummer and Johnny Williams opened their mouths full of fog, and showed Willis their pale drifting teeth.

The ancient Victorians of North Hill stared down at Willis as he walked home from the library. The streets and the buildings here had a uniform and vaguely comforting greyness. Willis did not know why he felt comforted, he just knew that he was.

Some people would want to change that greyness,

make it into something new, something "dynamic,"
like other cities. But those people weren't the true
inhabitants of Greystone Bay. Willis, and the other
true inhabitants of Greystone Bay, had a certain
reluctance about changing the old.

From time to time, they would come up to him and
whisper. The other children. They would drift up the
sidewalk and whisper something in his ear, the
blanched fullness of their faces creased by their perfectly linear smiles. Their faces were white and soft,
like wet dough, smoke, or cloud.

"It's like a dream come true," he'd overheard his
father tell his mother that one evening. He was glad to
be able to please his parents.

He could not imagine another life besides this one.
In this life he had friends, pale faces who drifted up
the sidewalk and whispered. They didn't need to
show their teeth. He'd been born in Chicago, and
reborn in Greystone Bay. He could not imagine.

He opened his eyes and closed his eyes. Either way,
it was the same.

DEAD POSSUMS

by Kathryn Ptacek

IT WAS RAINING AND NEARLY DARK AND ALREADY BEGIN-
ning to get foggy. Damn, how he hated the fog. Hank
Strasak was dead-dog tired after a workday that began
at five A.M., and now all he looked forward to was
kicking off his shoes and lying back on the lumpy
couch in the living room until Mary-Ann called him
for dinner.

That was, if Mary-Ann was home.

They'd been having a few problems lately. Big
problems. What an understatement. He tried to grin
and caught a glimpse of himself in the rearview
mirror. The grey light of dusk washed out his normally dark skin color, and he looked like he had a rictus.
He relaxed his facial muscles, and the frown that
formed looked far more natural on his heavy features.

189

A curl of untrimmed hair flopped into his eyes and he blew at it.

The car veered slightly, forcing his attention back to his driving. Damn, he'd better watch what he was doing. He'd nearly gone off the road back there.

Something grey flashed against the darker grey of the street, and without thinking he tapped the horn, then realized it wouldn't do any good. He applied the brakes, but the creature was already under the wheels. He felt the sickening thump, slammed on the brakes. The car fishtailed to a stop alongside a deserted orange traffic cone, and he sat there for a moment before getting out and walking back to the animal.

A possum. And it was about as dead as it could be. He stared down at the blood-flecked fur and felt a little sick. It was the first time he'd run over anything. The first time. He walked around to the front of the car and stared down at the splash of blood already beginning to wash away in the rain.

He got in the car and drove away. He would be home soon. Home.

"I'm home, hon!" he called as he walked into the house on Ashley Street. He was careful not to slam the door; Mary-Ann had told him many times before that she hated when he slammed the door, and since then he'd been very careful not to do it. Except, of course, when he was pissed at her and didn't care what got her angry.

Nothing. The house was silent.

No Mary-Ann. No Heather. Where was she? She should have been home from school by now. Christ, she should have been doing her homework. He knew she had a math test tomorrow, and they'd planned on him quizzing her the night before.

So where were they?

He walked through the hushed house, alien with its emptiness. He glanced in Heather's neat bedroom with its pictures of horses and cats salvaged from magazines and pinned on the walls, in their bedroom, in the kitchen. No one. Shrugging, he returned to the bedroom to get out of his damp clothing. As he changed, he realized how long it had been since he felt her presence there. Too long. Once in dry jeans and shirt, he returned to the kitchen to look out the window over the sink at the backyard. He could barely see it now in the early darkness, but that didn't matter. He knew each inch of that yard.

He was proud of it, that little space of greenery. He'd worked long hours on weekends to put in the lawn and the flower beds along the neat wooden fence, and almost every Sunday he was out there raking or trimming or just admiring his work.

At work they called him a farmer.

They also called him a Polack. Czech, he repeated he didn't know how many times, I'm Czech —Bohemian—and they just laughed and called him a Pole. And told him another insulting joke about a Polish couple on their wedding night.

God, how he hated them and that miserable job. The glass factory had been founded by his grandfather, who'd come to this country from Bohemia in the last decade of the previous century. He'd brought with him the fine technique of glassmaking that made Bohemia glass so famous.

Grandfather Heinrich Strasak had built the factory from the ground up, and it had become well known throughout the country, and then his father had inherited it. That's when the problems had begun. His father had no head for business, and by the time Hank was old enough to know what was going on, his father had lost the factory, and now the grandson of its founder was working in it, just like any other guy in town.

It wasn't fair, Hank thought, not for the first time; but that was the way it was, and there wasn't much he could do. Still, it galled him. Particularly as it remained the Strasak Glass Works, and each day when he drove under the wrought-iron arch proclaiming the name, he flinched.

He pushed away from the sink and sat down. Nearly six, and they weren't back. He made a sandwich of ham and cheese and drank a beer, and by the time the last crumb was wiped up, he was still alone. He hadn't bothered with the light, and sat in complete darkness watching the rain as it splattered down the window-panes, and thought of the possum. Poor thing.

He sighed and rubbed a hand over his face, then got another beer and trailed into the living room. It was dark here, too, and he wondered what Mary-Ann would do if she came home then and found him in a dark house. She'd know he was brooding again, and why had she married him when he was just a grumpy ol' Pole.

Czech, he would reply wearily, and wonder why she couldn't remember that after twelve years of marriage. He remembered that she was German and English. It wasn't hard.

But Mary-Ann, he knew, didn't have much time for him or for remembering such things as his birthday or their anniversary, or for sitting down in the evenings and just talking with him. Not since she discovered her new religion. When they were first married she'd worked in an office, but after Heather was born, she'd stayed home. He didn't mind, although it would have been nice to have two incomes. Still, he liked having her here for Heather. And she never complained, so he supposed she didn't mind, either.

But when Heather was four, Mary-Ann got interested in some really weird stuff. Restlessness, he thought. She bought those screaming-headline tabloids at the supermarket and read them to him at dinner. He laughed and said they were all made-up stories, and she got mad, and threw a plate at him. Luckily it missed. But it didn't stop there.

She took yoga lessons; that didn't last long before being replaced by est, and in turn by Gestalt, water therapy, Scientology, and nirvana-ism. A few years ago she announced she was "going" vegetarian and she refused thereafter to touch any meat—not only wouldn't she eat it, she wouldn't prepare dishes with meat in them. So he shopped after work and bought the hamburger and hot dogs and pork chops, and at Thanksgiving, when they weren't going to her folks' house, he fixed the turkey. Again, he didn't mind.

The beer can was empty, so he tossed it into the garbage and fetched another one. He sat down in the living room.

One day last year he got a phone call at work. He listened quietly, then went down to bail his wife out of jail. By the time he got back, everyone knew where he'd been and why, and they were laughing at him. Oh, not always outright, of course, but he could tell. As he went by his co-workers, they'd fall silent, as if they'd been talking about him, or a moment later someone would giggle. That's when he'd told them to stuff it, and Old Man Marsh's widow called him in and reamed him out on his attitude.

It was even harder on Heather, though. Her classmates laughed at her, called her names, and said her mother was a criminal and a nut and that she was just as nutty. She cried at night when he tucked her in and asked why her mother was different, and not knowing the answer, he said she was just being kind to animals. How could he say that her mother really was a nut?

The animal-rights group Mary-Ann had joined wasn't just any ordinary humane group, he had realized then. It was a militant organization not content in simply writing letters to senators and congressmen. It wanted action. Immediate action, and it didn't care how it got it. And it sure as hell didn't mind the headlines it got along the way. The group, Mary-Ann informed him, was prepared to take up arms in defense of the animals—and even to die in that defense.

Sure, he liked animals. He had a dog as a kid, but he wasn't about to treat it like a human. This group thought they were. Mary-Ann and her friends had gone to a medical laboratory just below North Hill to protest the use of animals in experiments. She was busted by the police for spray-painting "Thou shalt not kill" on the outside of the building, while her buddies were busy inside letting the rabbits and rats and cats and dogs out of the wire cages. Her friends got busted, too. "Liberating God's creatures," they'd claimed, and they chanted biblical verses from their cells. That's when he learned they were mixing religion with their politics.

He didn't talk to her on the drive home nor all of that night, and it was then he realized how far they'd grown apart. He thought once or twice about divorce, but wasn't sure he was ready for it. Most of the time everything seemed to go all right.

There was, of course, that time when they were at the Fletchers and their daughter Jill wanted to show the new trick she'd spent all week teaching her golden retriever. Before the little girl could start, Mary-Ann stood up and coldly announced that she didn't want to see the trick because it was cruel to force animals to do something they obviously didn't want to do. Jill's face darkened and she ran crying from the room, and that's when Hank stood and said they better be running along.

He yelled all the way home, and so had she, and Heather, crying, huddled in the back with her hands over her ears.

All that time he put up with the multitude of booklets strewn across the table at breakfast time and the stacks of photocopied fliers that the group put up in markets and utility poles and under windshield wipers of cars in parking lots, but which had to be stored someplace, and somehow his house got volunteered. He even put up with the occasional meeting held there, and when he knew the group was coming over, he'd take Heather out to a movie or to walk or to a special snack at one of the restaurants on the harbor.

They no longer made love. She lay on her side of the bed, and he on his, and whenever he rolled over and touched her, she flinched. Soon he stopped that. She didn't call him by name anymore, either, and strangely that bothered him more than the other. She called him "he" or "your father" when she talked to Heather. Never "Hank," and sometimes at night, when he couldn't sleep, he would think he had become a nonentity to her.

She stopped taking care of the house, and he would come home to find not only the breakfast dishes still in the sink, but those from the previous night, as well as an assortment of ants and roaches. He endured unmade beds, and mildewed towels and tiles, stacks of papers everywhere, a film of dust coating everything, and with Heather he made it an adventure on weekends to see what they could clean up next in the house. They managed to keep up with the housework most of the time, and if Mary-Ann was aware, she gave no indication. She continued making her phone calls and pounded away at their old Olympia typewriter by the hour, drafting one letter after another.

And he tried to understand. But he couldn't; not anymore. It was as if she'd crossed a line somewhere and was moving ahead, while he was standing still, watching her as she faded into the distance. The farther away she got, the less he understood. He didn't like the idea of experiments; no one did, but to actually destroy laboratory equipment worth thousands of dollars . . . to disrupt research . . . to get violent . . . that was incredible. And to upset a little girl because she taught her puppy a trick—he couldn't forgive her for that. Not ever. Nor had the Fletchers, apparently, because they were never invited back, even though he saw Jack at work almost every day.

And then there was the time the group started petitioning the City Council to outlaw the annual winter dogsled races because they were cruel to dogs. He'd blown up then, too, as he reminded her that dogs had always worked for humans—that's why they'd been domesticated, for God's sake, and one of their tasks had been to pull sleds across snow and ice. She'd countered that that activity was no longer necessary, and if a dog had a choice, it wouldn't pull a sled.

He argued; she countered. They got nowhere, and finally parted in silence. Silence kept them away from each other the next week, too, and that was when Heather began sucking her thumb again. Ten years old and she had a habit like that. Disgusted, he tried to stop her, but Mary-Ann told him to leave the girl alone. She was simply expressing herself.

He and his pillow and a ratty old afghan his mother had crocheted when he was nineteen moved out onto the couch that night and remained there.

Sometimes he thought he was living a nightmare. Sure, he knew he didn't have it as bad in some ways as other guys at work—like the guy who'd lost his family in the fire—but why had his life turned out this way? What had his marriage become?

He got another beer and clasped it lightly in his hands. Against his skin the cold metal tingled, awakening him, and he stood. He couldn't wait here all night; not when it looked like Mary-Ann wasn't coming home. She'd left him, then. But gone . . . where? He drained the can, then tossed it into the garbage and wondered with surprise where all those other cans had come from. The garbage can was completely full.

It didn't help, of course, that he suspected she was seeing some guy in the group. Suspected? Hell, he was pretty damned sure of his facts. And he bet right now she and Heather were over there.

And he was gonna get his family back.

It wasn't all that hard to locate them, after all. He just looked in her address book and when he found the name of the group's leader, he knew he had the right guy. He checked the address, then drove over there.

The rain sluiced over him as he got out of the car and went up the walk. The doorbell was one of those with a tiny light in it, and it stared like an orange eye at him. Grimly he thumbed it. The door opened, and a man he'd seen several times at his house stood behind the screen door.

"Oh, hi, Hank. I didn't expect to see you here."

"I bet not."

"Want to come in?"

"Yeah." Hank jerked the screen open before the other man could make a move. "Richard, isn't it?" he asked as his eyes searched the living room. The other man nodded. Hank didn't see anything out of the ordinary there . . . no hint of them.

Almost as if Richard had read his mind, he grinned. "The others are downstairs."

"Downstairs?"

"Basement," Richard called over his shoulder as he led the way. "Made it into a den a few years ago. Thought I'd need that for the kids to play in, but when my wife left me, she took the kids. So I just rattle around in this big house."

Yeah, until you rattle around with my wife.

He could hear the voices now, and knew that even now they wouldn't be socializing. Not these people. They were fanatics. They didn't have time for anything but their Cause. This was Business, after all.

They were there, both Heather and Mary-Ann. His wife looked up. Her blond hair was neatly pulled back, her face bereft of makeup. That was another thing he blamed on the group. She didn't style her hair now, or wear lipstick or eye shadow, and she wore dowdy clothes. She looked like she'd aged fifteen years.

The group members paused in their heated discussion as they recognized Hank. Heather, whose dark head had been bent studiously over a jigsaw puzzle, waved at him. He smiled at her.

"What are you doing here?" It was Mary-Ann.

No greeting. Hank repressed the belch he felt sprewing up from his stomach, even though he wanted to let it out so it would shock these people.

"I gotta talk with you."

"Can't it wait?"

"No."

She saw he meant it and excused herself and followed him back up the stairs. She glanced back once, and he knew Richard was watching them.

"What's this all about?" she demanded once they were in the living room. "How did you find me?"

"Why didn't you leave a note? I was getting worried. Something could have happened."

She folded her arms across her chest. "Well, nothing did, so what do you want? I don't have time to stand here. I've got to get back to work."

"I want you to come home with me."

"That's impossible."

"I want us to go home together and make love, and then talk afterward."

She stared at him coldly. "I can't."

"Hank." His voice was pleading. "Can't you even say my name?" She didn't answer and he moved away.

"You've been drinking again."

She made it sound like he got drunk regularly. Sure, he enjoyed a few beers after work, but he never drank the hard stuff. She knew that. But with her conversion, she'd also given up alcohol and smoking. He wondered when she would be nominated for sainthood.

"Just a few beers."

"You smell like an old wino."

"You on speaking terms with winos now?" The

humor was lost on her; on him, as well. Her foot
tapped. A bad sign. "Come on, Annie, come home
now. We'll put on some good music, snuggle a little."

"Don't call me Annie. You know I hate that."

"What does he call you?"

"What?"

"I said what does he call you?" He jerked his chin
toward the stairs. "I bet he doesn't call you Mrs.
Strasak. Are you having an affair with him?" He held
his breath.

Her gaze met his. "Yes."

He released the air. There, it was out in the open,
and surely now he would feel better. Why, though, did
he feel a knot twisting inside his guts, like the beer had
gone sour or something. Why did he feel like he
wanted to explode and yell and scream?

Instead, he shifted his weight from one foot to the
other, then said: "How long has it been going on?"

"A year."

"That's all?"

"Yes."

"Yeah, you wouldn't lie. You might get struck down
by a lightning bolt."

"I'm going back."

"No, you're not." He grabbed her arm before she
could turn around.

"Let go."

"No." His fingers tightened.

"You're hurting me."

"You've hurt me for years now, Annie, and you
didn't give a damn. I wish I could hurt you, but I don't
think there's any way." He released her arm just as
Richard walked into the room.

"Is everything all right here?"

The perfect host, Hank thought, and felt his head begin aching, as if a band were tightening around it. She was probably right; he had drunk too much.

"Go on back," he said wearily. "I don't want to keep you away from your little fuzzy critters any longer."

She left. Without a backward look.

Hank let himself out quietly, and when he got in the car, he sat in the front seat, staring at the house. He didn't see the car door open or close, and was startled to hear Heather's voice.

"I'm lonely, Daddy."

"Oh, baby." He pulled her to his chest and stroked her rain-dampened hair. And knew what he could do to hurt his wife.

He kissed the top of his daughter's head, then started the car and drove home. He told her to sit in the car while he was in the house just a minute. Inside, he first packed a little suitcase with some of her clothing and favorite toys, then pulled a large case down and began tossing his things into it.

When he was done, he turned off the last light and left. The house stood black in the fog.

He took the curve wide, the car swinging over the solid yellow line into the left lane of what in the town one mile back was Port Boulevard, and Heather squealed with fright. The windshield wipers squeaked as they scraped an arc across the glass.

"Daddy, please," she pleaded, "slow down."

For answer, he pressed down on the accelerator, and the car leaped ahead in the wet darkness, its twin lights raking the dense forest that pressed closely on both sides. A wisp of fog curled around some of the

tree trunks; leaves, plastered by the rain, slipped
silently to the forest floor. Something thumped under
the tires, and Heather twisted around on the seat to
look back at the dead creature, painted a hellish red
by the taillights.

"Daddy, you ran over an animal."

"It's just a possum," he said to the accusing tone,
and tried not to feel guilty. "Sit down, and put your
seat belt on like I told you."

Quietly she obeyed, and in the faint greenish light
from the dashboard he saw the tears on her cheeks.
She lifted one corner of her Sylvester and Tweety
T-shirt and rubbed her eyes.

He shook his head, then jabbed at the cigarette
lighter. She really liked animals; loved them, that is,
and that was beginning to worry him. She cried over
the horses getting killed in the westerns; didn't care if
the good guy got it. Just the goddamn horses. And
she'd leave the room if an animal on TV got hurt or
killed. That was too much like her mother. He lit his
cigarette. She was the only good thing that had come
out of his marriage, and he wondered if it was too late
for her. Had her mother already poisoned her?

Another thump under the tires jerked his attention
back to the road. That had to be a pothole, didn't it?
They would be reaching the interstate in a bit and
when they did, he would—they would—be leaving
Greystone Bay behind for good.

Rotten town, rotten job, rotten wife. Worse . . . a
rotten life.

It would be different up north. He'd go to Boston,
maybe, and look around. Boston would need good
workers. He'd had a lot of different jobs in his
lifetime, so he was qualified. God knows, he could

learn quickly, too. Ash dribbled down his shirt front, and he coughed, then wiped the back of his hand across his mouth. His stomach was sour from all the beer he'd drunk earlier, and he was beginning to feel pressure in his bladder.

"Daddy, slow *down*."

That was the tenth or eleventh time, and he was getting tired of it. He knew she was right, but he wanted to get as far away from Mary-Ann tonight as possible. And the faster the better. He hunched over the wheel, shifting his weight from one buttock to the other. He was already stiff and they hadn't been on the road for ten minutes yet. It was gonna be a long night.

He tried not to think about what he'd done. He knew the fault wasn't all Mary-Ann's. Two made a marriage; two unmade it. He knew he'd said and done things that had only made the situation worse, and sometimes he'd just baited her so that she got angry, and yet . . . was that just the end of it after all this time? Not a farewell? Not even a handshake? And she still hadn't called him by name. He felt tears at the corners of his eyes.

He glanced at Heather, saw she had her favorite toy, the blue rabbit, tucked under one arm. He didn't remember her bringing that with her. She was looking out the window, her forehead pressed against the glass, but he knew she was sucking her thumb.

He glanced left and saw the small bloody carcass on the shoulder of the far side. Another possum. Jeez. It was about the fifth one they'd passed so far. What was with these damned animals? Why did they feel obligated to throw themselves under a car's wheels? Why didn't they just stay in the woods? Why were they running out in front of him tonight? God, the first one had been that afternoon and since then it hadn't stopped.

He looked back at the slick length of the road and decided he'd better slow down. The alcohol had slowed his reflexes, and it was hard to see now. The fog—that blinding sound-sucking fog wouldn't be missed, that was for sure—was creeping in from the sea, only a few miles to the east, and he didn't want to end back up at Bay Memorial Hospital and then have Mary-Ann come in and demand to know just what the hell was going on. Or even worse . . . what if she didn't come at all?

Silently Heather pointed to something up ahead, and too late he saw the tiny pinpoints of light that meant eyes of some animal that had just strayed out onto the road. He tried to brake, but once again the car ran quickly over the animal, and Heather screamed, as if it had been her own body he'd hurt.

The car slipped to one side and as he straightened, he saw the possum ahead on the wet tarmac, the animal sitting in the middle of the road just staring at him as if it had nothing better to do, and he jerked the wheel around to avoid the damned animal because he didn't like the way it was looking at him. The car went into a spin; he tried to bring it out, but the wheels locked on the slick surface, and the car skidded, then heaved itself off the road, crashing into the wide trunk of an oak with a sickening smack.

When he woke, he could feel the rain splashing on his face. And from nearby he heard the undulating wail of an ambulance or a patrol car, or maybe both. He grinned, tasting the saltiness of blood on his lips.

He and Heather wouldn't be out here long, that was for sure. Someone was coming for them.

He saw the lights now strobing into the dark fog, and saw a stretcher being lifted into the back of the ambulance. Heather, then; God, he hoped she was all right. Kids generally were; they were young, healthy; she'd spring right back would his little Heather. There was nothing to worry about, was there?

He watched, though, in puzzled silence as the cop paused behind the ambulance to talk to one of the attendants. Why weren't they coming to get him? He wanted to go with Heather to the hospital. She was probably scared, probably crying, and he wanted to hold and comfort her.

"—not yet," the cop was saying as he tried to light a cigarette in the rain. Frustrated, he finally gave up, flicked the sodden mess to one side.

"—happened?"

"Looks like he might have gotten disoriented —maybe hit his head on the steering wheel—and crawled off into the woods. We're calling off the search tonight because of the fog. Can't see a thing. Hope it lifts by morning. See you back in town."

The cop slapped the attendant on the back, then they got back in their vehicles, and with sirens and lights flashing, they drove off. The only sound now was the drumming of the rain on the black pavement.

I'm here! Hank shouted, and only the wind soughing in the branches heard him. He struggled to move, but couldn't as pain like hot irons jabbed through his body. I'm here, he whimpered. Here. Alive.

The rain fell through the blinding fog, and it was only when the car was a few yards away that Hank saw the headlights glowing. He screamed for it to stop because he was lying stretched across the highway, but the driver didn't hear him, didn't see him.

Not in the fog.

The fog and blood wetly kissed his skin.

He screamed again when the second car came speeding down the highway, and the third only minutes later. He screamed long into the night, but no one heard. Not in the fog.

THE GRANDPA URN

by Bob Versandi

WHILE HIS GRANDMOTHER, SARAH CALDER, WAS IN THE barn filling her fruit basket with some of her best pie apples from the storage barrels, her young grandson, Sean, resumed his search of her bedroom, trying not to leave any signs of disturbance. Only the large cedar chest at the foot of the bed remained unchecked. Kneeling in front of the old wooden box, he raised the lid and uncovered stacks of neatly folded linens. He stuck his hand into the narrow spaces between the sides of the chest and the linens, but could feel or see nothing. Closing the chest, he looked about his grandmother's bedroom for any possible hiding places he might have overlooked. Satisfied that he hadn't missed anything, he left the bedroom, checking at the doorway that the room was as he had found it. As he

closed the door behind him, he wondered where he
should look next. Before he was able to decide, he saw
through the parlor window that his grandmother was
coming across the front yard with a heavily laden
basket of apples. He ran to the kitchen door and
swung it open as the old woman huffed and puffed her
way inside. She put the basket down in front of her
and removed her kerchief, brushing a few errant
strands of grey hair off her forehead.

"Soon as I catch my breath, child, we'll prepare the
pie fillin'," she said as she put a hand to her chest.
Sean knew that his search would have to wait.

"Grandma, the apples are so big."

"So's your appetite when one of my apple pies is on
the table," she chuckled.

"Get me my paring knife and the big wooden bowl
from the cupboard while I rest these old bones in the
rocker."

Sarah Calder watched the eleven-year-old boy move
to his tasks as she slowly settled into the oak rocker
that sat in front of the kitchen fireplace. The morning
fire had kept the hearth toasty and the old woman
luxuriated in the warmth as it eased the discomfort
her arthritic body suffered from the strain of her apple
gathering. Only her eyes and hands seemed to still do
her bidding without taking painful revenge.

Sean put the wooden bowl on her lap and placed the
paring knife in the bowl, then moved the basket of
apples to within easy reach of the old woman. She
smiled down at him as he positioned himself cross-
legged at her feet and handed her one of the larger
apples from the wicker fruit basket. She took the
offered apple and deftly began to cut a ribbon of green
skin from its surface, releasing the fruit's sweet fragrance. When the apple had been completely peeled,

she placed it in an earthenware porringer that was always kept on the small table alongside the rocker.

The boy watched as the old woman picked up another apple and swiftly repeated her skinning technique. He decided he'd ask his question now.

"How did Grandpa die?" he asked as his grandmother transferred the peeled apple from her hand to the porringer on the table alongside her rocker. The old woman adjusted her shawl about her shoulders as though the boy's words had left in a draft. She selected another apple from the basket at her feet and began to spin it against the sharp paring knife as she had done for at least sixty-six years of the eighty she had passed.

"Such a sad question for such a bright Sunday morning," she answered as the boy watched another green peel curl from the knife blade and drop into the wooden bowl in her lap.

"Mama told me the Pequots killed him and burnt the body. She says you kept the ashes and put them in an urn. What's an urn, Grandma?"

"An urn is a holy vessel, sorta like a large spice jar with a fancy lid that folks keep the remains of their loved ones in, after the bodies have been turned back into God's ash."

The boy handed his grandmother another apple from the basket while he prepared his next question.

"Do you keep Grandpa in an urn, Grandma?"

The old woman paused, put her knife and apple into the wooden bowl, and dried her hands on her apron. Grasping the arms of her rocker, she began to gently rock the chair and gazed sadly into the innocent questioning eyes of her grandson.

"Yes, child, I guess I do."

"How did Grandpa die?" he asked again.

The old woman rocked with an almost mechanical rhythm and turned her gaze to the kitchen window and the forested hills that lay beyond the farm.

"Your grandfather and I came to Greystone Bay in 1759 when his brother took ill and could no longer farm the land. Life was a whole lot harder then. The winter of '61 took your grandfather's brother and we decided to stay on permanently. Grandpa Jacob put in the orchards and built the barns. He loved the land and the land loved him back. Your grandfather worked them fields from sunup till sundown, taking time off only to sing God's praises on Sunday mornings.

"In '72, I gave your grandfather a son, your daddy, and in '74, your aunt Kathryn was born. Those were the happy times in Greystone Bay. Your daddy and your aunt were more joy than a woman deserves. They grew up fast, too fast. When your daddy was just a little older than you, Jacob takes him up into the northern quarter and shows him six acres of his richest farmland. He tells him that as of that moment it was now your daddy's land.

"The following summer, Jacob and your daddy began clearing a section for house buildin'. That's how your daddy come to find the mound."

"What mound?" Sean Calder asked.

"The Pequot burial mound. The Pequot Indians used to bury their dead in big mounds of earth. They buried them with all kinds of things. Spears, tomahawks, bracelets, bowls, goblets, and only God knows what else.

"Your daddy found the mound after cutting away some thick brush a few yards from the treeline. He didn't know what it was, but your grandfather knew it was a burial mound right off. His brother had warned him about them when we first come to Greystone Bay, but Jacob paid him little mind. Your grandfather had no time for superstitious twaddle.

"Since the mound was in the way of the house foundation, Jacob tells your daddy that it'll have to be leveled. Seeing as it was getting late, your grandfather decides to start clearing the mound the following morning. The next day, your daddy is feeling poorly, so Jacob heads up to the north quarter to start leveling the mound by himself."

The old woman paused. Sean kept respectfully quiet while waiting for his grandmother to continue.

"Jacob commenced to diggin' away that Pequot mound. After twenty or thirty shovelfuls, your grandfather uncovers some bones. Just a few at first, then more and more. Pretty soon, each time he pulls the shovel out of the mound, bones fall out like grain spilling from a sack with a hole. He was too busy diggin' to notice the Pequots watching him from the treeline. Lord knows where they come from, or how they knew the mound was being dug out. There ain't been a sign of Pequots in this region for years.

"Well, one of the Pequots comes a-running and a-hollering down from the treeline and your grandfather figures he better defend himself. Jacob raised the shovel like a club and as soon as that Indian got close, he sent that heathen soul to hell. When they saw your grandfather kill their companion, the rest of them Pequots come a-hootin' and hollerin' out of the forest and Jacob figured that his time before God had come. But then, just as the Indians got close enough for your grandfather to pick off their fleas, they looked at the dug-out mound, the bones, and the dead Indian bleedin' all over it and they run back into the trees even faster than they run out.

"Jacob watched them disappear into the trees, not believing his eyes. He gave thanks to the Lord for sparing his life and for Indian superstitions. It was then that your grandfather decided to leave the mound intact for another season, and began to fill in the dug-out section. Before he had finished, that heathen Pequot had joined his ancestors inside the burial mound. Once the mound was back together, Jacob headed back to the farm.

"Later that night, he told me what had happened and I was fearful of what them Pequots might do next. Your grandfather chuckled and said from the way they were runnin', it would take years for them to double back.

"We put your daddy and your aunt to bed early so's we could get some extra sleep. Jacob needed it more than me, but I never let your grandfather go to sleep alone.

"There was no moon that night so I have no idea how it all happened, but sometime during the time we slept, them Pequots come back. I remember hearing a noise in the bedroom, and when I turned over to wake your grandfather, something hit me on the back of the neck and I fell to the floor unconscious.

"It was morning when I woke up, and the bedroom was a shambles. Your grandfather must have fought them very hard. There was a lot of blood. One thing was a bit peculiar though, your daddy and your aunt never heard a thing and slept peacefully through the raid. I never could make sense of that.

"As soon as I was sure we were safe and my neck needed no doctorin', I went lookin' for your grandfather."

The old woman paused again.

Sean noticed that his grandmother seemed to have

gotten older looking as she relived the events she was describing. Her forehead seemed more furrowed and her eyes had grown squinty and wet. He was sorry he had pressed her for the truth of his grandfather's death. As he waited for her to continue, he almost wished she wouldn't.

"I gave your daddy Jacob's pistol, and told him to hide with his sister in the root cellar if he heard anything other than my call in the next few hours. Then I took the muzzle loader and went off to search for your grandfather.

"Indians can be cruel. Some have ways that are more like beasts than men. Jacob's brother told us stories of Pequot savagery that gave me many a sleepless night, but nothing could have prepared me for what I found when I got up to the north quarter where your grandfather had been taken.

"They fixed it so's he couldn't see how they were going to torture him to death and then they killed him, a piece at a time. Jacob Calder was almost six foot, but when I found him, he could've been buried in a child's casket.

"I decided that nobody would ever see him like that so I went back to the farm for kerosene and matches. I told your daddy to stay in the root cellar with little Kathryn until I returned. Back where they had left your grandfather, I soaked what remained of his body in the kerosene and set it afire.

"I kept the fire going until only ashes remained. Then I scooped the warm ashes from the earth with my hands and placed them in my kerchief. I brought your grandfather's ashes home and put them in an urn so he'd always be here with me."

The old woman ceased her rocking and rested her head against the back of the wooden chair. Sean watched as the tension left her face and her appearance brightened.

"Where is the urn, Grandma?"

"Down in the darkness, where good souls can rest quiet and easy," she answered without looking at him.

Then he knew. The urn was in the root cellar. It had to be there; he had looked everywhere else.

"Can I see it?" he asked.

"Not now, child, maybe later," the old woman answered. "My poor old mouth has gone cotton-dry from all this talk, how about you fetchin' us two cups of cider before I start the piecrusts?" she added.

The boy nodded and went to the other side of the kitchen to get down the cider jug his grandmother kept on a shelf above the woodbox. It was always at least half full of fresh cider whenever he came to visit. He poured two cups of the thick sweet liquid and drank his on the spot. The second cup he carried back to where his grandmother waited, only to discover she had fallen asleep. He was about to waken her for her drink, but decided not to.

Now he could search the root cellar and find his grandpa's urn.

Placing the cup of cider on the side table by the rocker, he tiptoed from the kitchen and quietly opened the door of the hall pantry. The entrance to the root cellar was through the floor of the pantry. He lifted out the rectangle of wood floor that concealed the stairs that led down into the cellar. A strong smell of earth and damp wood flooded the pantry. The cellar was so dark he couldn't even see the top stair.

On the lowest shelf in the pantry was a candlestick and matches, obviously placed there for use in the cellar. He struck a match and lit the candle. It caught immediately and he lifted the light in order to see the stairs. There were six of them leading down to an earthen floor and he could even make out part of a wooden rack that held jars of homemade preserves. He stepped down into the opening, carefully testing the first stair as he eased his weight onto it. He stepped down again and the candle flickered as the second stair creaked under his weight.

The candlelight now revealed more of the root cellar and the boy searched the illuminated section for what might be his grandfather's urn. He could see nothing that looked like it might contain Jacob Calder's ashes. He stepped down again.

"Sean!"

The boy turned and saw his grandmother glaring down at him.

"You get up here this instant."

Sheepishly he made his way back up through the cellar entrance and handed his grandmother the burning candle.

"I'm sorry, Grandma, I only wanted to see Grandpa."

The old woman took the candlestick and shook her head in disappointment. "You'd best go back to the kitchen, child. I'll fetch Grandpa's urn and show it to you there."

The boy did as he was told, and the old woman descended the stairs into the cellar. He rehearsed another apology for his behavior while he waited for her to return.

Moments later, his grandmother came back into the kitchen carrying a small ceramic jar with a dome lid. It was quite ordinary and almost looked like the kind that honey was kept in. Climbing back up the stairs had left the old woman short of breath, and it took a few minutes before she could speak easily.

"This is your grandpa's urn. If you want, you can hold it and look inside."

The boy hesitated, then wiped his hands on his shirt and took it from her. It was warm from her touch and reminded him of how she had scooped the ashes from the fire she had made. Poor Grandpa. He lifted the lid and on the bottom he could see a cake of hardened ash that was almost black. He quickly closed the urn and handed it back.

"I'm sorry, Grandma."

The old woman ran her hand through the boy's flaxen hair and down his cheek.

"I know you are, child. Now, I'm puttin' Grandpa's urn back in the cellar and while I'm doin' that, I want you to get me a new sack of flour from the shed out back."

"You gonna make the piecrusts now?"

"As soon as you bring the flour."

The boy ran from the kitchen, and the old woman smiled after him. Once he was out the door, she pushed herself out of the rocker to put the urn back in the cellar. As she descended the stairs, a feeble voice whispered from the darkness.

"Sarah, did the boy see me?"

"God help him if he had, Jacob."

CONFESSION OF INNOCENCE

by Melissa Mia Hall

IN THE YEARS BEFORE THE GREAT WAR WE WERE BEAUTI-ful. We had long flowing hair and stricken, silken eyes. We met in secret, six sacred ladies that called themselves the Greystone Sisterhood, and in our meetings we worshiped one another with surpassing ease, staging tableaux vivants inspired by paintings done by the Pre-Raphaelite Brotherhood and their followers. We had seen various paintings on trips to England either taken separately or together with one or the other. All of us had seen a picture in person, except for Mary Alice Marsh, who looked so much like the ill-fated Elizabeth Siddal we took to calling her "Lizzie" whenever she could not hear us and sometimes when she could.

It is true about our beauty, as vain and as preten-

tious as that may have sounded; it is most assuredly
true. My name is Jenny Lorcaster and I looked rather
like Jane Morris, the dark-haired Pandora that en-
chanted Dante Gabriel Rossetti. My specialty was
reenacting her brooding portraits, careful to reproduce her clothes with meticulous skill. I, like Jane
Morris, had much skill with the needle and an exact-
ing, artistic eye.

The other women were also lovely, although not at
all exact replicas of the women who figured so promi-
nently in the tempestuous lives of the PRB. Edith
Williams, who loved the delicate Botticelli softness of
the Edward Burne-Jones paintings, often liked to
think she looked like his wife, Georgiana Burne-
Jones, but she could only vaguely suggest the mystical
quality of Georgie's round, penetrating eyes.

Violet Grey did have the dark Latin looks of Mary
Zambaca, the model Burne-Jones was also fascinated
by, but although she tried constantly to reproduce the
tragic expressions and the lush pensiveness Burne-
Jones so obviously admired, she could only manage a
certain wistfulness broken too quickly by a tendency
to laugh too much, a quality shared by Bethany
Campbell, who had the audacity to specialize in the
Rossetti portraits for which the notorious Fanny
Conforth sat. But she also enjoyed duplicating the
poses of Alexa Wilding, whose reputation was never
quite as tarnished as that of Fanny, a former prosti-
tute.

Lisa Galton preferred to re-create an assortment of
artist models. Her favorites oscillated between
women who had modeled for Millais, Brown, and
Holman Hunt on occasions when she felt especially
religious, since her father was a minister and his
influence had a way of tempering her choices.

During the spring of 1912, our secret meetings became more urgent and eloquent, our tableaux more elaborate and lovely. The success of "Spring," inspired by John Everett Millais's painting of the same name and staged in Galton's apple orchard, urged us to share it with others. We engaged Edward, Edith's brother, to photograph it. This boastful pride in our own beauty perhaps set the wheel of fortune to spinning. I cannot know, only speculate. Edward, of distant blue eyes and sliding smile, agreed most eagerly. He was home from Harvard for the summer and only too ready to indulge his photographic interests, already becoming more than just a hobby to him, much to his father's dismay. Edith told him a bit about our society, not everything, but enough to disturb the tranquil nature of our meetings. And enough to tear great gashes in the canvas of our loveliness. For Edward then told Jacob Cushing, a childhood friend and someone also interested in photography. He was sworn to secrecy and he promised, as Edward did, not to spread it around town that our meeting twice monthly, ostensibly under the name Greystone Needlework Society, had anything else to do aside from displaying current experiments in embroidery, tatting, or crochet. Jacob promised not to say anything and he did not, not at first. Still, the pattern of our peace came undone the moment they came to the orchard, Edward with his bulky camera and plates, Jacob with his Brownie and film. Edward, harboring artistic dreams, and Jacob, more arcane dreams all twisted around his passion for pale Mary Alice and her red-gold hair. Mary Alice was always battling an illness of some sort. That spring her skin was almost translucent and her limbs exceedingly slim and delicate. All of her life seemed to have been punctuated by coughs and sighs. But that spring she was well, her eyes bright and lips often curved by a secretive smile. And Jacob fell in love with her.

It must be said, however, that Mary Alice Marsh was rather an outsider to Greystone Bay. She never quite belonged in North Hill society, to the extent the rest of us did, all coming from undiluted old families. Her father was an upstart, a southerner who came to the Bay through the invitation of Orson Campbell, whom he met at the World's Fair in Chicago. It is probable, however, that the invitation of Orson's sister, Susan, carried more weight. For it was her Andrew Marsh married after a scandalous whirlwind courtship of three weeks. Marsh came from old money; his grandfather had been a plantation owner in Georgia, and his father, the owner of a chain of mills scattered throughout the South. Why he left his family for the North has always been shrouded in mystery but he quickly asserted himself here and established a banking concern which still flourishes today. His wife, Susan, had Mary Alice straightaway and two sons followed, John and Theodore. After the youngest was born in '98, she died of childbed fever. Mary Alice was then sent away to finishing school at an early age. An exceptionally bright pupil, she entered a ladies' college when she was only sixteen and I think she planned to return in 1913 if she could not convince her father to allow her to go abroad. She wanted to be an artist and showed some skill with chalk and charcoal. She could only attend our meeting sporadically, being away so often, and brought her color box. She sketched us once in a while, but seldom showed us her efforts, being usually unhappy with her amateur renderings.

I must say I was a little envious of her talent, as

were we all. Mary Alice was the youngest of our sisterhood, and unlike Edith and Bethany, who were both affianced, Bethany to the aforementioned Edward, she was unmarried and without a special suitor. Quite alone in the world except for her father and her two brothers, whom she hardly knew at all.

I remember her as a gawky child taken to telling morbid, ghostly tales preferably in dark places like under the bed. Bethany, her cousin, has even recalled the time she spent at her house forced to listen to her stories in the wardrobe of Mary Alice's bedroom buried under a pile of clothes. Bethany has also attested to constant overindulgence of her father. She remembers how cluttered that bedroom was, festooned with dolls and gewgaws brought from all over Europe and Asia. But Bethany also has recalled to me, more than once, how unaffected Mary Alice was by that overindulgence. She seemed unimpressed by almost anything and was ever more fascinated by her tales and her sketches than by anything her father gave her. Or even by her father himself. We have never recalled an outwardly show of affection passing between them. We often think that it was the lack of a mother in Mary Alice's formative years that caused this peculiarity.

I wish often that Edward had not told Jacob about our meetings. It's as if, I think, the tragedy would've been averted by this omission. The intrusion of males upon our meeting profaned them, reduced them to eccentric parodies of beauty. Perhaps it was our collective vanity that made us long to be memorialized for eternity. If so, then it was our own fault. Our re-creation of Millais's "Spring" or "Apple Blossoms," including Lisa Galton's two charming daughters, Doris and Daphne, turned out so splendidly we all wanted to remember it. The trees in Galton's orchard were in full bloom and the careful arrangement of our bodies echoed the original painting so eloquently we wanted a souvenir. As if I needed one. I still feel the sun seeping through our clothes, the touch of the faintest breeze in our hair, Lisa's two girls watching us raptly, Edith humming Mozart, and Bethany trying not to laugh. And our Lizzie stretched out on the ground in golden yellow, chewing on a blade of grass, trying not to let her large eyes fall closed on a longing to sleep. The fragrance of that day lingers more strongly in my heart than the picture produced from Edward's plates or Jacob's Brownie. But we had to have a souvenir. And we got it. Even now, Edward's photograph hangs above my highboy and I see Edith pouring the water into her bowl, the dribble of water a streak of silver. I outstretch my hand toward the water.

Jacob has dark hair like me. He has a distinctive face, attractive, a little too intense, expressive. His feelings rush to the surface of his face. One reads his face like a densely written page. He had not seen Mary Alice since she was thirteen or fourteen. She had blossomed. He studied her sprawled out on the grass, oblivious to all except to the sky and horizon, the herd of trees across the way, the white fence. I remember him standing there, watching alongside the intent Edward, his slender hands fumbling with his clumsy apparatus. It was as if someone with a torch had passed too near Jacob and set his coat on fire but he was too entranced to be aware of the smoke rising. All of this I saw from the corner of my eye, unable to move from my position until the pictures were taken.

But I saw him and felt, oh, poor Jacob, because Mary Alice could not see him the way I did. She was not the sort to notice men's awe of her, or even how we appreciated her unusual looks. Those of us securely married especially felt at ease in admiring her, never worrying about her stealing away our men. She never seemed attached to the world and seldom, if ever, spoke of any romantic attachments.

After we finished, we had a picnic in the orchard that lasted an hour or more before we scattered to our homes, each of us promising to have a tableau ready for the next meeting. The young men had begged to be in attendance, and with some trepidation, it was agreed they could come. However, we all shared a restless presentiment that their attendance might inhibit us from portraying our heroines to the best of our ability.

"I'm afraid Jacob will tell my husband," Lisa said in the midst of doing up her hair. She was more afraid of Jacob telling her father, but her fear was assuaged by my own, perhaps too quick, reply, "We've done nothing undecorous or unseemly."

"He's not fond of art. He calls it the devil's playground," Lisa said softly, but she smiled, the lines of worry upon her brow relaxing.

Violet stretched and stood, frowning at the grass stains on her hem. "Maybe it's time we went public anyway; we've done nothing to be ashamed of."

I was shocked. "I don't think the town would think admirably of a bunch of young women who sit around and play like they're artist models, bohemian Trilby tarts!" I laughed, unable to keep a straight face. "It's not exactly correct behavior. My mother would be appalled and so would yours!"

"One has to do something around here. The Bay is not exactly the most exciting place to be," Bethany said. We stared at her for a moment, a little startled.

"I don't mean I dislike the Bay, it's just not very much fun. One has to do"—her voice trailed off into a whisper—"something." She glanced away from us.

"I like our gatherings," Mary Alice suddenly said. She shook out her skirt and shivered a little. "They're jolly, truly fine. But my goodness, that grass was damp."

"Oh, I hope you don't catch cold!" Edith said. We all suffered a pang of conscience. If Mary Alice fell sick again, we'd all feel terribly guilty. She sneezed as if hearing our collective thoughts. "Sorry!"

"Oh, no, Mary Alice, we're the ones that are sorry. You'd best be getting home and into bed."

"Lord, don't be silly. I'm wonderfully well." She tugged on her light wrap, sun-warmed and of apple green. She waltzed across the grass for a few moments and giggled. "It was pure bliss having the men about. They all had men, you know, our sisters of the PRB. One had to, then. And now, even now."

We all looked down to the ground, in unison. Mary Alice had a way of saying things we didn't exactly know how to reply to.

"Edward's so meticulous. And Jacob, Jacob's quick like. I wonder if, for all his care, Edward's photographs are any better than Jacob's. He's awfully handsome, Jacob is."

She had noticed. Her coppery eyelashes caught the afternoon sun. I looked away, my heart thumping. Even then, I heard voices in the air singing out warnings. That summer settling in, the peace of spring melting away. She had become the sort that noticed, after all. I felt abashed at the loss of innocence, or what I suspected to be one. It was going away to school all of the time, I thought, and some of the others agreed with me.

Before the next meeting of our society, Lisa and Violet stopped by for tea, and they told me they thought they had seen Jacob and Mary Alice walking down by the sea. It was from a considerable distance, but how could they not identify Mary Alice's brilliant hair? When the sun touched it, it caught fire. Whether this sighting was true, it was common knowledge that Jacob and his mother, Daisy Cushing, went to Sunday dinner at the Marshes'. It didn't startle us then, when suddenly it became common knowledge that Jacob was courting Mary Alice officially. That Andrew Marsh cared so little for his daughter's reputation amazed us.

Jacob had worked for my husband for several years. Ben owns a shipping concern. Jacob was a ladies' man, the sort that flies from one flower to another. A bee. It's not hard to understand my natural concern back then, my anxiety for any woman underneath the light of his fascination. He was fast, a dangerous type. Bethany told me about the woman in Boston he goes to visit occasionally. There's a rumor of a child or two. And there's the case of the chambermaid who worked for his mother who's since disappeared after an incident at the Cushing household. I can imagine what sort of incident.

But I'm getting away from the point of this. What we did.

The tableaux. They were harmless, truly harmless, and very lovely. They began, or rather, our sisterhood began, as I have stated earlier, as a homage to the women the Pre-Raphaelites painted. It began as a game, an enjoyment. We were beautiful, ranging in age from nineteen or eighteen (our Lizzie) to around thirty. I am twenty-eight and although Lisa says she's twenty-nine, I know for a fact she's almost thirty-one.

She has Doris and Daphne, eight and ten. I have a boy who's three years old. Violet has a four-year-old girl.

It is true we were grown women, responsible women, but the tableaux allowed us to express something of beauty, of passion. Ben even knew of my especial fondness for Rossetti. On our last visit abroad he surprised me with a small chalk sketch, a head modeled after Jane. It is the treasure of my life. I spend hours studying it and myself in the mirror. Jane is still alive at this time and I have thought of writing to her to express my admiration for her. But whenever I try to do so, I fall short of completing the task. I am not sure it is Jane I admire so, but Gabriel. And he is dead.

On occasion, one of the others has proposed doing tableaux inspired by other artists. Bethany, in particular, wanted to do a Gibson Girl, but of course, I resisted this proposal, as did the others. Gibson is, I don't know, too American. His women are already so old-fashioned. It's true the Pre-Raphaelite women are much older, but their age strikes the heart with the timelessness of their entrapment. Languishing adored ones, they are enigmatic with secret wisdom. Their pallid faces and flowing hair inspire me to whisper, "You must not think; you must not." Was our obsession healthy? I don't know, but when I was attired in the proper costume, my whole attention fixed on portraying Jane, I felt a member of a sisterhood that stretched forth and past, a link in a long golden chain festooned with red roses and sharp black thorns.

It was, perhaps, a discontent with my own world that made me get so involved with our little society. I married Ben when I was sixteen. He wanted children and I did not. I had two miscarriages and then no success at all in handing him a son. Until three years ago when I finally bore one and gave it to him, a sacrificial offering. I am not happy, though.

Do good works, be a good Christian, and help the poor. That was my mother's advice when I told her about my discontent with Ben. It wasn't that he was terrible or, better still, horribly cruel. I thought I loved him when I was sixteen but I am now afraid I loved getting away from my parents' house still more.

I have lost myself in fantasies of other lives. Beautiful dreams. My imagination is rich with visions of how I would like it to be, my life. An unending idyll of love. I love the Brontës, some Tennyson. I have read most of Sir Walter Scott and other books about King Arthur. I am a Lady of Shalott.

I am very good at acting. There were dreams of running away to New York at one point, after the first miscarriage.

We are rich. Aside from the shipping business, we own much land. He is a land baron. Once I asked him why we did not take a house far away from here, as we could afford it. He said no, but we could take long visits abroad. Which we have done. But he will not leave the Bay for too long at a time. It is his heritage, he is wont to say. And I am from here, too, and know it would be wrong to move away. But I think about it.

Our Lizzie has spent much time away from the Bay. That's perhaps one of the reasons why she is different. She really had intentions of becoming an artist and living in Paris. It's too bad she couldn't do so but her father would never have approved of it, anyway.

They were lovers. I know that. I feel that. When we met the second time to do a program of two or three scenes, Mary Alice had grown taller, if such a thing is possible in a scant two weeks, and her wax-candle pallor was lit from within, so she glowed. When Jacob came with Edward to once again record our efforts for posterity, he followed her about, his movement shadowing hers, a material echo. We all saw it. I caught them in a dim hallway between changes of set, kissing. I withdrew silently, wondering if Ben would come home early and catch us in our summer masquerade. I envisioned the town discussing the goings-on at the Lorcaster house and I returned to spy upon their boldness. In my house.

His lips were on her slim white neck, his body enclosing hers with ownership. She stood very still. I returned to my parlor with the marble floors and expensive Turkish carpet. In a few minutes Mary Alice came running. Jacob's laughter surrounded her and she was smiling.

"I've decided what I want to do for my next tableau!" she announced. We all turned in unison and waited breathlessly.

"Ophelia! John Everett Millais's dear dead Ophelia!"

I was suitably horrified and noticed Violet's shared apprehension. She pressed my hand and shook her head. "Isn't it just like her to pick such a morbid theme?"

Behind me Edith was preoccupied with rearranging her costume for the Burne-Jones piece she was about to portray. Her hands kept returning to her hair nervously and she kept opening her eyes wider and still wider, thinking that in doing so, they would at last grow rounder. "I have the perfect pond behind my house," she said, "and Mother's in Europe and will not be back till the end of August."

"Oh, no, Mary Alice, that's such a dreadful picture, not at all what you should do."

"Lizzie did it," Mary Alice said defiantly.

"You're liable to catch cold. Lizzie did, if you'll remember."

"How could I remember? I wasn't there," Mary Alice said.

I fell quiet.

There are people in this world who are born bent, fated to stand apart from others. I believed this. I still do when it's a long night and I can't sleep and the moon is sufficiently bright. Mary Alice was bent. She had an air of fatality about her, a manic gaiety. She laughed at the wrong things.

Bethany told me about the time they were playing on the front porch of Bethany's house when a small cat brought Bethany a tiny dead squirrel, thinking, no doubt, to impress her with his hunting prowess. Bethany had been devastated, bursting into tears. Mary Alice had only laughed and said, "Well, am I impressed!"

There was no dissuading her. It was agreed that Mary Alice could portray Ophelia. She clapped her hands with delight and quoted from Shakespeare:

"Our cold maids do dead men's fingers call them;
There, on the pendent boughs her coronet weeds
Clambering to hang, an envious silver broke;
When down her weedy trophies and herself
Fell in the weeping brook. Her clothes spread wide,
And mermaid-like, awhile they bore her up;
Which time she canted snatches of old tunes,
As one incapable of her own distress—"

Mary Alice finished speaking and Jacob shouted out hurrahs and Edward took her picture standing before a wide window where the curtains were pulled back and the full light of day poured in on her face like a flood.

We watched on, jealous of Edward's admiration, so complete as to forget his only photographs were to be of our costume pieces and not of Mary Alice striking a humorous declaiming pose that seemed to poke fun at our intricate stagings.

"Let it be Ophelia, then," Bethany huffed, for she did not like the impassioned show of attention toward Mary Alice by her supposedly devoted suitor.

Who did? This was in late June, and by late July, worn out from the festivities of the Fourth, we postponed the next program. It was getting more and more difficult to contain the membership of our sisterhood since the men had invaded—by invitation, surely, but still, invaded. My husband had caught rumor of it from Jacob as I had feared and he teased me about it unmercifully but indulgently as if what we did was completely harmless and of no notice. It angered me. I didn't want to feel as if we were children at play, just children amusing themselves in an idle, holiday way. It was that, I suppose, in most people's eyes.

But not in mine. I was preparing "Mariana" by Rossetti, not difficult to do, since by now I had mastered most expressions by Jane Morris, ever troubled, ever sad. My husband kept asking if he could come to see the program and why we could not make it a social event. It outraged me.

I remember the times before when it was just the sisterhood and in our silent worship of ourselves and those who came before, uplifted us, made us special.

There was a weariness now within me and I could find no delight in those heavy summer days now descended upon the Bay and its environs. A deep lassitude settled in. I could hardly lift my limbs. My little boy, Ramsey, became insufferable, getting into things and places he did not belong. I took walks in the cool of the evening, trying to get away from myself as well as from Ben and Ramsey. At twilight, when things turned blue-grey, I felt calmer, but still uneasy about the upcoming meeting. Our Lizzie would do the Millais, I, with Bethany's help, the Rossetti, and Edith, with the others, a Holman Hunt piece. Or was it Burne-Jones? My memory blurs because it was never done. At the next meeting only my and Mary Alice's pieces were completed.

It was in one of my walks that I again came upon them. It surprised me and I held silent, unable to announce myself. They were in each other's arms in the garden of a neighbor's home. Out for a breath of air and a kiss before dinner. It was nothing untoward and I'd heard they were unofficially engaged. I don't know why it struck me with such sadness, spying them through a clutch of rosebushes. I felt old.

We had a spell of rain the first week of August. The program was scheduled for the next weekend. I had not given my consent for Ben to come because then the other husbands would insist upon coming and soon the whole town would've pressed on attending. Mary Alice rang me up several times, chattering on about her costume and how excited she was about marrying Jacob in the spring. A child she was, noisy and so eager. I wanted to shake her, box her around the ears, pinch her hard. "Wake up!" I wanted to say. "It's not like that; it's not that agreeable!" But I began to believe it was all jealousy. Jacob loved her. He reeked of love and tenderness. Ben had even noticed it. "They're going to be very happy," he said one night over dinner. Ramsey knocked over his mug of milk and I silently cursed his big brown eyes. "So they shall," I agreed.

"Lucky swell, that Jacob, lucky—luckier—"

"That me?" I said, straightening up. Ramsey started to cry. I wanted to kill him. Instead, I wiped his gravy-stained mouth and blinked back my own tears.

"Jenny—"

"Ben, you're getting fat," I said, just to say something cruel.

Ben looked out the window through lace curtains we had brought from Belgium. He wasn't listening.

The last three days before it happened went by so slowly, each day lasting a lifetime, and the heat held. I began to sense the inevitability of it all. I picture their sweet faces and the men's. Jacob had such dark eyes. On the night before, I had vivid dreams. I dreamed we were all going up stairs, up and down, tirelessly. The women were naked and carried garlands. I thought we were reenacting "The Golden Stairs" but there were men with us, wearing white garments and carrying dripping paintbrushes. I kept thinking I'd trip on a splatter of paint. We were all singing the same song but in the dream I kept thinking, "It's not the same," and wondering where she was. Lizzie, I mean, Mary Alice. I woke up sweating and confused. Ben got on top of me and began thrusting and pushing. He was asleep. I pushed him aside and got up. I went to the window. Our bedroom is on the second floor. I looked down and thought I saw a ghost, the ghost of my child. But he wasn't dead so it could not be a ghost. I hate Jacob for what he has done to me.

I chew a strand of hair and think of her. She's just a child. I picture her painting in Paris. I see her old and stooping over canvas. I had his child and he did not want it. I thought I had it for Ben, not Jacob. I did this. I stood the rest of that night thinking about her.

As dawn arrived I finally became cool enough to get back into bed. But not to sleep.

In the morning I wrote a note to her. I sent it with the grocery boy. I paid him to deliver it to her before she left for Edith's house.

I am not Jane, I am Jenny Lorcaster and I am remembering. I "performed" my "Mariana" and Edward took an excellent photograph of it. I did it in the sun-filled conservatory. While I did my piece, Mary Alice prepared hers in the backyard by the pond Edith had earlier helped festoon with nettles and wildflowers. When we all went out to see our Lizzie's piece, we were all in a festive mood. I'd pushed away all thoughts of the note I'd sent to her. We strolled down to the pond where she floated, the perfect reenactment of Millais's Ophelia. Her face appeared through the water imbued with an unearthly light. A robin flew out from a drooping branch and nearly tangled itself in my hair. Mary Alice's mouth fell open and her eyelids slid halfway down. She was the picture of death and madness. We were all astounded and impressed. I held my breath, waiting. Clouds crossed the sun. I felt chilled. Violet murmured something intelligible and sad.

Edith screamed out, "Oh, bear her up, Edward; oh, save her, please."

"She's only acting," I said, "let her be."

In unison, we came still forward, pushing to the edge of the small pond. A man's arms pulled me back. I saw the dark hairs, the brownish-white skin, the muscle. He went past me. "Mary Alice!" He looked back at me, as if I could do something. "She's dead! She's dead!"

I shook my head but they all rushed still farther,

sliding into the muck. I clutched at his sleeve. All was still. We were transfixed and transformed into figures of a painting.

"Millais knew she would die young," Bethany said in a strained voice.

At last, Edward came unfrozen and with Jacob's help, pulled the poor wretch from her muddy death. I pulled the flowers from her cold hand, expecting at any moment to hear her shrieking laugh.

I did not kill her.

I did not.

I did.

DOOM CITY

by Robert R. McCammon

HE AWAKENED WITH THE MEMORY OF THUNDER IN HIS bones.

The house was quiet. The alarm clock hadn't gone off. Late for work! he realized, struck by a bolt of desperate terror. But no, no . . . wait a minute; he blinked the fog from his eyes and his mind gradually cleared, too. He could still taste the onions in last night's meat loaf. Friday night was meat loaf night. Today was Saturday. No office work today, thank God. Ah, he thought, settle down . . . settle down . . .

Lord, what a nightmare he'd had! It was fading now, all jumbled up and incoherent but leaving its weird essence behind. There'd been a thunderstorm last night—Brad was sure of that, because he'd awakened to see the garish white flash of it and to hear the gut-wrenching growl of a real boomer pounding at the bedroom wall. But whatever the nightmare had been, he couldn't recall now; he felt dizzy and disoriented, like he'd just stepped off a carnival ride gone crazy. He did recall that he'd sat up and seen that lightning, so bright it had made his eyes buzz blue in the dark. And he remembered Sarah saying something, too, but now he didn't know what it was . . .

Damn, he thought as he stared across the bedroom at the window that looked down on Baylor Street. Damn, that light looks strange. Not like June at all. More like a white, winter light. Ghostly. Kind of hurt his eyes a little.

Brad got out of bed and walked across the room. He pushed aside the white curtain and peered out, squinting.

What appeared to be a grey, faintly luminous fog hung in the trees and over the roofs of the houses on Baylor Street. It looked like the color had been sucked out of everything, and the fog lay motionless for as far as he could see up and down the street. He looked up, trying to find the sun. It was up there somewhere, burning like a dim bulb behind dirty cotton. Thunder rumbled in the distance, and Brad Forbes said, "Sarah? Honey? Take a look at this."

She didn't reply, nor did she stir. He glanced at her, saw the wave of her brown hair above the sheet that was pulled up over her like a shroud. "Sarah?" he said again, and took a step toward the bed.

And suddenly Brad remembered what she'd said last night, when he'd sat up in a sleepy daze to watch the lightning crackle.

I'm cold, I'm cold.

He grasped the edge of the sheet and pulled it back. A skeleton with tendrils of brittle brown hair attached to its skull lay where his wife had been sleeping last night.

The skeleton was wearing Sarah's pale blue nightgown, and what looked like dried-up pieces of tree bark—skin, he realized . . . *her* skin—lay all around, on and between the white bones. The teeth grinned, and from the bed rose the bittersweet odor of a damp graveyard.

"Oh . . ." he whispered, and he stood staring down at what was left of his wife as his eyes began to bulge from their sockets, and a pressure pulsed in his head as if his brain was about to explode. Blood trickled from his lower lip where his teeth had pierced.

I'm cold, she'd said, in a voice that had sounded like a whimper of pain. *I'm cold.*

Brad heard himself moan, and he let go of the sheet and staggered back across the room, tripped over a pair of his tennis shoes, and went down hard on the floor. The sheet settled back over the skeleton like a sigh.

Thunder rumbled outside, muffled by the fog. Brad stared at one skeletal foot protruding from the lower end of the sheet, and he saw flakes of dried, dead flesh float down from it to the deep-pile aqua-blue carpet.

He didn't know how long he sat there, just staring. He thought he might have giggled, or sobbed, or some combination of both. He almost threw up, and he wanted to curl into a ball and go back to sleep again; he did close his eyes for a few seconds, but when he opened them again, the skeleton of his wife was still lying in the bed and the sound of thunder was nearer.

And he might have sat there until Doomsday if the telephone beside the bed hadn't started ringing.

Somehow, he was up and had the receiver in his hand. Tried not to look down at the brown-haired skull and remember how beautiful his wife—just twenty-eight years old, for God's sake!—had been.

"Hello," he said in a dead voice.

There was no reply. Brad could hear circuits clicking and humming, deep in the wires.

"Hello?"

No answer. Except now there might have been —*might* have been—a soft, silken breathing.

"Hello?" Brad shrieked into the phone. "Say something!"

Another series of clicks; then a tinny, disembodied voice: "We're sorry, but we cannot place your call at this time. All lines are busy. Please hang up and try again later. Thank you. This is a recording . . ."

He slammed the receiver down, and the motion of the air made flakes of skin fly from the skull's cheekbones.

He ran from the bedroom, barefoot and in only his pajama bottoms; he ran to the stairs, went down them screaming, "Help! Help me! Somebody!" He missed a step, slammed against the wall, and caught the banister before he broke his neck. Still shouting for help, he burst through the front door and out into the yard, where his feet crunched on dead leaves.

He stopped. The sound of his voice echoed along the street. The air was still and wet, thick and stifling. He stared down at all the dead leaves around him, covering brown grass that had been green the day before. And then the wind suddenly moved, and more dead leaves swirled around him; he looked up, and saw bare grey branches where living oak trees had stood before he'd closed his eyes to sleep last night.

"Help me!" he screamed. *"Somebody please help me!"*

But there was no answer; not from the house where the Pates lived, not from the Walkers' house, not from the Crawfords' nor the Lehmans'. Nothing human moved on Baylor Street, and as he stood amid the drifting leaves on the seventh day of June he felt something fall into his hair. He reached up, plucked it out, and looked at what he held in his hand.

The skeleton of a bird, with a few colorless feathers sticking to the bones.

He shook it from his hand and frantically wiped his palm on his pajamas—and then he heard the telephone ringing again in his house.

He ran to the downstairs phone, back in the kitchen, picked up the receiver, and said, "Help me! Please . . . I'm on Baylor Street! Please help—"

He stopped babbling, because he heard the clicking circuits and a sound like searching wind, and down deep inside the wires there might have been a silken breathing.

He was silent, too, and the silence stretched. Finally he could stand it no longer. "Who is this?" he asked in a strained whisper. "Who's on this phone?"

Click. Buzzzzzz . . .

Brad punched the 0. Almost at once that same terrible voice came on the line: "We're sorry, but we cannot place your call at—" He smashed his fist down on the phone's two prongs, dialed 911. "We're sorry, but we cannot—" His fist went down again; he dialed the number of the Pates next door, screwed up, and started twice more. "We're sorry, but—" His fingers went down on about five numbers at once. "We're sorry—"

He wrenched the telephone from the wall, threw it across the kitchen, and it broke the window over the sink. Dead leaves began to drift in, and through the glass panes of the back door Brad saw something lying in the fenced-in backyard. He went out there, his heart pounding and cold sweat beading on his face and chest.

Lying amid dead leaves, very close to its doghouse, was the skeleton of their collie, Socks. The dog looked as if it might have been stripped to the bone in midstride, and snowy hunks of hair lay about the bones.

In the roaring silence, Brad heard the upstairs phone begin to ring.

He ran.

Away from the house this time. Out through the backyard gate, up onto the Patcs' front porch. He hammered at the door, hollering for help. No one answered. He smashed a glass pane of the door with his fist and, heedless of his gashed knuckles, reached in and unsnapped the lock.

With his first step into the house, he smelled the graveyard reek. Like something had died a long time ago, and been mummified.

He found the skeletons in the master bedroom upstairs; they were clinging to each other. A third skeleton—Davy Pate, once a towheaded twelve-year-old—lay in the bed in the room with posters of Prince and Quiet Riot tacked to the walls. In a fishtank on the far side of the room there were little bones lying in the red gravel on the bottom.

It was clear to him then. Yes, very clear. He knew what had happened, and he almost sank to his knees in Davy Pate's mausoleum.

Death had come in the night. And stripped bare everyone and everything but him.

But if that were so . . . then who—or *what*—had

dialed the telephone? What had been listening on the other end? *What?*

He didn't know, but he suddenly realized that he'd told whatever it was that he was still on Baylor Street. And maybe Death had missed him last night; maybe its scythe had cleaved everyone else and missed him, and now . . . and now it knew he was here, and it would be coming for him.

Brad fled the house, ran through the dead leaves that clogged the gutters of Baylor Street, and headed east toward the center of Greystone Bay. The wind moved again, sluggishly and heavily; the wet fog shifted, and Brad could see the sky had turned the color of blood. Thunder boomed behind him like approaching footsteps, and tears of terror streamed down Brad's cheeks.

I'm cold, Sarah had whispered. *I'm cold.* And that was when the finger of Death had touched her, had missed Brad and gone roaming on through the night. *I'm cold,* she'd said, and there would never be any warming her again.

He came to two cars smashed together in the street. Skeletons in clothes lay behind the steering wheels. Farther on, dead leaves cushioned the bones of a large dog. Above him, the trees creaked and moaned as the wind picked up, ripping holes in the fog and showing the bloody sky through them.

It's the end of the world, he thought. Judgment Day. All the sinners and saints alike turned to bones overnight. Just me left alive. Just me, and Death knows I'm on Baylor Street.

"Mommy!"

The sobbing voice of a child startled him, and he stopped in his tracks, skidding on leaves.

"Mommy!" the voice repeated, echoing and warped by the low-lying fog. "Daddy! Somebody . . . help me!"

It was the voice of a little girl, crying somewhere nearby. Brad listened, trying to peg its direction. First he thought it was to the left, then to the right. In front of him, behind him . . . he couldn't be sure. "I'm here!" he shouted. "Where are you?"

The child didn't answer. Brad could still hear her crying. "I'm not going to hurt you!" he called. "I'm standing right in the middle of the street! Come to me if you can!"

He waited. A flurry of brown, already-decaying leaves fell from overhead—and then he saw the figure of the little girl, hesitantly approaching him through the fog on his right. She had blonde hair done up in pigtails with pale blue ribbons, and her pallid face was streaked with tears and distorted by terror; she was maybe five or six years old, wearing pink pajamas and tightly clasping a Smurf doll in her arms. She stopped about fifteen feet away from him, her eyes red and swollen and maybe insane, too.

"Daddy?" she whispered.

"Where'd you come from?" he asked, still shocked at hearing another voice and seeing someone else alive on this last day of the world. "What house?"

"Our house." Her face looked like it was about to slide off the skull. "Over there." She pointed through the fog at a shape with a roof, then her eyes came back to Brad.

"Anyone else alive? Your mother or father?"

The little girl just stared.

"What's your name?"

"Kelly Burch," she answered dazedly. "My

tel'phone number is . . . is . . . 663-6949. Could . . . you help me find . . . a p'liceman, please?"

It would be so easy, Brad thought, to curl up in the leaves on Baylor Street and let himself lose his mind; but if there was one little girl still left alive, then there might be other people, too. Maybe this awful thing had only happened on Baylor Street . . . or maybe only in this part of town; maybe it was a chemical spill, radiation, something unholy in the lightning, a freak of nature. Whatever it was, maybe its effects were limited to a small part of town. Sure! he thought, and when he grinned, the child abruptly took two steps back. "We're going to be all right," he told her. "I won't hurt you. I'm going to walk to Main Street. Do you want to go with me?"

She didn't reply, and Brad thought she'd truly gone over the edge but then her lips moved and she said, "I'm looking for . . . for my mommy and daddy. They're gone." Her face was expressionless, but new tears ran down her cheeks. "They just . . . they just . . . left bones in their bed and they're gone."

"Come on." He held out his hand to her. "Come with me, okay? Let's see if we can find anybody else."

Kelly didn't come any closer. Her little knuckles were white where she gripped the smiling blue Smurf. Brad heard thunder roaming somewhere to the south, and electric-blue lightning scrawled across the crimson sky like a crack in time. Brad couldn't wait any longer; he started walking away again, stopped and looked back. Kelly stopped, too, dead leaves snagged in her hair. "We're going to be all right," he told her again, and he heard how utterly ridiculous that sounded. Sarah was gone; beautiful Sarah was gone, and his life might as well be over. But no, no—he had to keep going, had to at least *try* to make some sense out of all this. He started off once more and he didn't look back, but he knew Kelly was following about fifteen or twenty feet behind.

At the intersection of Baylor and Ashley Streets, a police car had smashed into an oak tree. The windshield was layered with leaves, but Brad saw the hunched-over, bony thing in the police uniform sitting behind the wheel. And the most terrible thing was that its skeletal hands were still gripping that wheel, trying to guide the car. Whatever had happened —radiation, chemicals, or the Devil striding through the streets of his town—had taken place in an instant. These people had been stripped to bones in the blink of a cold eye, and again Brad felt himself balanced precariously on the edge of madness.

"Ask the p'liceman to find Mommy and Daddy!" Kelly called from behind him.

"There's a police station at the Plaza," he told her. "That's where we're going to go. Okay?"

She didn't answer, and Brad set off.

They passed silent houses. Near the intersection of Baylor and Hilliard, where the traffic light was still obediently blinking yellow, a skeleton in jogging gear lay sprawled on the ground. Its Nike sneakers were too small for Brad's feet, too large for Kelly's. They kept going, and Kelly cried for a few minutes but then she hugged her doll tighter and stared straight ahead with eyes swollen almost shut.

And then Brad heard it, and his heart pounded with fear again.

Off in the fog somewhere.

The sound of a phone ringing.

Brad stopped. The phone kept on ringing, its sound thin and insistent.

"Somebody's calling," Kelly said, and Brad realized she was standing right beside him. "My tel'phone number is 663-6949."

He took a step forward. Another, and another. Through the fog ahead of him he could make out the shape of a pay phone there on the corner of New Hope Road.

The telephone kept on ringing, demanding an answer.

Slowly, Brad approached the pay phone. He stared at the receiver as if it might be a cobra rearing back to strike. He did not want to answer it, but his arm lifted and his hand reached toward that receiver, and he knew that if he heard the silken breathing and the metallic recorded voice on the other end he might start screaming and never be able to stop.

His hand closed around it. Started to lift it up.

"Hey, buddy!" someone said. "I wouldn't answer that if I was you."

Shocked almost out of his skin, Brad whirled around.

A young man was sitting on the curb across the street, smoking a cigarette, his legs stretched out before him. "I wouldn't," he cautioned.

Brad was oddly dismayed by the sight of a flesh-and-blood man, as if he'd already forgotten what one looked like. The young man was maybe in his early twenties, wearing scruffy jeans and a dark green shirt with the sleeves rolled up. He had sandy brown hair that hung to his shoulders, and a couple of days' growth of beard darkened his jaw. He pulled on the cigarette and said, "Don't pick it up, man. Doom City."

"What?"

"I said . . . Doom City." The young man stood up;

he was about six feet, thin and lanky. His work boots crunched leaves as he crossed the street, and a patch on the breast pocket of his shirt identified him as a Sanitation Department workman. As the young man got closer, Kelly pressed her body against Brad's legs. "Let it ring," the young man said. His eyes were pale green, deep-set, and dazed. "If you were to pick that damned thing up . . . Doom City."

"Why do you keep saying that?"

"Because it is what it is. Somebody's tryin' to find all the strays. Tryin' to run us all down and finish the job. Sweep us all into the gutter, man. Close the world over our heads. Doom City." He blew a plume of smoke into the air that hung between them, unmoving.

"Who are you? Where'd you come from?"

"Name's Neil Spencer. Folks call me Spence. I'm a . . ." He paused for a few seconds, staring along Baylor Street. "I *used* to be a garbageman. 'Til today, that is. 'Til I got to work and found skeletons sittin' in the garbage trucks. That was about three hours ago, I guess. I've been doin' a lot of walkin'. Lot of pokin' around." His gaze rested on the little girl, then moved back to Brad. The pay phone was still ringing, and Brad felt the scream kicking behind his teeth. "You're the first two I've seen with skin," Spence said. "I've been sittin' over there for the last twenty minutes or so. Just waitin' for the world to end, I guess."

"What . . . happened?" Brad asked. Tears burned his eyes. "My God . . . my God . . . what *happened*?"

"Somethin' tore," Spence said tonelessly. "Ripped open. Somethin' won the fight, and I don't think it was who the preachers said was gonna win. I don't know . . . maybe Death got tired of waitin'. Same thing happened to the dinosaurs. Maybe it's happenin' to people now."

"There've *got* to be other people somewhere! We can't be the only ones!"

"I don't know about that." Spence drew on his cigarette one last time and flicked the butt into the street. "All I know is, somethin' came in the night and had a feast, and when it was done it licked the plate clean. Only it's still hungry." He nodded toward the ringing phone. "Wants to suck on a few more bones. Like I said, man. Doom City. Doom City here, there, and everywhere."

The phone gave a final shrilling shriek and went silent.

The child was crying again. Brad stroked her hair to calm her. He realized he was doing it with his bloody hand. "We've . . . we've got to go somewhere . . . got to *do* something . . ."

"Do what?" Spence asked laconically. "Go where? I'm open to suggestions, man."

From the next block came the distant sound of a telephone ringing. Brad stood with his bloody hand on Kelly's head, and he didn't know what to say.

"I want to take you somewhere, my friend," Spence told him. "Want to show you somethin' real interestin'. Okay?"

Brad nodded, and he and the little girl followed Neil Spencer north along New Hope Road, past more silent houses and buildings.

Spence led them to a 7-Eleven store, where a skeleton in a yellow dress splotched with blue and purple flowers lolled behind the cash register with a *National Enquirer* open on its jutting knees. "There you go," Spence said softly. He plucked a pack of

Luckies off the display of cigarettes and nodded toward the small TV set on the counter. "Take a look at that, and tell me what we ought to do."

The TV set was on. It was a color set, and Brad realized after a long, silent moment that the channel was tuned to one of those twenty-four-hour news networks. The picture showed two skeletons—one in a grey suit and the other in a wine-red dress—leaning crookedly over a news desk at center camera; the woman had placed her hand on the man's shoulder, and yellow sheets of the night's news were scattered all over the desktop. Behind the two figures were three or four out-of-focus skeletons, frozen forever at their desks.

Spence lit another cigarette. An occasional spark of static shot across the unmoving TV picture. "Doom City," Spence said. "Not only here, man. It's everywhere. See?"

The telephone behind the counter suddenly started ringing, and Brad clamped his hands to his ears.

The phone's ringing stopped.

Brad lowered his hands, his breathing as rough and hoarse as a trapped animal's.

He looked down at Kelly Burch. She was smiling.

"It's all right," she said. "You don't have to answer. I found you, didn't I?"

Brad whispered, *"Wha—"*

The little girl giggled, and as she continued to giggle, the laugh changed, grew in intensity and darkness, grew in power and evil until it became a triumphant roar that shook the windows of the 7-Eleven store. "DOOM CITY!" the thing with pigtails shrieked, and as the mouth strained open, the eyes became silver, cold, and dead, and from that awful crater of a mouth shot a blinding bolt of blue-white lightning that hit Neil Spencer and spun him like a top, throwing him off his feet and headlong through the 7-Eleven's plate-glass window. He struck the pavement on his belly, and as he tried to get up again the flesh was dissolving from the bones, falling away in chunks like dried-up tree bark.

Spence made a garbled moaning sound, and Brad went through the store's door with such force that he almost tore it from its hinges. His feet slivered with glass, Brad ran past Spence and saw the other man's skull grinning up at him as the body writhed and twitched.

"Can't get away!" the thing behind him shouted. "Can't! Can't! Can't!"

Brad looked back over his shoulder, and that was when he saw the lightning burst from her gaping mouth and hurtle through the broken window at him. He flung himself to the pavement, frantically trying to crawl under a parked car.

Something hit him, covered him over like an ocean wave, and he heard the monster shout in a triumphant voice like the peal of thunder. He was blinded and stunned for a few seconds, but there was no pain . . . just a needles-and-pins prickling settling deep into his bones.

Brad got up, started running again. And as he ran he saw the flesh falling from his hands. Pieces of skin drifted down from his face; fissures ran through his legs, and as the flesh fell away he saw his own bones moving underneath.

"DOOM CITY!" he heard the monster calling. "DOOM CITY!"

Brad stumbled. He was running on bones, and had left the flesh of his feet behind him on the pavement. He fell, began to tremble and contort.

"I'm cold," he heard himself moan. "I'm cold . . ."

She awakened with the memory of thunder in her bones.

The house was quiet. The alarm clock hadn't gone off. Saturday, she realized. No work today. A rest day. But Lord, what a nightmare she'd had! It was fading now, all jumbled up and incoherent. There'd been a thunderstorm last night—she remembered waking up, and seeing lightning flash. But whatever the nightmare had been, she couldn't recall now; she thought she remembered Brad saying something, too, but now she didn't know what it was . . .

That light . . . so strange. Not like June light. More like . . . yes, like winter light.

Sarah got out of bed and walked across the room. She pushed aside the white curtain and peered out, squinting.

A grey fog hung in the trees and over the roofs of the houses on Baylor Street. Thunder rumbled in the distance, and Sarah Forbes said, "Brad? Honey? Take a look at this."

He didn't reply, nor did he stir. She glanced at him, saw the wave of his dark hair above the sheet that was pulled up over him like a shroud. "Brad?" she said again, and took a step toward the bed.

And suddenly Sarah remembered what he'd said last night, when she'd sat up in a sleepy daze to watch the lightning crackle.

I'm cold, I'm cold.

She grasped the edge of the sheet and pulled it back.

THE PLAY'S THE THING

by Bob Booth

SCOTT RICHARDS LOOKED AT HIS DOCTOR AND NODDED. Their conversation had not gone the way he would have liked, but then again conversations with one's physician rarely did at his age. He thought of himself as being in fairly decent shape; but what was fairly decent for a fifty-year-old was not the same thing as what was fairly decent for a thirty-year-old, and the operative word was "fairly."

"I'm going to have to give you The Speech," Dr. Resnik said with a sigh. "I don't expect you to listen but when I go to your wake I want to be able to stand beside the coffin with a clean conscience."

Scott nodded. One of the things he had always liked about Resnik was his no-nonsense approach to medicine.

"Simply put, you're killing yourself," he went on,

tapping a pencil against his teeth. Then in an apparent effort to look more serious he put the pencil down and folded his hands in front of him like a preacher.

"How many packs of cigarettes do you smoke a day?" the doctor asked.

"One."

"You're lying," he said calmly.

"Two."

"And you're about twenty pounds overweight. Strike two."

Scott nodded silently.

"You've reached the big five-oh and you have high blood pressure."

"Hmm," Scott said between clenched teeth. He hated his blood pressure. It was the one thing he could not control. His physique, the cigarettes, the booze which the doctor had not yet mentioned were all burdens he chose to carry around with him. Blood pressure was different. Blood pressure was like kissing your uncle and finding out later that he has AIDS.

The doctor raised his hands slightly and put them back down on the rich mahogany desk, as if to say, "What are we going to do about it now that I've told you?"

Scott was silent. He wasn't waiting for the doctor to tell him how to cure all his ills; he knew there was no magic prescription forthcoming. He was still thinking about his blood pressure. No amount of beta blockers or diuretics could keep it within the normal range as long as he kept abusing himself. Avoid stress. That was going to be Resnik's next topic, of that he was reasonably sure. Avoid stress, get out of the theater, lead a calm, ordinary, dull life, and maybe you'll live a little longer.

He wasn't sure he wanted to live that way, but the

alternative was a little frightening. When he was twenty he had believed in the "brighter flame" theory of poetic existence. It was a theory, shared by many young people, postulating that those who died young lived better for a shorter time; like Keats, Shelley, and Byron. He had also believed that it was noble to kill yourself when the "juice" ran out like Hemingway had done. He even had found a certain nobility in an interview he'd read with Kurt Vonnegut during which the writer stated that his two-packs-of-Pall-Malls habit was actually a planned slow suicide. There was something darkly romantic about a man who could kill himself that way because of the uselessness of human life as he perceived it.

That was at twenty. At fifty those theories didn't seem so airtight. It was like saying whatever else happens in a war you're going to die well. Just you try it.

"What do you suggest I do?" he asked after the long silence that had grown up between them like a thick English hedge.

"Drink less, eat less, smoke not at all, retire, and move out of the city. Do all that and you *might* live a little longer. I stress the might."

"We're that far down the road, are we?"

"Around the bend," Dr. Resnik said, rising, his hand thrust out in a gesture of concern and friendship. In reality it said that he had got his fifty bucks' worth and there were others with more treatable ailments waiting to be seen.

Richards shook the doctor's hand with his right hand and buttoned his shirt with his left. He was still not completely dressed as he headed out the back door of the doctor's office toward the elevator.

* * *

Scott had been in Greystone Bay over a month, and each morning he walked. He walked out the front door of Mrs. Trumbell's weathered clapboard boardinghouse and north on Harbor Road. He liked the sound of the sea and the whirling screech of the gulls as he made his way toward Port Boulevard, where he turned left and sacrificed the tangy salt air for the pleasant expansiveness of the boulevard with its island of green. Mrs. Trumbell, though charming and anxious to please, was an awful cook. Scott had known by the second day that if he took many meals with her he would be dead before very long, and had got into the habit of walking to one of the department stores on Port Boulevard. There were three of them and each had a snack bar that opened at ten o'clock; a good, civilized time for a semiretired invalid to have breakfast. There were certainly better restaurants in Greystone Bay, and Scott was rich enough to eat in them if he wanted; but too many years of city life had made eating something more utilitarian than pleasurable. Cafeteria food was quick and cheap, designed as a convenience for busy shoppers, and that suited him just fine.

After breakfast he wandered the downtown area aimlessly seeking out bookstores or antique shops that might harbor some unknown treasure. Though he had been too busy in the city to build much of a library or furnish his various apartments in anything but the latest fad furniture, still he kept hidden within him a thirst for the finer things in life. Not cars or yachts or expensive jewelry, but the true "classics" of our culture. There was something pleasing about the dusty smell of an old bookstore or the weathered, substantial bulk of antiques squeezed into a small, beaten storefront. They were the artifacts of a culture that had lasted hundreds of years and would be around long after their creators had returned to dust.

Kevin Lochner was the one acquaintance aside from Mrs. Trumbell that he had made since coming to Greystone Bay. He ran Attic Books, a used bookstore on the lower end of Port Boulevard. Scott felt a kinship with Lochner right away. Formerly a heavy smoker, Kevin kept an inhaler on the old desk next to his filing cabinet. He suffered from emphysema and it was an effort for him even to feed the cats that lived in the store. He had close-cropped white hair and looked comfortable in the flannel shirts he wore winter and summer. He could speak softly and intelligently on any topic you'd care to name and unlike many of the high-priced book dealers Scott had met in New York, actually read a lot of what he sold. A customer could spend hours of Lochner's time and walk out without a purchase. There would be no hard sell, only a smile and a thanks for the conversation. It was how God must have meant bookstores to be, thought Scott, though he didn't believe in God and he suspected that Lochner didn't either.

Scott nodded to Kevin, placed the coffee he had brought for him on the desk, and went back through the stacks to the drama section. He knew there would be nothing he hadn't seen the day before but it was his excuse to come into the shop. He suspected that if anything new and unusual had come in, Kevin would have kept it at the desk to show him just as he came in the front door; but it gave him pleasure to keep up the little fiction that their fast-forming friendship needed a business base, so he did. When a suitable interval had passed he walked back to the desk and lit a cigarette. It was only his third of the day. In the city he would have been through a pack by this time.

"Thought about what you're going to do yet?" the book man asked him, sniffing the air like a hound who used to eat steak but now has no teeth.

Scott shrugged and glanced at the book sale notices that were pinned to the wall over the cash register. He had seen them all before and most of them were out of date, but it was a good place to look when you didn't want to answer a question.

"Why don't you open a theater?"

"In Greystone Bay?"

"Culture won't get you rich in Greystone Bay," he said, sweeping his hands out across the shelves of books that were his livelihood. "But it'll pay the rent."

"It's a big job," Scott said. The idea had occurred to him before but he had spurned it. Theater had already ruined his health and broken his heart more than once.

"Weren't you a producer in New York?"

"Sometimes. Sometimes actor, sometimes director."

"Then you know what needs to be done," Lochner said, raising the Styrofoam coffee cup to his lips. "All you need is the will to do it."

Scott made a face, but said, "I'd need a stage."

"Well, the movie theaters won't do, and they're both in operation anyway. How about the Elks Hall?"

"The Elks Hall?"

"Sure. It has a stage and a curtain and they don't use it that often. People in Greystone Bay aren't joiners. Some junior executives from the wire and cable plant started it about twenty years ago but membership has always been low to nonexistent. I'm sure they'd appreciate some help with the rent."

It was an intriguing idea. Every community of any

size needed a theater or repertory company. There were always enough talented kids or schoolteachers who wished they'd had the guts to head for New York when they were young enough to put on a creditable production. He could keep his hand in, at a much lower level, it was true, but just enough to keep the equipment from rusting. The Elks Hall wasn't a bad idea. They probably didn't have permanent chairs. Maybe he could put some tables in, hire a local caterer who made a passable roast beef or chicken, and do dinner theater. Light comedy, maybe a musical now and then.

Kevin gave him directions to the Elks Hall and he left, smiling for the first time in a month.

Bob Flowers was the Grand Poobah of the Elks. He was also into real estate, landscaping, and keeping tabs on the attendance at the two Greystone Bay cinemas for the film distributor in New York. He got paid six dollars an hour plus expenses to sit in the back of the theater with one of those hand-held steel counters and keep track of how many people watched a certain movie, as opposed to how many tickets the theater management said they sold. Flowers didn't do it for the money, certainly. He did it because he enjoyed going to a lot of movies for nothing and it was a good excuse to get out of the house for a few hours three times a week. Then, too, Peter McClelland, who owned both theaters, was a Moose.

"Being—how would you put it?—peripherally connected with show business myself, I quite understand your desire to bring good, clean entertainment to the citizens of Greystone Bay . . ."

Scott nodded.

"It is going to be good, clean family-oriented entertainment, isn't it?"

"We haven't decided what we're going to do yet," he answered, carefully using *we* instead of *I*. It always paid to let your adversary think he was dealing with a mob of indeterminate size, possibly well connected. "But I don't anticipate doing *Caligula*, if that's what you're asking."

"Yes," Flowers replied, shifting his weight in the swivel chair behind his desk at the real estate office. He had not offered Scott, a stranger after all, a seat. "Nothing of that sort would do, not at all . . ."

"How often would you need the hall, Mr. Richards?"

"We'd want to schedule performances for Friday and Saturday nights, with at least one run-through per week once we were into production. I was thinking of a dinner theater arrangement so that chairs and tables could be folded and stored if you needed the hall for a dance or a wedding or something."

"What were you thinking of paying us, Mr. Richards?"

"What is your normal rental?"

"Three hundred per evening."

"Take two on a volume buy basis. After all, we're guaranteeing you three nights a week, probably ten months a year if all goes well."

"I don't think the board would approve of two . . ."

"You have a liquor license, don't you?"

"Yes, we do, but . . ."

"You can have the liquor concession. People are going to want to drink with their meals and maybe one or two during intermission. Liquor profit will more than make up for the extra hundred."

"All right, but your people will have to pay for any renovations needed before you go on and for any damages incurred during or because of a performance. Fair enough?"

"Fair enough," Scott said, sticking out his hand. He didn't mind giving up the liquor concession. It was a pain in the ass and it brought with it the necessity of a large liability insurance premium. He had seen the hall and it didn't look to his practiced eye that much had to be done. A little cosmetic carpentry work could turn it into a respectable little theater. Besides, the people of Greystone Bay had been without live entertainment for nearly twenty years and probably wouldn't be too picky. He was counting on that for a lot of things.

The next morning he skipped breakfast and went to Lochner's for the opening of the doors. Kevin just smiled.

"Come to look over my stock of musical comedy?" he said gleefully as Scott stood before him, smiling for the first time since he left New York.

"Sure thing."

"Do *Gypsy*," Kevin said, but he didn't elaborate.

"*Gypsy*?"

"Flowers has a little daughter you could use for Baby June. It would etch your lease in stone for as long as you wanted it."

Scott smiled appreciatively. Kevin was demonstrating the prime quality of a good producer—the ability to manipulate people.

"And there's a part for a middle-aged woman who can sing."

"Yes."

"Get Peggy Jepson. She'd fill the hall."

Peggy Jepson would fill the hall, all right. Peggy Jepson had filled half the theaters on Broadway at one time or another. She'd won awards and made a pile of money, all in about five years. Then abrubtly, she had dropped out. Disappeared was more like it. Reporters were always greeted by shrugs from her agent and blank stares from those who had worked with her. She had moved into the realm of legend, with Le Gallienne and Bernhardt.

"She's here in Greystone Bay," Kevin said softly, his expression expectant.

"Peggy Jepson—*the* Peggy Jepson—in Greystone Bay? I thought she was dead."

"She came here on vacation twenty years ago and never left. There was a terrible accident. She's locked herself in that house up on North Hill and never leaves. Young Dr. McKenna used to go up daily, but that stopped some time ago. Has a housekeeper she sends into town for shopping. Orders things over the phone from Saltmarsh's."

"How do you know all this?"

"She sends her maid in for books now and then. Buys the *Best of Broadway Annual* every year when it comes out."

"Son of a bitch," Scott said. He knew he probably would have no luck talking her into a part in a fledgling dinner theater; but it was an excuse to talk to her, see how she had held up, maybe get some answers to questions that had puzzled him for years.

"Was her retirement connected with the accident you mentioned?"

Kevin shrugged. Who knew for sure?

"It was a little girl. Eva. They were doing a benefit

for the Greystone Bay Veterans Fund or something. The little girl fell off the stage. It wasn't much of a drop but she was small for her age and she landed wrong. Died instantly."

"She blamed herself?"

"Don't know. She went up to the cottage on North Hill and hasn't been seen since."

"Give me the address," Scott said, more determined than ever to talk with Peggy Jepson.

Peggy Jepson's house on North Hill was a large one and commanded a sweeping view of Greystone Bay, both the town and the ocean. It was an old grey Victorian badly in need of a paint job. Yellowing lace curtains hung in the windows like old, tear-stained handkerchiefs. The lawn was not well kept, but not too long either; Scott suspected Peggy Jepson hired a village kid to cut it once or twice a year, when it occurred to her. There was no doorbell, only an old brass knocker that looked like it might have come out of "A Christmas Carol." Then he remembered she had played in a musical version of the Dickens story and he wondered if this might have been the very knocker that had graced the stage. It was unlikely, but not impossible.

An Irish maid, whom Peggy always referred to as Mary Teresa, answered Scott's insistent knocking with a scowling visage that had been practiced at driving away intruders.

"I'd like to see Miss Jepson," he said as pleasantly as he could.

"And who should I say is callin'?"

Scott wasn't sure how to answer that. His name and Broadway reputation opened a lot of doors, but might just slam this one in his face. On the other hand, announcing himself as Mr. Richards, a new neighbor, probably wouldn't do him much good either.

"Just say an admirer," he finally answered.

"Hasn't been many of the likes of that lately," the old woman said, turning to report to her mistress.

"The Mistress will give you five minutes," Mary Teresa said when she returned. She did not look happy about it. She motioned Scott to follow her and led the way across a wide expanse of maroon carpeting in the spacious hallway and off to the left to what could only be called a sitting room.

The room was small, but elegantly furnished. There were lace doilies on the arms of the chairs and underneath the lamp on the small end table and there was a copy of a Whistler on one wall, a gilded mirror on the other.

"Why have you come to tell me lies?" a voice came from the doorway behind him.

She was beautiful. Of course she was pale and there were small wrinkles at the corners of her mouth and her eyes; but her face had retained that classic angularity that had made her the object of his youthful fantasies many years before. She had not put on weight, as he had feared, and she was nicely if rather oddly dressed.

"My name is Scott Richards," he said, holding out his hand after an awkward sort of half bow.

"The director?"

He was pleased. That this great woman knew his name was a surprise; that she should refer to him by the title he liked best of the many he had held was an indication of her sensitivity.

"I'm surprised you know me."

"I still read the trades, though I don't know why."

That was a good sign. Someone who has been retired for twenty years and still kept up with the scene was not psychologically ready to give up the ghost just yet.

"Sherry?" she asked.

"Please," he said, and sat down where she pointed.

"Mary Teresa," Peggy said softly. "A bit of the Bristol."

In a moment the Irishwoman entered with a bottle of Harvey's and two crystal glasses on a small silver tray. She poured, then silently left the room.

"I've come to talk you out of retirement," he said.

Scott couldn't wait until the next morning to tell Kevin. He called him from the phone booth on Harbor Road as soon as he got to the bottom of the hill.

"It wasn't as hard as I'd thought it would be," he said, his face grinning childishly over the mouthpiece of the phone.

"Must have been your boyish charm," Kevin said.

"No, I really think this is something she's wanted to do for a long time. Maybe she was just waiting for someone to ask."

"Plenty have asked."

"Yes, but that was twenty years ago when it first happened. I don't think anyone has approached her lately."

"No," the bookseller said after a pause. "I'll wager no one has spoken to her about the theater in at least ten years."

"Theater people have short memories. Once they had her pegged as a dead issue, no one cared to revive her."

"Did you mention me?"

"No, should I have?"

"I was afraid you might, since I told you to go and bother her."

"Do you want the credit?"

"Absolutely not," Lochner said vehemently. Then, after a pause during which Scott could hear the hiss of the inhaler, he continued. "She's a steady customer, as I told you. If this thing flops and she finds out it was I who put you on to her . . ."

"I understand," Richards said, laughing.

They spoke some more and finally Kevin invited Scott over for tea and some more conversation, but Scott had a lot on his mind and politely refused. He hoped Lochner wouldn't be too upset that their morning conversations would be cut off for a couple of months. There was an enormous amount of work to do and he had no idea who else in the community he could count on.

One mention of Peggy Jepson had set the old woman off, and for an hour Scott was regaled with town gossip. Peggy had a lover in Greystone Bay; that's why she returned to the town from time to time. Peggy was drunk most of the time. Peggy had a sports car that she drove at unreasonable speeds out on the highway. They knew Peggy would come to no good one day. There was also much talk of the little girl's unfortunate death, and Scott was a little sick of hearing about it.

"That was an accident, Mrs. Trumbell," Scott said. "A terrible tragedy this town would do well to forget."

"It was no accident, Mr. Richards. No accident at all."

"What are you saying!"

"I'm saying I was in the front row that night. They

were doing *The Bad Seed* and little Eva was in control of that stage. The audience was reacting to everything she did and she knew it. The woman from New York was jealous, Mr. Richards, I could see it in her eyes. Here she was, the big professional from Broadway, and this little tyke was stealing her show. Whenever Eva got a laugh or a gasp she would look over at Miss Jepson, like they were in some kind of competition. Then, at the end of the first act Miss Jepson had to back her toward the audience while accusing her of murdering the little boy in the lake."

Scott was spellbound, and despite his better nature thought he detected a twinge of truth in the woman's story. Actors are the most jealous breed on the face of the earth. He nodded for her to continue, though he need not have. She was just sipping her tea and gathering her thoughts. She had every intention of going on.

"She made it look like she was trying to grab the little girl and pull her back. With all the lights on a stage, as I'm sure you know, it's often hard to tell where the edge is."

He nodded assent.

"But really, Mr. Richards, she pushed her. As sure as I'm sitting here and was sitting in the front row that night, she pushed her."

"Do you think she wanted to kill her?"

"Who's to say? Probably she wanted her to fall and look foolish. It was only about a four-foot drop and normally the child would have had maybe a bruise or two, but it would have stopped the momentum of the play and broken the spell the girl had cast."

"Yes."

"But she landed wrong."

"Where was the performance?"

"At the Elks Hall," Mrs. Trumbell said with a shadowy grin. "It used to be the Strand. It was where the whole ghastly thing took place."

He was startled, but then pieced it all together. After the accident, there was little appetite for live theater in Greystone Bay. Some time later the newly arrived junior executives needed a place to hold their lodge meetings. No wonder Lochner said it would be the perfect place to stage a play.

The rehearsals went uneventfully enough. There was little trouble finding actors. There never is in community theater. Everyone wants to be a star. Everyone assumes that the talent is there, if only they'd had the breaks. There are always ex-cheerleaders and class presidents crying for the attention they were used to getting in school; and surprisingly enough, there are always a few who can really act.

When the word got out that this particular director was from New York and had talked Peggy Jepson out of retirement, there were any number of aspiring cast and crew members available for the least rewarding duty. In a restaurant Scott overheard two middle-aged matrons discussing the possibility of talent scouts from the city descending upon Greystone Bay. It only made sense. There was bound to be curiosity about Miss Jepson, and a man like Scott Richards doesn't come to Greystone Bay for his health.

He said nothing to spoil the illusion.

In a week the casting was done and he began blocking. There had been the usual flood of mothers with their bratty daughters who had neither looks nor talent. Nor were they particularly well behaved. What they did have were hundreds of dollars' worth of voice and tap lessons and parents who were busy living out their fantasies through the children. Scott dispatched these as quickly and as kindly as he could. Other than that, the auditions went pretty well.

They were going to do *Gypsy,* as Kevin Lochner had suggested. A crew was assigned to build the sets and another to procure lighting and sound equipment. There were a lot of donations. Greystone Bay had been without theater for a long time and local philanthropists decided the project was apolitical enough to support unhesitatingly.

A caterer was found who would serve a good roast beef dinner for ten bucks a head. Scott charged fifteen per ticket and quickly sold out. The only problem now was to produce a product professional enough to keep the audience coming back for future productions. He could foresee an organic entity of which he was the creative head. He would choose the productions and look in from time to time, but the work would be left to three or four young directors who wanted to build careers or hobbies for themselves and would be willing to put in all the hours necessary to do so.

There were the usual mishaps and accidents that come naturally when twenty or thirty people who don't know each other try to work at once in a confined space meant for half that number. Scott particularly watched Peggy's reactions. They were normal, and she got on with the cast right away.

Dressing rooms were scarce and the cast got to know each other much more intimately than they'd expected. That was all right with Scott. It built teamwork and caring and it was the glue that held the whole thing together. It was why theater on any level was always more alive than cinema.

Opening night. It was warm and festive both inside and outside the theater. The Elks were happy with the amount of drinks they were selling, Scott was happy with a sellout and a cast and crew he really thought were ready for the unbelievably frightening aspect of a first opening night, and Greystone Bay seemed unusually happy. It was a town with not much public personality. A town whose very private citizens had turned out in droves for Scott's experiment. He was grateful and he only wished to give them their money's worth.

Backstage you could see the tension in the air. Scott was going from actor to actor offering counsel and encouragement. They worried about the fine details of their makeup and he reminded them that there was no camera, no close-up shots. Onstage the makeup needed to be heavy and pronounced. From twenty feet or more no one would notice the line of the lipstick. Costumes that fit perfectly before now seemed as clumsy as football uniforms and actors couldn't remember what their character names were, let alone their lines.

Peggy reassured them. She was all smiles and soft touches and she told them the value of all their rehearsals. When the curtain went up they would go through their roles as if by magic. They might not remember a thing afterward, but it would be all right if they had put the work into it; and she assured them they had. Scott asked her out to dinner. Of course there would be the traditional opening-night party though there would be no reviews to wait for. Greystone Bay's only paper was an evening rag and the review might not appear until the "Weekender" section on Saturday. No, he meant afterward, maybe the next day. He wanted to be alone with her and just talk. Though she was no older than he was, she had worked with people who were only legends to him as he came up. Besides, he was lonely and she was a lovely, intelligent woman.

During the first scene Peggy's eyes scanned the audience and for a second that seemed to last far too long she paused. Scott followed her gaze and saw that she was looking right at Kevin. He was sitting about halfway back in the center of the room. He was at a table with a group of people Scott didn't know. He didn't think Lochner knew them either as they weren't any of the people he had seen hanging around the bookstore. Peggy went on but Scott's professional ear detected a slight quaver in her voice.

In the darkness that accompanies scene changes Lochner moved up to an empty seat at a table in the front row. He was sitting and, to Scott's surprise, smoking. Peggy saw him immediately and looked a bit startled. Kevin smiled.

Scott wanted to talk to him during intermission, but could not find him. He checked the men's room and the bar without any luck. He watched Peggy's entrance. When she saw Kevin's chair empty, she was visibly shaken for a moment, but the well-trained professional in her took over and she went on without missing a cue. Scott moved down the side of the theater and through the door that led backstage. He cut through the dressing room, where the stage manager was surprised to see him, and headed for the wings. He wanted to catch Peggy and reassure her when she exited.

Standing in the wings, Scott felt cold. It was summer and he was the kind of man who felt warm in December. The cold he felt was not the icy blast of a winter wind or the deadening numbness of a hard snow but the cold dread of fear moving, not up and down his spine as in the movies, but across his shoulders and down his left arm. He took one of the Valiums that Dr. Resnik had prescribed. It was the first one he had taken since his arrival in Greystone Bay.

There was a scene in the play during which Peggy had to open a door. The door was hung perpendicular to the line of sight of the audience so that they would see her reaction first and then the profile of the entering actor as he came through the door. From his position in the wings Scott could see what Peggy was seeing but at a much greater distance. He was not prepared for what he saw.

Kevin Lochner was sitting in a wooden chair in the doorway, facing Peggy. He seemed to be younger and more robust. There was a Victorian nightstand next to the chair and on top of it were a drink and a smoldering cigarette in an ashtray. Scott recognized it as the furniture from the sitting room he had been in on the first visit to the Jepson house and on many occasions since. Lochner looked strangely at home, as did the little girl who was standing beside the chair, gently caressing the back of his neck. She was beautiful and charming. She had short, bobbed blond hair and a twinkle in her blue eyes that captivated Scott from across the expanse of the stage. There was something radically wrong, however, and it took Scott a few moments to figure out what it was. Her head just didn't sit right. It was ever so slightly askew.

He looked over at Peggy and saw her grab for her

chest. He knew what was happening but was power-less to do anything about it. The actors onstage and the stagehands behind the curtain were all staring at Peggy, aware that something was wrong, but apparently unaware of what was behind the door.

Things seemed to be happening in slow motion. The girl was speaking to Lochner, and Scott didn't know if he actually heard her speak or was just reading her lips, something a director gets very adept at doing.

"Who's better, Daddy?" she was saying, a wicked smile darting across her face. "Me or Mommy?"

"Why, you are, of course," Lochner answered her, hugging her paternally around the shoulders. She turned her head to look straight at Peggy, who was busy crumpling to a dead-looking heap on the stage.

Scott didn't remember much of what happened after that. There were sirens and paramedics and those horrible-looking paddles that make the corpse leap off the ground with a poor imitation of life. The theater emptied slowly until the police arrived to clear everyone out. Scott made some vague noises about refunds in the morning but he wasn't paying much attention to what was coming out of his own mouth. He toyed briefly with the idea of going to the book-store but he was no longer sure it even existed. Finally, he just thought maybe he'd go back to New York and let it kill him.

SHE CLOSED HER EYES

by Craig Shaw Gardner

SHE DIDN'T WANT TO COME BACK TO GREYSTONE BAY.

Cheryl took a long drag on her cigarette and thought, in the same instant, how she had to give up smoking. But, then, she wanted to do lots of things, and somehow always ended up doing something else.

She looked out of the window of the coffee shop, out across the road to the town's short boardwalk and the beach beyond. In summer, this view could be idyllic, the sun high in a cloudless sky, the water a postcard blue. She remembered, when she was a girl, skipping stones on that beach at sunset. If you found just the right ones—flat and round bits of shale were best—you could skim them across the water three, four, even half a dozen times, making your mark on the still harbor as the skipping stone sent ever-expanding circles through the gold and crimson water.

Somehow, though, that sunset beach seemed like a different place from what she looked at now, just as she felt she was a different person from the girl who had stood by the water and skipped stones across the reflected dusk. How many years had it been? Five? Ten? It felt like a hundred. And it wasn't summer now. It was the end of March, and the sky and sea were an endless grey as the clouds roiled overhead and it rained, day after day after day.

She shivered as she felt a hand on her shoulder.

"Honey?" Joe's voice cut through her thoughts. "Are you cold?"

She looked up at her lover and tried to force a smile. "No, Joe," she lied. "I was just thinking how it used to be, when I used to live here."

Joe frowned for an instant before his face reestablished his constant grin. "Hey." He punched her shoulder gently. "What did we talk about? No sad faces around here, remember? We didn't come back to this place to lick old wounds. We're here to take Greystone Bay by storm!"

Cheryl stood up and let Joe's smile take some of the chill away. He was such a big, lovable jerk! She let him hug her tight and, a moment later, hugged him in turn. Maybe he was right. Maybe everything would work out, after all.

"Listen," Joe said as he pulled away. "I finally got through to Old Man MacDougal. He can show us the property this afternoon." His hand darted in to tossle her bright red hair. "Come on. It's time for us to take a little drive."

"Joe, my hair—" Cheryl began, but he was already

opening the door that led to the parking lot. Honestly! she thought as she wrapped her scarf around her head. Sometimes he could be so exasperating.

The world had looked very bleak from the seat by the window. It looked no better as she stepped outside, and she remembered just how cold the wind could be when it came off the ocean. A slight, freezing rain fell as they ran across the parking lot to Joe's new silver sports car. It had looked so bright and shiny the other day when he picked it up from the dealer. Just the thing, he had said, for "somebody who was going to make it big in real estate." Now, in the freezing drizzle, it just looked grey, the same color as everything else in this town.

Joe jumped in the driver's side and leaned over to unlock the other door. Quickly Cheryl climbed into her bucket seat, glad to be out of the freezing drizzle. March was always the worst time of year in Greystone Bay. Moisture swept down all month from Canada, but the marginally warmer ocean currents turned what might have been snow into endless weeks of sleet and freezing rain.

Joe started the car. "Prosperity, here we come!" he declared as he turned right onto Harbor Road and headed up to the rocky South Hill. Out here, driving through the rain, Cheryl couldn't share Joe's enthusiasm. Somehow, she didn't think prosperity could ever come from Greystone Bay.

She had closed her eyes, and in that instant, she had seen the sea; an angry sea, swept about by a raging storm. But the storm was high above her. She was far below the surface, so far that no light penetrated through the water, and she had to sense her surround-

ings in a different way. She had not realized, until
now, how deep that harbor was, and how much
deeper still was the channel that led to the Atlantic.

She was startled to realize that she had physical
form, that she was swimming through the water,
slowly rising to the surface. Her form was strange to
her, totally alien, like nothing she had ever seen
before. She was immense, and, she realized after a
moment's pause, she was hungry. It was such a
strange feeling. She was so seldom allowed to be
hungry.

She rose rapidly, her hunger giving her movements
an urgency she scarcely remembered. There was a
boat above her. And on that boat there was an
offering.

Her form thrust itself above the waves. The offering
screamed.

Cheryl tried to breathe evenly and watch the road.
The freezing rain changed as they climbed the hill
road and left the warmth of the harbor. The wind
swept tiny ice crystals to pound against the windshield and hood, beating against the car with such
force she thought that the wind itself was trying to
push them away from their destination.

She had to be careful. Her imagination was getting
out of control.

Joe seemed oblivious to her feelings. He watched
the road with a determined smile and talked on and
on about how glad he was to have the new car with its
new front and rear window defrosters and those
hard-rubber windshield wipers with the variable
speeds. He would have had to stop driving by now if
he still had the Chevette. It was doubly lucky he had
been able to get that front money.

Cheryl looked away from him, back out through the windshield. The wipers Joe was so proud of pushed back and forth, back and forth, leaving a white frame of ice crystals surrounding their path. Somehow they distanced the scene outside and made her think she was looking at a picture of the road rather than the road itself. The light was all wrong, too grey for this time of day. The ice crystals were too insistent.

Since coming back to Greystone Bay, Cheryl didn't know what was real anymore.

Joe laughed as the car slid to one side. He turned the wheel toward the skid and pushed down on the accelerator, straightening the wheel as the tires left the ice.

He glanced at Cheryl. "Storm or no storm, we're going to get there. You know that once I put my mind to something, it always gets done. There might be a problem or two along the way, but, sooner or later, everything works out just fine."

Cheryl sat silently in the passenger seat. She just kept staring out the window. Joe reached over and squeezed her knee.

"Whoops!" he quipped in mock alarm. "That's not the stick shift!"

"Joe, please!" Cheryl's voice was as cold as the world outside the car. She thought better of her words as soon as they were out. He was only trying to cheer her up, after all. She glanced at him with the slightest hint of a smile, hoping it took the bite from her tone. Joe shrugged and turned back to look at the road.

"So much for dumb jokes," he mumbled.

"I know you don't want to be here," he added, but his voice faded away before he could finish the thought. They'd had this talk before, about things in Greystone Bay that she'd just as soon forget. But she had also told him about the undeveloped land up on the South Hill overlooking the harbor. "The opportunity of a lifetime," Joe had called it. They couldn't let an unpleasant memory or two stand in the way of their success, now, could they?

She sighed. What more was there to say?

The car reached the top of the hill. There was a sign, partially obscured by the snow and ice, on the left-hand side of the road. Joe slowed the car down to a crawl so they could read it.

"MacDougal Farm," Cheryl said before she could make out the letters. Did she remember this place from before?

He took the turn slowly, careful to follow the half-filled tire tracks that were the only sign where the road led through the snow. The road curved again, skirting the edge of a forest, the mass of dark trees to his left, their branches covered with white. Joe maneuvered the car carefully, a steady hand on the wheel as they moved across the frozen ground.

"Nothing's going to stop us now," he said, more to himself than to Cheryl.

The car climbed to the top of a small rise. There, about fifty yards distant, they saw a cluster of buildings, dim grey in the swirling snow.

"Joe pulls through and gets us there again," he added in that same, soft voice, another one of his little "jokes," remarks Cheryl thought he believed in more than he liked to admit. He stopped the car next to a battered pickup, a large, ramshackle farmhouse to his left, a grey, sagging barn to his right. He turned off the ignition and pocketed the keys.

He reached for the door. "All ashore that's going ashore," he added.

"Joe?" Cheryl asked. "Would it be all right if I didn't go in with you?"

"What? I don't want you going all moody and depressed on me—" Joe paused and sighed. "Look, Cheryl, I know you don't want to be here. I asked you to come and do this for me. Old Man MacDougal's expecting both of us, so you've got to come. Trust me. If we put a little bit of effort into this, we're both going to make out like bandits."

"Okay," Cheryl said after a moment's pause. "Let me take a couple of puffs on a cigarette, and I'll be fine."

She had closed her eyes, and she was sitting in front of a window, in a rocking chair that never rocked, looking out over Greystone Harbor. She let her new thoughts fill her, and found that, while her body was withered by age, her mind was that of a young man, fresh from college, who had become curious about another man who had sat in this room, unmoving, and always looked out over the harbor.

Why had he been so curious? Why did he have to look at the man who never moved? He had thought about it, over and over, as the days had turned to weeks and months, and the seasons had drifted by his window. Some things had been revealed to him, some not. He suspected that he had had no choice. Greystone Bay had needed him. There were pacts to be kept, as old or older than the town itself, and he had been made the keeper.

Now his young body was gone. What was left of his consciousness dwelt inside this withered shell and watched. Someday, a year from now or a hundred years from now, some other curious soul would climb the stairs and peek in at the man who never moved. And should he be curious enough and step into the room where the old man watched, the newcomer would become the watcher, and the one who watched before would finally be free.

He sat in the rocking chair that did not rock and listened to the everyday noises of the street below, which he could not see, and the faint, steady rhythm of the harbor waves as they broke against the docks.

He knew by now that death was the only freedom.

He stared out over the harbor and kept the pact.

If only someone would come soon—this moment, this instant—and free him.

She threw her cigarette into a snowdrift and followed Joe up the recently shoveled path that led to the house. There was a light in a small window at the corner of a porch, a rosy glow that seemed to beat the winter chill away. She smiled. It reminded her of her mother, always leaving a light on for Cheryl when she was a girl, a spot of warmth that beat away the chill of the outside world. This light was the first real sign of life Cheryl had seen since she had come back to Greystone Bay.

The door opened as they approached. A tall man with a full shock of white hair and beard appeared in the doorway.

"Mr. Summers, I presume." The tall man smiled. "You must really want to see me."

"Oh, you know I do, Mr. MacDougal. It is Mr. MacDougal, isn't it?" Joe was talking rapidly, using his salesman's voice. Cheryl hated it when Joe started to talk that way. "I think, once I tell you my idea, you'll see how much I want to get started. I'm really glad you agreed to see me. I don't feel we have a moment to lose."

Cheryl followed Joe into the house. They were in the kitchen, a large, well-lit room dominated by a great oak table that Cheryl was sure could seat a dozen or more around it.

An older woman dried her hands on a dish towel as she walked toward them across the room. She smiled at Cheryl. "Why don't you take off your boots and let them dry out?" She pointed to an old blue square of carpet next to a large Franklin stove. "That way they'll be dry when it's time to leave."

Cheryl started to object. She wasn't sure she'd feel comfortable walking around in stocking feet in a strange household.

The older woman waved her dish towel in Cheryl's direction before she could speak, as if to disperse her visitor's reservations in the warm kitchen air. "Oh, don't worry," the woman added. "We don't stand on ceremony in the MacDougal household." She paused to pick up Cheryl's boots. "Oh. And you can call me Kate."

Cheryl thanked her and introduced herself, then dutifully handed Kate her boots. She glanced over at Joe. He had already managed to maneuver Mr. MacDougal into a corner by the kitchen table and was shooting facts and figures at the older man in a verbal barrage. MacDougal, for his part, seemed rather bemused by the whole thing, using Joe's monologue as an opportunity to fill his pipe. But when Joe stopped at last to catch his breath, the older man spoke instantly:

"I hate to see such enthusiasm go to waste." He nodded at the window. "The storm's slowing down out there. Why don't you and I go and take a look at the hill?"

Joe was speechless for an instant. Cheryl was sure he had never thought it would have been this easy. MacDougal lit his pipe in the silence.

"Sure," Joe said at last, his salesman's grimace replaced by a genuine smile. "Mr. MacDougal, that sounds like a great idea." He turned to Cheryl. "Hey, honey! Want to take a little trek in the great out-doors?"

"Oh," Cheryl answered, taken by surprise. She had been looking forward to sitting for a few minutes in this warm kitchen, perhaps having a cup of tea with Kate. Joe seemed to need her in everything. How important was it for her to go? Did she have to be included in everything?

The door outside opened before she could reply. Another man walked inside, much the same height and build as MacDougal, but much younger, perhaps in his twenties, close to Cheryl's age. He stamped his snow-covered boots on the mat just inside the door, then looked straight at her.

"Hello, Cheryl," he said.

Cheryl looked at him more closely. There was something familiar about him. She tried to picture him without his scruffy beard. "I'm sorry—" she began, then stopped herself. "Robbie?" she asked.

He smiled and looked even more like the cheerful, hyperactive teenager Cheryl used to know. "So you remember?"

Cheryl laughed. "How could I forget somebody like Robbie MacDougal?" When Joe had told her the name of the farm, she had pushed all thoughts of something like this happening from her mind. It would have been too much of a coincidence, like something out of a dream. Besides, hadn't the MacDougals she knew lived somewhere near the harbor?

"Joe Summers." Joe had walked over to Robbie during his exchange with Cheryl. Joe practically stuck his outstretched hand in Robbie's face. Robbie dutifully shook it.

"Seems like old home week here today, doesn't it?" Joe added. "We were on our way out, your father and I, to look at some property I'm interested in buying. I think there's some opportunity to develop the land around here. I'm willing to give your father here a piece of it if he's reasonable about the price."

Robbie smiled. "Terry here's not my father. He's my uncle. And he's got a good head for business."

Joe laughed, a short, barking sound. "I'm sure he has. I'm sure he has." He had reached the door outside. "Cheryl, are you coming?"

Cheryl glanced at Robbie. "No, Joe," she said after a moment's pause. "I think I'll stay here where it's warm. You can tell me all about it when we get back."

Joe chewed his lip and shook his head. "That's the trouble with women these days. No spirit of adventure." He glanced back at MacDougal. "Shall we go and inspect the property?"

"After you," the old man remarked as he shrugged on a red-and-black-checked coat. He followed Joe out of the kitchen. Kate smiled at the two of them, then turned and busied herself at the sink.

Robbie walked over to Cheryl as soon as the door had closed.

"So how are you?" he asked. "It's been a long time."

Cheryl didn't know what to say. She looked away from Robbie's blue eyes. "I'm fine," she began at last.

"I—I moved to Boston, you know. I wanted to try life in a big city."

"Do you like it?"

"Oh, it's not bad," she replied vaguely. She looked back at Robbie's face. "It's better than it was in Greystone Bay."

Robbie's mouth twitched downward, as if he wanted to frown but wouldn't let himself. "We were a lot younger then, Cheryl. I didn't know what to do." He paused and ran his fingers through his sandy hair. "I'm glad you came back."

Cheryl smiled at that. "I'm glad to see you again, too. Besides that, I'm not too sure."

"About Greystone Bay?"

She nodded. "You know my problem. It went away when I lived in Boston. Now that I'm back here, though"—she laughed without humor—"it's happening all over again."

"I'm not surprised, not at all." Robbie reached out to let his hand rest lightly on Cheryl's shoulder. "Do you mind if we sit down at the kitchen table? I'd like to tell you about some things I've been doing."

Cheryl followed Robbie's broad-shouldered frame across the room. She couldn't believe he was here, that the two of them were together again. How often had she thought about him, so long ago? He didn't look that different. Oh, he'd grown a beard, but the eyes and the smile were the same.

It all was a bit like a dream. She had stopped thinking about Robbie a long time ago, had left him behind with the rest of Greystone Bay, a parcel of unpleasant memories that she had stored away for good, memories foreign to her new life in Boston.

She only realized now how much she had wanted to

see Robbie again. He turned, smiling, and offered her a chair. She sat and smiled in return.

"So you and Joe are something of an item, huh?" Robbie began. Kate, who was in the midst of fixing tea for the three of them, yelled at her nephew for being an insensitive twit. Robbie laughed.

"Oh, I know it's none of my business," Robbie continued. "Joe seems like a nice enough fellow. How long have the two of you known each other?"

"Oh, not very long at all, really," she replied. "It was sort of a whirlwind thing. We don't really know each other all that well, I guess. At least not yet. I'm afraid I told him about Greystone Bay, and he got all excited. And here we are."

Robbie nodded. "Uncle Terry told me all about his condominium plans. It looks like the South Hill will finally be civilized."

"It will if Joe has his way." Cheryl shook her head. "And Joe likes to have his way."

"I understand he knows of some new building methods which will allow him to build out on the rocks."

"I'm afraid you're asking the wrong person." Cheryl smiled defensively. "I don't know that much about it."

"Why should you? It's up to Joe and Uncle Terry now." He glanced up as Kate brought over a pair of steaming mugs. She placed one in front of each of them, then muttered something about finding her sewing and left the room.

Robbie paused and looked down at his hands. There was a long moment of silence between them.

"Cheryl, about what happened before—" he blurted at last. "Well, what's done is done. But what I wanted to tell you now is that I believe you. I believe in everything you saw."

Cheryl stared at him, He had managed to take her breath away for the second time in a matter of minutes. If she wasn't dreaming before, she most certainly was now.

Robbie laughed, a friendly, easy sound. "It surprises you, huh? Well, the boy who ran away when you needed him most hereby admits his mistake at last. I'm sorry, Cheryl."

"It wasn't your fault, Robbie—"

"Well, it wasn't your fault, either. But we all treated you like it was, didn't we?"

He smiled at her and took her hand. She felt she was going to cry. Memories flooded her from all those years ago: the derisive laughter of her former friends; how alone, so completely alone she had felt: and what happened when she closed her eyes.

She closed her eyes, and this time, there was darkness. But it was not the darkness of sleep. Rather, she was in a place that had no light, someplace underground.

There were many of them there, put in this place long ago, so long ago that they were eventually forgotten. But still they had a purpose; a purpose they waited to fulfill.

There was movement. She was aware of hands, many hands, perhaps a hundred, rising through the frozen earth as if the hard-packed ground were water.

They had waited so long and watched in their way, with sightless eyes, from their home within the earth. It was time again for the waiting to be fulfilled.

Her hands broke through to the surface and felt the barely remembered caress of the open air. They were searching. What they wanted was very near.

But someone she knew was calling to her. She recognized the voice. She heard someone call her name.

She paused in her search.

Someone was calling. She had to stop it. She had to pull the hands away.

Someone was calling.

"Cheryl!"

She opened her eyes and saw Robbie's face, full of concern, only inches away.

"It—happened again, Robbie," Cheryl whispered.

"The visions?"

Cheryl nodded. "I've only been back in Greystone Bay a couple of hours. They've started already!"

"I'm not surprised," Robbie told her. "And I think I know why you have them." He offered her his hand. "Let's get you back up into a chair."

Cheryl realized she was on the kitchen floor. She let Robbie pull her up, then, after a couple of shaky steps, sat down on the straight-backed chair she had fallen from.

Robbie took her hand.

"You know, I cared about you very much, back in high school. I imagine that might be difficult for you to understand, the way I rejected you, just like everybody else. There was something about those visions, Cheryl. You had everybody scared. Did you know that?"

Cheryl stared at Robbie's hand where his fingers intertwined with hers. The visions were getting as strong as they were before.

"You were very important to me back then," Robbie continued, "even though I was as scared as everybody else. I may have slammed a door in your face, screamed at you along with the other kids, but I still thought about you all the time." He squeezed her hand gently. "I had to find out why I had run away, and just what I was running from. In doing that, I learned a lot about Greystone Bay. And I think I learned something about you as well."

Cheryl looked back up at Robbie's face. His blue eyes looked directly back into hers.

"I went to college for a while, you know," he continued, "until I realized I couldn't find out any more through ordinary channels, and had to start looking elsewhere." He made a whoosing sound, not quite a sigh, with his tongue and lips. "How do I start? You know about Stonehenge, don't you? And Easter Island? Well, there are other places like those, special places, that ancient man, with methods different from those we use today, would discern were focuses of power, you know, mystical power, the power of the elements. Things modern science dismisses, because they are not easily categorized. But these things exist nonetheless." He pulled his hand free to scratch at his sandy hair. "I think Greystone Bay is one of these places."

"So Greystone Bay is somehow special, somehow different?" Cheryl asked. "But what does that have to do with me?"

"I think you tap into that power somehow. You've probably thought about your visions all your life as a curse, but I think, if they were used the right way, they might turn out to be a gift, like some ancient Greek oracle or something."

Cheryl laughed in disbelief. "I think you're going to have to explain this to me a little more slowly."

Robbie took her hand again. "I'd like to do that. Very much." It was his turn to laugh. "I had to come back here, you know, to find out if my theories were right. I hardly even hoped, though, that I'd ever see you again."

Kate poked her head in the door that Cheryl guessed led to the dining room. Robbie smiled at her. Kate smiled back and disappeared.

"Wait a moment," Cheryl protested. "Is this some kind of conspiracy?"

"Well," and Robbie smiled sheepishly, "a little bit of one. I had to talk with you again, alone. Both Aunt Kate and Uncle Terry understand that. You see—"

The door outside opened with a crash. Cheryl pulled her hand away from Robbie's.

"Hello, the house!" Uncle Terry's smiling face appeared around the sill. "We've got a casualty of the great outdoors here."

Joe pushed past the older man and stepped into the kitchen. "Oh, I'm all right!" he protested.

One look at him, and Cheryl knew there was something wrong. He looked paler than she had ever seen him, and his perpetual smile was gone. He walked unsteadily across the room and sat at the kitchen table.

"Joe?" Cheryl asked. "Are you really all right?"

Old Man MacDougal laughed good-naturedly.

"Your friend here's a little afraid of heights."

Joe laughed uneasily in response. "I don't know what came over me. There I was, almost at the edge, just this little bit of woods between me and the cliffs, and something—" He laughed again and shook his head. "It was too long a drive from Boston, I guess. Never try to do business when you're tired."

Kate frowned. "Are you sure you feel all right now? You're not driving back to Boston today, are you?"

Joe shook his head. "No, we're staying at a place in

town, the Atlantic View Hotel. My partners back in Boston want me to look into a couple of other properties in Greystone Bay. When I'm a little more rested, I'll come back and look at this one as well. Who knows? Maybe the weather will clear up, too."

"Would you like some tea or something?" Kate asked. "Maybe a little brandy."

Joe shook his head. "No, thanks. We've imposed on you folks far too long. I think I just need to get to the hotel and get some shut-eye." He stood, pushing his chair back.

MacDougal began to fill his pipe. "Well, feel free to come back, anytime you are up to it."

"I'll give you a call." Joe grabbed Cheryl's hand. She hesitantly followed him toward the door.

"Well, it was nice seeing you again, Robbie. I guess we'll run into each other again."

Joe pulled her outside before Robbie could answer.

"Come on," he said. "Let's get into the car."

Cheryl pulled away from him on the path outside and walked quickly to her side of the car.

Joe unlocked her door from the inside. She opened it and slid into the passenger seat.

"You needn't be so rude," she said, looking out the front window. "How do you ever expect to get a sale acting like that?"

"All I expect now is a good night's sleep." Joe's voice was cold as he started up the car. "That, and maybe some peace and quiet on the ride into town."

"Joseph Summers!" Cheryl replied angrily. "What is the matter with you?"

"Don't get holier-than-thou here." Joe gunned the car into reverse, sending clouds of snow aloft to either side. "What's wrong with me is my own business."

"Your own business? I thought you always said we

were doing things together. That's why you made me come to Greystone Bay, wasn't it? I just don't understand you!"

"Oh? And I expect that big fellow with the blond beard understands you a lot better than I do!"

"What?" So that was it! "You're not even worth talking to!" Cheryl turned away from Joe to look out of the passenger side of the car. Joe had managed to turn the car away from the MacDougals' house and was slowly retracing his path, following his own tire tracks back to the main road.

The new-fallen snow was so white and the trees beyond so dark that they reminded her of a very old photograph, full of sharp contrasts, like some she had seen once of the Civil War. It gave her the feeling that these woods, and this snow, had been here for a hundred years or even longer, that this forest and field and the hills around had been here forever, and never, ever changed.

She stared out the window as they reached the main road and the pristine white was replaced by asphalt and dirty snowbanks. She didn't want to look at Joe, because she knew he was right. At this moment, she wished that Joe was nowhere around. She wished she had come back to find Robbie a long, long time ago.

She wondered if she had ever seen some of Robbie in Joe. They were similar in superficial ways. But where Robbie was energetic, Joe was pushy. Robbie's cheer was natural; Joe's was often forced. Maybe, through her relationship with Joe, she had been trying to find Robbie all over again.

They reached the top of a hill and, for a moment, saw the town before them, as grey as its name implied. Neither of them spoke. Joe turned on the radio.

Cheryl stared out the window at bare trees and dirty snow.

"I need a drink," Joe said as they parked in the lot behind the hotel.

"Joe," Cheryl replied, trying to keep her voice calm. "It won't do you any good to turn away from me like this. Don't you want to talk to me at all anymore?"

Joe looked at her, but for once didn't give her a clever reply. The snowstorm had begun again in earnest when they had started down the hill for town, and the swirling snow seemed to unleash their emotions inside the car as well, so that the last ten minutes had been one long argument. At first, Cheryl had thought Joe was just jealous of Robbie. Joe had denied it vehemently and had turned the conversation to complain about other arguments the two of them had had some weeks in the past. He went on, she thought, to list everything she had ever done to annoy him.

So why didn't she get out of the car and leave him? Partly it was because she had done her fair share of arguing as well, with her own set of accusations. But more than that, she had the feeling that, no matter how much Joe yelled at her, he was really angry at something else, as if he was afraid to tell her about what was really upsetting him.

"Yeah," Joe said at last. "Yeah. Maybe you're right. But I still need a drink. Let's get a bottle and go up to the hotel room."

Joe remembered a package store just down the street from their hotel. It wasn't much of a walk, he said, even in the snow. Cheryl dutifully followed him around the side of the hotel and down past a dozen seaside stores. The wet snow and slush lay half an inch deep on the sidewalk. Most of the businesses were closed for the season. Another, the Greystone Smoke Shop, had a hastily rendered "Closed Due to Weather!" sign in the window. There were no other people on the street, nor any cars. Cheryl wondered what Joe would do if the package store was closed, too.

Joe turned abruptly and pushed open a glass door with a wooden frame. A bell tinkled overhead as the door closed behind them.

"Afternoon." A small man, bald save for a few wisps of white hair above each ear, looked up from where he read a newspaper at the counter. "What can I do for you today?"

Joe said he needed a bottle of good Scotch. He was about to seal a big business deal. It was time to celebrate.

As the shopkeeper turned to fetch the bottle from the shelf behind him, Cheryl remarked that she was surprised he'd stay open on a day like this.

The shopkeeper smiled as he turned back to face them. "Oh, I always do business." He told Joe the price. Cheryl was surprised by how cheap it was. "Even in blizzards." He took Joe's money and rang it into an ancient cash register. "Think about it." He nodded out at the snow. "Not much else to do, is there?"

Joe tried to laugh, but it sounded no more genuine to Cheryl than one of his sales pitches. She wished he could just step back and really talk about what was bothering him. Well, maybe tonight, she told herself. We can have a couple drinks, and maybe, just maybe. She wouldn't give up on him just yet.

Joe grabbed the bag and told Cheryl it was time they got back to the hotel. She followed him outside.

Joe drained his glass and smiled a genuine smile at last.

"That's better," he said, pouring himself another.

Cheryl took a sip from her Scotch and water. She really didn't feel much like drinking.

"Do you want to talk?" she coaxed. "You know, you haven't been the same since we left Boston."

"Yeah. Yeah." Joe rolled his glass between his hands. "I know. I wanted to show you more of a good time. It's just that I've got so much riding on this. The guys back in Boston fronted me a lot of money. I don't know how I could pay them back—" He hesitated. "No, that's not the way Joe Summers thinks. I knew I could do this in Boston, I know I can do it now. Anybody can foul up a little. I was tired from the drive, this damned snowstorm—" He took another drink.

"Joe?" Cheryl asked. "Why don't you tell me about it? If you don't, we're just going to start fighting again."

"Yeah," he replied. "Okay." He poured more Scotch into his glass.

"Everything was fine," he began tentatively. "Well, it wasn't fine, but I was doing well enough. I should have worn higher boots. You should have seen how much snow was out there! I had to walk in Old Man MacDougal's boot prints to keep from getting my shoes soaked through, and he was getting way up ahead of me. He moves pretty fast for an old geezer." He raised the glass to his lips, only sipping at it this time. "It's all woods between the farmhouse and the cliffs, probably only a five-minute walk when there isn't a foot of snow. I think MacDougal would have covered it in five minutes, anyway, if I didn't keep getting lost behind him. Still, I did my best to keep up, and I made a couple little jokes about us city slickers. We were getting along all right."

He paused to take another, deeper drink.

"Well, I'd lost MacDougal again, and he yelled back that he was up ahead, on the cliffs overlooking the South Hill. I hurried to meet him, figured I could keep him excited and maybe make the sale right there. I came up to a little clearing and started to cut across it." He stopped and looked down at his Scotch on the rocks. "That's when things got funny."

"Funny?" Cheryl prompted after a moment's silence.

"Yeah," Joe replied. "Yeah." He drained his glass again. "It seems stupid now. I walked into this little clearing, there wasn't much snow there. The trees grew together overhead, that's probably why the spot was bare. But first thing I did, I tripped, almost fell. Thought I'd hit a hidden root. But when I looked down, there was nothing there."

Joe put his drink down and stood up. "Now, this just gets crazier." He paced across the worn carpet. "The next thing I knew, I felt like something grabbed my pant leg. I thought I was caught on a bush or something and tried to shake it loose. That's when it grabbed my ankle." He staggered as he turned to look at Cheryl, and had to put out a hand to steady himself against the overstuffed chair that sat in the corner. "That's when I got scared. Whatever got me hurt like hell. It wasn't an animal, I can tell you that. It was hard and sharp, and dug into my skin. Like it was made of rock, or maybe bone." He closed his eyes and leaned against the chair. He seemed to be shaking.

Cheryl stared at him and thought about her vision. About the hands, reaching out of darkness and finding what they sought. They wished to possess it, to take it with them—but there had been a voice. A human voice had called her name.

"Joe?" she asked softly. "Did you cry out?"

"What?" He opened his eyes again. "Of course I did. I didn't care what MacDougal thought of me anymore. I screamed bloody murder!"

"Joe? Did you call my name?"

He laughed sourly. "I called everybody. MacDougal. My mother. You had to be in there somewhere."

That was it. It was his voice she had heard. Suddenly, all those things Robbie had told her about started to make sense.

"No, you had to call my name. I heard you."

He looked at her dully. "What are you talking about?"

She tried to explain to him about the darkness, and the hands, about what she had seen.

Joe sat in the overstuffed chair. "I think we've both had too much to drink."

"Joe!" Cheryl insisted. "Listen to me. I know it sounds crazy, but I think I know what happened. You see, this afternoon, Robbie told me—"

"Oh!" Joe yelled. "I knew we'd get back to Robbie!"

"Would you shut up!" Cheryl exploded, surprised at her anger. "I can tell you what happened!"

"No." Joe rose unsteadily to his feet. "No. I don't want your help anymore. You and that Robbie creep." He laughed as he lurched in her direction. "You know what MacDougal said to me? He only agreed to see me because I was with you! Good old trustworthy Cheryl!" He sat heavily on the edge of the bed. "And after all the work I put in on that geezer." He reached over and grabbed the Scotch. This time he drank straight from the bottle.

"Joe, you're upset," Cheryl said softly, trying to restrain her anger. "If you'd just calm down a little bit—"

Joe shook his head. "I know I can do it. I've got that deal. I can taste it. I don't care what kind of mumbo jumbo you let the big blond stud feed you. I don't care if the old man worships at your feet. I'm going to get what I want!"

Joe took another swig from the bottle. When he spoke again, his voice was much quieter. "Shouldn't look a gift horse in the mouth," he muttered. "That's what you are, Cheryl, a real gift horse." He waved the bottle in her direction. "I can't stop talking. I told myself to just shut up. I'd shut up if I wasn't drunk."

He sat back heavily in the chair. "Hell, I'm drunk. Maybe none of this happened at all. Or maybe crazy things happen to me because I have a crazy girl-friend."

"I am not crazy!" Cheryl yelled. To her surprise, she found she was on her feet.

"God!" Joe was on his feet, too. "You can't take a joke, can you?" He pushed past her and grabbed his coat. "I'm getting out of here. I've got to think."

Cheryl didn't turn to see him leave. The door slammed behind her. She hunched forward and stared at the wallpaper: faded yellow flowers on a sea of dingy grey.

Her visions had cursed her before, when she lived in Greystone Bay. Now they seemed to curse her again. She was so sure, listening to the reassuring sound of Robbie's voice, that she had an answer at last. Now she wasn't so sure. Maybe Joe was right.

Maybe she was crazy, after all.

She sat back in her chair and cried.

She glanced at her watch one more time. It was almost ten. Where could Joe have gone?

Cheryl stared at the phone, expecting it to ring and give her some answer. But if it finally rang, and if she picked it up, did she want it to be Joe on the other end? Part of her wished it would be Robbie instead.

She was being foolish. She and Robbie hadn't seen each other for years. They were completely different people from the two kids who had known each other in Greystone Bay.

But she didn't want to leave Joe this way, after a drunken argument that both of them would probably regret in the morning. Besides, in a strange way, she felt responsible for Joe. He had come to this seacoast town because of something she had told him. Now he had run away from her, drunk out of his mind. He could get hurt if he wasn't careful.

She had been too angry to follow him right after he had left. Sitting in the hotel room with the snow raging outside for the better part of an hour had given her a chance to cool down and think things through. One way or another, she wasn't doing any good staying here brooding.

She grabbed her coat. There couldn't be that many places open on a night like this. She'd go out and look for Joe, even if she had to trek up and down Ocean Street through the snow.

*   *   *

He hadn't made it as far as the snow.

He was sitting in a booth at the back of the hotel bar. Across from him was another woman, with long dark hair pushed back behind her shoulders. She was dressed well, although, as Cheryl approached her from across the room, she seemed more and more like one of those rare women who would look good in anything they wore. Cheryl was surprised someone so sophisticated would spend her winters in a backwater like Greystone Bay. She wasn't so surprised to find her sitting across from Joe.

"Hi, Joe. Why don't you introduce us?"

Joe looked up at Cheryl's voice. He didn't seem to be any more sober than before. "Sure," he said. "Yeah." He waved at the woman across from him. "Valerie, this is Cheryl."

The two women murmured pleasantries. Valerie asked if Cheryl didn't used to live around here. Yes, Cheryl responded in surprise. How did she know? Valerie worked for the local library and knew almost everybody around town.

Valerie suggested that Cheryl sit down and join them. Cheryl had the feeling that it had somehow slipped Joe's mind to tell this woman he had come to the town with a female companion. Cheryl was surprised how calmly she was accepting all this.

"Actually," she said, "I need to talk to Joe about something private."

Joe shook his head vehemently. "You can talk in front of Valerie! She understands me."

And I don't, Cheryl thought. She felt a pang of hurt and anger rise in her chest.

Valerie looked at Cheryl, then at Joe. She didn't say a word.

"The two of us have been talking," Joe continued. "I know just what to do." He cleared his throat. "I think," he said after a moment's consideration, "I think that a vacation community like Greystone Bay needs to continue growing. I think the South Hill is underutilized. It's ripe for development. I think the Condominium Town Houses we were discussing are just the thing. I'm going to go up and tell that to Old Man MacDougal first thing in the morning." He toasted Valerie with his empty glass. "I think it'll make a brighter future for all of us!"

"Joe," Cheryl began, but she didn't know what else to say.

"Maybe I'd better go," Valerie said, reaching for her coat and slim black bag. "I don't think I quite realized the situation here."

"Oh, you've realized everything!" Joe insisted. "You've told me just what to do!"

Valerie smiled apologetically as she stood to leave.

"I'm going to go right back out there! MacDougal wants me back. The old geezer can smell a sale. I might even go out there a little early. Farmers get up at dawn, don't they? That'd impress the bastard. One real look at that property, and I've got a sale!" Joe clenched his hand into a fist.

"Joe," Cheryl said, "I think you should come upstairs and go to bed."

"With you?" Joe laughed derisively. "I never want to go to bed with you again! I've found somebody who really understands me. I'm going to be a winner soon, you'll see. I was tired when I went out to MacDougal's place before, and you were making me crazy. But not again! Never again! I'm going to be around Greystone Bay a long time."

Joe grabbed his coat. He pushed Cheryl roughly aside as he strode from the bar.

She turned around. The bar was almost deserted. The three other patrons and the bartender didn't seem to have any interest in Joe's outburst. Valerie had disappeared. When had she gone? Cheryl didn't know, and she didn't care. She didn't know if she cared about anything anymore.

Cheryl went back to her hotel room. She couldn't think of anywhere else to go.

Being here was a lot like being nowhere at all. The snow still fell outside, muffling what few noises there were so that the entire world was silent. She was angry with Joe; no, more than that, she was furious. How could a man act like that? She had had other relationships fall apart, but never like this.

The Scotch she had drunk before had given her a headache. It just made everything worse. She couldn't bear to watch television or listen to music. She turned out the lights and smoked three cigarettes in a row, her eyes following the bright red embers in the dark.

Exhaustion got the better of her at last. She stubbed out the cigarette and closed her eyes.

She was something that lived beneath the sea and waited for sacrifice. She was the young man that stared from the window and kept the pact. She was a hundred other things, some human, some not. And she was a pair of hands in darkness, reaching through the cold earth for sustenance.

They sensed his presence above them. They had expected him. Now that they knew of him, they knew he would return. They could hear his voice muttering softly, feel his footprints in the snow.

He had used that voice to escape them once. It would not happen again. They rose quickly and broke through the frozen earth.

Their victim was slow, dull-witted. He screamed as they took his ankles, his knees and waist and chest and shoulders. He opened his mouth to speak, but they had his throat before his mind could form the words. They squeezed, and his voice was gone.

They were satisfied.

She had had a dream.

She opened her eyes. The room was filled with that pale glow that comes just before dawn.

She rubbed her eyes, trying to come fully awake. What had she dreamed? It had been something unpleasant, but in the dawn light, she could no longer quite remember it.

Cheryl got out of bed to light a cigarette and walked to the window. The snow had stopped finally, and lay as a pure white blanket over the shoreline until it met the grey water of the harbor. The clouds were breaking up overhead, and there were patches of blue sky here and there. It looked like it might be a nice day.

She thought of Joe. But only for a moment. She doubted he bothered to think about her anymore. There was no use in worrying. Whatever they had had together was gone. After last night, they were both on their own.

She stubbed her half-smoked cigarette out in the ashtray and stared in the mirror above the bureau. Her eyes were circled with smudged mascara. It made her look a bit like a lost waif.

Well, she said to herself, this waif is about to be found. She picked up the thin Greystone Bay phone book and looked up the number for Terrance

MacDougal. There was a phone call she had to make.

Unless it was too early; she found her watch. It was only half past five. She had better wait a few minutes before changing her destiny. She propped up the pillow and sat back on the bed, trying to relax.

She closed her eyes and saw the darkness beneath the earth. She was a pair of hands, one of a hundred such pairs of hands, all of them grasping at the newcomer, pulling him toward them until he could become one of their number. The newcomer struggled, but their grip was firm. They pulled him down into the soft earth—

No! Cheryl opened her eyes. She didn't need to see the vision if she didn't want to. Robbie had called it a gift, and when he had done so, she realized she might have control over that gift, and rule the visions rather than have them rule her.

She had opened her eyes, and the vision had stopped. One more thing to be thankful for. A little while more, and she'd make that call. Maybe she would have breakfast with Robbie. Maybe they would talk about just what her visions meant. Maybe they would talk about other things.

Sometimes, Cheryl admitted, Greystone Bay took care of its own.

The Chroniclers

NANCY HOLDER is the author of over a dozen novels, and her stories have appeared in many anthologies of horror and dark fantasy. She lives in San Diego, where she's teaching her border collie to herd ducks.

NINA KIRIKI HOFFMAN lives in the Pacific Northwest, and her offbeat and superior stories have appeared in most major anthologies and magazines.

F. PAUL WILSON, whose latest novel is *The Touch*, lives in New Jersey, where he practices medicine just like Doc Johnson.

ROBERT E. VARDEMAN is the author of the popular Cenotaph Road series, and the coauthor (with

Geo. W. Proctor) of the equally popular *Swords of Raemllyn.* He lives in New Mexico, where he contemplates bonsai.

KIM ANTIEAU is adjusting from her move to Arizona from Oregon, but her stories, which have appeared in *Shadows* and other anthologies, do nothing but improve.

THOMAS SULLIVAN lives in the Midwest, teaches English, and spends his royalty checks on things best not mentioned here.

GALAD ELFLANDSSON's stories have appeared in *Shadows, Greystone Bay 1,* and most of the genre's major magazines and anthologies. He lives and sometimes works in Ottawa, Canada.

LEANNE FRAHM lives and works in Australia, is impossible to get hold of by anything short of personal messenger, and continues to write some of the most disturbing stories in the field.

JOSEPH PAYNE BRENNAN's latest collection is called *The Borders Just Beyond.* And as the saying goes, he doesn't get older, he just gets better.

STEVE RASNIC TEM lives in Denver and has become one of the most prolific and brightest talents in the field.

KATHRYN PTACEK's latest novels are a historical Chinese fantasy, *The Phoenix Bells,* and a dark fantasy, *In Silence Sealed.* She is convinced that all the possums in New Jersey are dead.

BOB VERSANDI is a writer and director of television commercials, lives on Long Island with artist wife Jill Bauman, and is determined to turn in his camera for a typewriter. This is his first story.

MELISSA MIA HALL is a Texan, which explains more than anything why her stories are so strange. She is also a photographer, poet, and soon-to-be-published novelist.

ROBERT R. McCAMMON is the best-selling author of *Swan Song, Usher's Passing* and *Mystery Walk.* He lives in Alabama, where he's currently working on his new novel.

BOB BOOTH, a typesetter by trade, book collector by inclination, lives in Rhode Island, where he's trying to convince his daughter not to practice too hard for her part in *The Bad Seed.*

CRAIG SHAW GARDNER, whose stories have appeared in nearly every major magazine and anthology in the field, is the author of the best-selling trilogy, *A Malady of Magicks, A Multitude of Monsters,* and *A Night in the Netherhells.*

THE BEST IN HORROR

Ramsey Campbell

☐ 51652-4 DARK COMPANIONS $3.50
   51653-2   Canada $3.95

☐ 51654-0 THE DOLL WHO ATE HIS $3.50
   51655-9 MOTHER   Canada $3.95

☐ 51658-3 THE FACE THAT MUST DIE $3.95
   51659-1   Canada $4.95

☐ 51650-8 INCARNATE $3.95
   51651-6   Canada $4.50

☐ 58125-3 THE NAMELESS $3.50
   58126-1   Canada $3.95

☐ 51656-7 OBSESSION $3.95
   51657-5   Canada $4.95

Buy them at your local bookstore or use this handy coupon:
Clip and mail this page with your order

TOR BOOKS—Reader Service Dept.
49 W. 24 Street, 9th Floor, New York, NY 10010

Please send me the book(s) I have checked above. I am enclosing
$_____ (please add $1.00 to cover postage and handling).
Send check or money order only—no cash or C.O.D.'s.

Mr./Mrs./Miss _____
Address _____
City _____ State/Zip _____
Please allow six weeks for delivery. Prices subject to change
without notice.

GRAHAM MASTERTON

☐	52195-1	CONDOR		$3.50
	52196-X		Canada	$3.95
☐	52191-9	IKON		$3.95
	52192-7		Canada	$4.50
☐	52193-5	THE PARIAH		$3.50
	52194-3		Canada	$3.95
☐	52189-7	SOLITAIRE		$3.95
	52190-0		Canada	$4.50
☐	48067-9	THE SPHINX		$2.95
☐	48061-X	TENGU		$3.50
☐	48042-3	THE WELLS OF HELL		$2.95
☐	52199-4	PICTURE OF EVIL		$3.95
	52200-1		Canada	$4.95

Buy them at your local bookstore or use this handy coupon:
Clip and mail this page with your order _____

TOR BOOKS—Reader Service Dept.
49 W. 24 Street, 9th Floor, New York, NY 10010

Please send me the book(s) I have checked above. I am enclosing $_____ (please add $1.00 to cover postage and handling). Send check or money order only—no cash or C.O.D.'s.

Mr./Mrs./Miss _____

Address _____

City _____ State/Zip _____
Please allow six weeks for delivery. Prices subject to change without notice.